PHILIPPA GREGORY

ORDER OF DARKNESS

DARK TRACKS

VOLUME IV

PHILIPPA GREGORY

ORDER OF DARKNESS

DARK TRACKS

VOLUME IV

SIMON & SCHUSTER

First published in Great Britain in 2018 by Simon and Schuster UK Ltd
A CBS COMPANY

1 3 5 7 9 10 8 6 4 2

Simon & Schuster UK Ltd
1st Floor, 222 Gray's Inn Road
London WC1X 8HB

www.simonandschuster.co.uk

Simon & Schuster Australia, Sydney
Simon & Schuster India, New Delhi

A CIP catalogue record for this book
is available from the British Library.

HB ISBN 978-0-85707-742-4
TPB ISBN 978-0-85707-743-1
eBook ISBN 978-0-85707-745-5

This book is a work of fiction. Names, characters, places
and incidents are either the product of the author's imagination or
are used fictitiously. Any resemblance to actual people living
or dead, events or locales is entirely coincidental.

Typeset in the UK by M Rules
Printed and bound by CPI Group (UK) Ltd, Croydon, CR0 4YY

MIX
Paper from
responsible sources
FSC® C020471

Simon & Schuster UK Ltd are committed to sourcing paper that is made
from wood grown in sustainable forests and support the Forest Stewardship
Council, the leading international forest certification organisation. Our
books displaying the FSC logo are printed on FSC certified paper.

NEAR LINZ, AUSTRIA, MARCH 1461

There was an angry bellow from inside the woodcutter's hovel; the woman, struggling up from the stream with a heavy bucket of icy water in each hand, raised her head and shouted back. Something in her tone enraged him – he was always on the brink of fury – and, as she put down one of the slopping pails in the muddy patch before the tumbledown building, the rough wooden door banged open and the woodcutter surged out, his dirty shirt half open, his thick trousers flapping. He grabbed her free arm to hold her steady and slapped her hard, across the face. She reeled back from the blow, but gritted her jaw against the pain, and stood, head bowed, like a beaten ox.

He brought his head close to hers and shouted, his spittle spraying into her impassive face. He let her go, and impulsively kicked over both pails into the mud; she would have to go to the stream again, and haul more water. He laughed, as if the thought of her pointless labour was the only funny thing in this bitterly hard world. But then his laughter died as he looked at her.

She was not pressing her slapped cheek with the cold palm of her hand, nor bowing her head in sobs. She was not shrinking from him, nor picking up the rolling, empty buckets. She had spread out her hands wide; she was snapping her fingers as if to a drumbeat that only she could hear.

'What are you doing?' he demanded. 'Woman? Fool? What d'you think you're doing?'

Her eyes were closed as if she could sense nothing but a smooth wooden floor and clean limewashed walls and candlelight, and the fresh smell of a swept barn ready for a midsummer dance. Her head was tipped, as if listening to the rattle of a tambourine and the tempting, irresistible saw of a fiddler. As he watched, quite bemused, she lifted the hem of her ragged dress, spread it wide, and started to dance, as pretty as a girl.

'I'll dance you!' He started towards her, but she did not shrink from him. She took three steps to the left and did a little jump, then three steps to the right. She turned round as if she were being spun by an attentive partner. Ignoring the icy mud on her bare feet, she started the part of the dance where the women circle the room, as if she was being watched by admirers, her head held high, her eyes blind to the leafless branches of the trees and the cold sky above them.

He laid heavy hands on her shoulders and felt her jig beneath his grip as if he were about to dance with her. He tried to drag her into their hut, but she only danced towards the open door, bowed to the dirty interior, and danced back out again. He drew back his fist to thump her into unconsciousness, but something in her smiling, bland face made him hesitate: suddenly powerless, his hand fell to his side.

'You've gone mad,' he said wonderingly. 'A madwoman you've always been, but now you've lost your wits, and you'll be the ruin of us all.'

LIEZEN, AUSTRIA, APRIL 1461

A robed and hooded traveller turned his weary horse into the stable yard of a good inn in the town of Liezen, threw the reins to a lad who came running to his piercing whistle, and eased himself down from the saddle with a sigh.

'Is there a Luca Vero staying here?' he asked the boy, tossing him a coin. 'And his clerk?'

'Why, who wants him?' came a disembodied voice from inside the darkness of a stable, and then a tall, square-faced, smiling young man of about twenty looked over the half-door of the stable. Behind him, his horse came and rested its nose on his shoulder as if they would both like to know who was looking for Luca Vero.

'I am sent from his lord to bring him a message,' the man said briefly. 'I suppose you are Freize, Luca's manservant?'

Freize bowed his head, slightly surprised that his name was known. 'That's me. And this is my horse, Rufino.'

The horse seemed to incline his head also, and regard the traveller with a matching polite curiosity.

'And you are?' Freize asked.

'I am Brother Jerome,' the stranger said. He turned to the stable lad. 'See that my saddlebag is taken indoors and get me the best room available. I sleep alone.'

'There are rooms available,' Freize volunteered. 'Enough space for a man to take a room just for himself, if he can afford it, if someone else is paying for him. And a very good common table. They eat well here. I have discovered the pleasure of dumplings. Do you know them? Take two and you need little more for hours, several hours; take three and you will need a nap. I doubt anyone can eat four. And you should try the stewed chicken. They have a way with stewed chicken that you would ride from Rome to taste.'

The man smiled slightly. 'I am not here for the chicken,' he said. 'Or the dumplings.'

'But you have ridden from Rome?' Freize confirmed.

The stranger smiled, acknowledging that Freize had guessed his journey.

'Well, you've ridden a long way to look down your nose at a treat,' Freize said, not at all abashed. 'I'm assuming that you are being paid to come all this way, that you are the messenger that we were told would come here?'

'Yes. I've come to meet Luca Vero, your master. I am honoured to be a member of his Order.'

'Tasked with the same sort of work?' Freize gently pulled his horse's ear in farewell, and then let himself out of the stable, bolting the door carefully shut behind him. 'Are you another Inquirer? Sworn to ride around in uncomfortable places, finding evidence for the end of the world, signs of the end of days, to sit in judgement, when required, on poor fools who have frightened themselves to death already, and report back to Milord?'

The stranger nodded at this jaundiced description of his work. 'I am a member of the Order of Darkness tasked to examine these terrible times,' he said. 'Since the fall of Constantinople, the Devil is here, daily walking the world. Everywhere I go, I find more horrors. Everywhere I go, I record them for Milord, and he reports to the Holy Father himself. There is no doubt that there are more and more events and they are growing stranger all the time.'

'My very point!' Freize exclaimed, delighted to at last find someone who agreed with him. 'I cannot tell you what happened to me in Venice! Alchemists and wealth, and the destruction of all gold so that we could not buy Luca's father out of slavery; the strangest of people; troubled weather; even odd animals. On this very journey we have been followed – I swear we have been followed – by some sort of a Being. A little thing, you never catch it in plain sight, but it is there – out of the corner of my eye – moving from the bridles when I go to tack up, slipping away behind the feed buckets. Never fed, never sleeping and not a thing of this world, for sure. So what is it, this little thing? And so I say to my friend and lord: why don't we go back home and watch events unfold from there? Since there are so many unnatural people in this world, since strange things are happening all the time, why do we need to go seeking them out? Let them come to us! Lord knows there are enough bad and unknown events occurring in this dangerous world without us having to look for trouble!'

Freize led the way through the arched gateway towards the inn as Brother Jerome disagreed: 'Your master has to go and search out these things because he is an Inquirer of the Order of Darkness. It is his work and his duty to go wherever there is danger or a mystery, and discover it.'

Freize looked unconvinced. 'But what is the point of it all? What happens to his report?'

'Of course, Milord considers it,' the man said. 'As the Lord of our Order, he reads everything that we send to him. If it is serious and urgent, he takes it at once to the Holy Father, and the Pope himself studies it. And, when they put together the report from your friend with the signs from all the other Inquirers, then they know . . .'

'Exactly! They know what?' Freize demanded, pushing the inn door. 'They know that dozens, perhaps hundreds, of terrible things are happening all over the world, and we, poor fools, are dashing around from one dreadful place to another to catch sight of them as they happen. As if anyone would want to see them. As if anyone of good sense would not run in the opposite direction!'

'By gathering all the reports they then know that these are the signs of the end of days. That this is the end of the world.'

Freize hesitated. 'You think so too?' he asked, as if he still hoped the answer would be no. 'You really think it is happening? The end of the world?'

'It is a certainty,' the man said gravely. 'It has started already, God help us all. It started with the fall of Constantinople, with the infidel Ottomans at the altar of the Eastern Church. Now we have to fear for ourselves. For if they reach the altar of the Western Church at Rome, the home for the Pope of the West, then it is all over for us. Your master, and I, and everyone serving Milord in the Order, must discover when the darkness will fall on us. It is not a question of 'if', it is a question of how long do we have? Perhaps it is as soon as tomorrow.' He looked at Freize's aghast face. 'You should say your prayers, for perhaps it is even tonight.'

~

'A very jolly visitor bringing the best of news.' Freize gloomily reported the arrival of Brother Jerome to his travelling companions: Isolde and her friend, Ishraq. He looked from one smiling face to another, one of them as blonde as a Saxon, the other as dark as a Spaniard. 'Here comes another Inquirer, just as we were promised, turning up out of the blue, come to give us our mission and warn us of the Devil walking through our days,' he said glumly. 'As if I were not afraid enough already.'

'Poor Freize,' Ishraq teased him, giving him a hug, briefly resting her head against his broad shoulder. He looked down on her smooth black hair, her hijab headscarf casually thrown back, her upslanting black eyebrows, the curve of her olive-skinned cheek, and his arm tightened round her waist.

'You are a comfort,' he conceded. 'At least I will die in the company of a beautiful girl.' He looked across at the fair-headed Isolde and bowed to her. 'Two beautiful girls.'

'Surely the world won't end before dinner, so you've got that to look forward to,' Isolde pointed out.

'And there are certain to be dumplings,' Ishraq added.

'Yes, but he'll want us to go somewhere,' Freize

complained. 'To some terrible place that is sliding into hell, and find out why. And I don't want to go anywhere. I'm done with travelling. I want to go home.'

'At least you've got a home to go to,' Isolde remarked from her seat by the little window. 'If I don't get to my godfather's son and raise an army, I'll never win back my castle and lands. I can only come with you if the Inquirer sends you east because that's my route. If your orders take you in another direction, we'll have to part ways here.'

'I go with you,' Ishraq, her childhood friend, reminded her. 'Wherever.'

'This Inquirer didn't tell me anything,' Freize said. 'Just that he would meet with Luca.'

'Let's go down,' Ishraq suggested, 'and find out for ourselves.'

'But are we supposed to be seen?' Isolde hesitated. 'Luca might not want it known that we are travelling with him.'

'Surely, everyone knows by now,' Freize said cheerfully. 'Since Milord used you to disguise the inquiry in Venice, everyone knows that his Inquirer Luca Vero is travelling with a lady and her companion. Brother Jerome came into the yard and knew my name at once. I should think that the whole of Rome knows that you two are travelling with Luca and me and Brother Peter the clerk. Ishraq is right: we need to know if we can stay together. Let's go and see.'

~

It was Isolde, as the Lady of Lucretili, the grandest member of the party, who led them into the hall, to find Luca and

Brother Peter seated at the dining table with the new arrival. 'We wondered if we might join you?' she said politely to Luca. 'We wanted to know your new destination, and if our journeys still lie together.'

He jumped to his feet at once, his smile warm and intimate. 'Of course,' he said. 'Please come in, your ladyship, take a seat, take my chair.'

To the stranger he said: 'This is Isolde, Lady of Lucretili. Did Milord tell you that we are all travelling together?'

'He said that you had companions,' the man said, rising to his feet and bowing. 'But I had no idea ...' His bemused gaze took in the beautiful young woman, her conical headdress standing tall on the coiled plaits of her thick blonde hair, her rich dress of dark blue velvet with fashionable sleeves slashed to show the bright turquoise silk underneath, and her air of confidence.

Ishraq came in behind Isolde. 'This is my friend and companion, Ishraq.'

Now the stranger flinched back and crossed himself, for the girl before him was unlike anyone he had ever seen before. Her skin was as brown as a beech nut, but completely smooth, her eyes dark and ringed with kohl, her black hair hidden under an indigo silk scarf tied around her head. What startled him most was her tunic, like an Arab woman's, and her billowy pantaloons which she had strapped to her slim legs for riding. His gaze flicked to Luca almost accusingly: 'An infidel?' he asked. 'You are travelling with a Moor?'

'Ishraq is a most true and loyal friend.' Luca started to defend her, but Ishraq only laughed at the man, showing little, perfectly white teeth.

'I'm no harm to you, Inquirer,' she said. 'So you need not cross yourself at the sight of me. I was raised in a Christian household by a great crusader lord and I serve his daughter, the Lady of Lucretili.' She nodded towards Isolde who looked challengingly at the stranger, and stepped closer to stand shoulder to shoulder with her childhood friend. 'I have been in a Christian household since I was a baby, but my mother was a Moor and I am proud of my inheritance.'

'Even so,' Brother Jerome said, still shocked.

'I have met your Milord already, and I can't say that I was impressed with him,' the young Arab woman went on, startling the Inquirer even more with her bold speech. 'Now you have met me, I see that you are not impressed either, so we are equal in our prejudices. But I remind you that the people of my race now command half of Christendom and are advancing on the rest of it, so, if I were you, I would prefer me as a friend rather than an enemy. We're rather dangerous as enemies, as you can see. Certainly, I wouldn't be insulting on sight.'

'The advance of the Ottomans is a disaster – one of the great signs of the end of days,' the man bridled. 'The fall of our sacred Constantinople confirms the end of the world – a tragedy.'

'Only to you,' she said shortly. 'From the point of view of the Ottomans, everything is going rather well. Not that I am on their side. But I do think that if you are going to spend your life in the pursuit of knowledge, you had better consider how different something looks from another point of view.'

In the stunned silence, Luca and Isolde carefully

avoided each other's gaze for fear of laughing out loud at the shocked expression on the Inquirer's face.

Brother Peter, the clerk, intervened. 'I, too, was surprised when we found ourselves escorting these two ladies,' he remarked. 'We met on the road after our first inquiry, and since then we have travelled together. Of course I would prefer to avoid women, all women, but our ways have run together so far, and not even I – a celibate monk who has devoted my life to our Order – can deny that these are exceptional young women who are courageous in danger and helpful in inquiry. But, in any case, they are going east and have their own reasons for travelling, and Milord has ordered that we must travel together until our roads part. Then I shall be sorry to say goodbye to them. Perhaps our new destination will take us apart tomorrow?'

A swift glance between Luca and Isolde showed that they hoped they would stay together. Ishraq smiled at Brother Peter. 'Well, I hope not,' she said. 'I have learned much from you, Brother. But how d'you feel, Luca?' She turned her attention to him, her eyes sparkling with mischief. 'As a younger celibate monk travelling with us, shall you be pleased to part or shall you be sorry to lose us like Brother Peter?'

'I am a novice,' Luca said with quiet dignity. 'As you know. I have not yet taken my vows. But I could not have completed my inquiries without you both. I owe you both a debt of gratitude.'

'If Milord has no objection to you all travelling together then I can have none,' the visiting Inquirer said hastily.

'That's very independent of you,' Ishraq observed sarcastically.

'And you already know Freize, our general factotum,' Isolde said as Freize opened the door a little wider and came into the room from where he had been listening outside.

'General . . .?'

Isolde nodded firmly. 'It's how he prefers to be known,' she said quietly. 'And we admire him and respect his preferences.'

'Not just a servant, you see,' Freize pointed out. 'Indispensable.'

'We're a motley crew,' Brother Peter conceded. 'But we have seen some things on this journey! Milord has been pleased with our reports and even came out to visit us in the middle of one of our inquiries.'

Brother Jerome was impressed. 'He did?' he exclaimed. 'Why did he do that?'

Brother Peter was bland. 'Of course we don't know why.'

'Perhaps you would know?' Isolde asked Brother Jerome. 'It was when an Ottoman galley came on shore for repairs and the owner, Radu Bey, insisted on dining with Luca. Milord said that Radu Bey was the greatest enemy to Christendom. He tried to capture him.'

Brother Jerome looked away. 'I couldn't say,' he said shortly. 'I know of the Moor Radu Bey – he is second in command to the sultan himself, a danger to every Christian and every Christian community in the world.'

'He's not a Moor,' Ishraq pointed out. 'He's fair-skinned.'

'But why is he a particular enemy to Milord of the Order of Darkness?' Isolde prompted.

'Every Moor is our enemy,' the Inquirer ruled. 'For it is their advance which signals the end of days. But this Radu Bey is not part of my inquiry, nor is he mentioned in your

14

orders. I don't speculate about him.' Brother Jerome closed the conversation by reaching into his pocket and drawing out a rolled manuscript.

Freize nodded towards Luca as if this confirmed his worst fears. 'More sealed orders,' he said. 'And so adieu to the stewed chicken and dumplings.'

'We like to speculate,' Ishraq remarked dulcetly and earned a swift reproving grin from Luca.

'Do you share the orders with everyone?' the Inquirer asked, looking at Luca.

The young man nodded. 'Without everyone's insights and skills, we would have been lost over and over again.'

The stranger raised his eyebrows as if he found this a most odd way of going about an inquiry and then he broke the seal and spread the rolled paper on the dining table.

They all sat. They all waited.

'There seems to be an outbreak of what is called *dancing sickness*,' he started. *'La maladie de la danse.* Milord wants you to take the the old road north, and then go east along the banks of the River Danube. Somewhere along the road you will hear reports of dancers, there is an outbreak in that area, they are travelling downriver, I don't know where they are right now, you will have to ask for them and find them. You are to meet them and examine them as they dance together. Those who can speak should be interviewed individually. You will consult with the local priest and see if any exorcism or praying has worked on them. You may experiment with cures. You may test individual dancers with anything that you think might work – but only if they are people of no importance whose death or destruction does not matter. You will address the local landowner, Lord Vargarten, who rules north of the river, and speak with the bishop to see if they have had previous outbreaks, and if so what was the cause, and how it ended. And you will report back to Milord as soon as you know whether this is some kind of frenzy or poisoning or madness, or something worse.'

'Worse?' Freize asked anxiously. 'In heaven's name, what sort of a world do you people live in? What do you imagine can be worse than a frenzy, a poisoning or madness?'

'Possession,' Brother Jerome said shortly. 'If they have been invaded and taken over by demons. And if it is the demons who are making them dance.'

'Demons?'

'Possibly. Yes.'

Freize's horrified face spoke for them all. 'Demons?' he said again. 'You want us to go among people who may be possessed by demons?'

The man bowed his head. 'It is, of course, the work of the Inquirer to see the terrors of the world and discover their nature. You are free to decide that you don't want to accompany him. That must be between him and all his companions.'

'But to go looking for them?' Freize asked. 'If they are demons? What if they want to possess us?'

The Inquirer exchanged a smile with Brother Peter at the simplicity of the servant. 'We will not be affected,' he said. 'We are men of education; we are men of the Church.'

'Then what about the girls?' Freize demanded.

At once, the Inquirer lost his pompous confidence. 'Ah, now that: I don't know,' he said. 'Women are known to be more vulnerable to madness and to fits. Their minds are

16

frail, they have little determination and they are not strong. Perhaps these young women should be left behind for their own safety.'

'It's our road. We can follow the River Danube east,' Isolde said drily. 'The journey we have undertaken so far is proof enough of our determination and strength; and we both have had an education. If schooling makes you safe then we should be fine.'

'I don't mean singing and needlework,' the man said, smiling at the pretty young woman.

Isolde looked at him with such disdain in her deep blue eyes that for a moment he gasped as if he had been winded by a blow. 'No, neither do I.'

'Lady Isolde was raised by her father, the Lord of Lucretili, in Italy, to inherit his great estates, and to take his role in council,' Luca explained. 'She ruled his castle and lands during his illness. She is a *midons*, a lord of the castle. She has studied a lot more than singing and needlework.'

He bowed his head. 'But may I ask, why is her ladyship not at home, ruling her lands at Lucretili?'

'My brother stole my inheritance on the death of my father and I am going to find my godfather's son, and ask him to raise an army for me to win it back,' Isolde said simply. 'I am planning a battle to the death. I won't be stopping on the way to dance.'

'But what about your slave?'

'I'm not a slave, I'm a free woman,' Ishraq corrected him. 'The Lord of Lucretili allowed me to attend the universities of Spain and I studied there.'

'Do Moorish universities admit women?'

'Oh yes,' she said with a little smile. 'Some of their finest philosophers and scientists are women.'

Brother Jerome tried to nod as if this were not startling and unsettling news to him. 'They are?'

'I studied philosophy, and astronomy, geography and mathematics, and I trained as a warrior,' she said, smiling as his wonderment grew. 'The Lord of Lucretili was generous enough to give me a wide education. I should be safe enough.'

The priest bowed his head. 'And I am learning much right now. You have studied things that I am forbidden to learn: banned books, heretical knowledge. Astronomy alone is limited, some men have said the wildest things, heretical things ... well, I can see that your learning will protect you, and it is your decision. But I am bound to warn you that there may be danger.'

'But what about Freize?' Isolde asked. 'Will he be tempted to dance? He's a young man of great courage and enterprise, but you had no schooling, did you, Freize? Will he be all right?'

'I can't really read,' Freize pointed out. 'I can sign my name and reckon. But nobody would call me a scholar. Will that mean that I'll dance about when we get wherever we're going, God help us?'

'I don't know,' Brother Jerome said frankly. 'That is the danger you face. We don't know what causes the dancing sickness, why it stops, why it starts. That's the reason for the inquiry: to discover the cause and the cure and to save the people from the sickness and send them home.'

'Has anyone ever cured it before?' Luca asked.

'Of course many people claim to have cast out demons,

but the dancing sickness seems to start and to stop for no reason. That's what makes us think it is a sign of the end of days. Surely it cannot be that people just take it into their heads to dance till they die. It must mean something. Perhaps you can find out why. I will pray for all of you.'

'I thank you for your prayers,' Freize said unhappily. 'But then what? After we have danced about with madmen?'

The Inquirer looked up and allowed himself to smile. 'Then your master Luca will make his report and I, or another messenger, will deliver your next mission,' he said. 'In the meantime, I think you are carrying a quantity of gold from Venice which belongs to Milord?'

'We are,' Brother Peter said. 'And we would be glad to be relieved of the burden.'

'You can give it to me in the morning when our ways part,' the Inquirer said. 'I am going west. I will hand it over to another Inquirer who will take it to Rome and to Milord himself.'

'Why, how many Inquirers are there?' Ishraq asked curiously.

The man looked at her as if she were an enemy spy, trying to worm secrets from him. 'Enough to learn of all the dangers that face Christendom and all the signs of the end of the world,' he said grimly. 'Some who report on the rise of your countrymen, who warn of the Ottoman forces who come closer and closer with every victory to the heart of Christendom. They have won Constantinople, the greatest Christian city in the East; they threaten all of Greece; undoubtedly, they are planning to conquer the whole of Europe; and when they reach Rome then we know – it has been prophesied – that it will be the end of days. But we, the guardians of Christendom, are everywhere. We watch everywhere. The Ottomans think that they are unstoppable, but we are always vigilant. We watch and we warn, we inquire and we report.'

'My godfather's son stands against them,' Isolde remarked. 'Who is he?'

'The third Count Vlad of Wallachia,' she replied.

He bowed his head as if to acknowledge a powerful general. 'He stands against them,' he confirmed. 'And we keep constant watch.'

'But still they come onward,' Ishraq remarked.

He nodded. 'Satan advances,' he said. 'And the world is ending.'

~

Brother Jerome left at dawn, taking the donkey loaded with the gold that had washed out from the dross they had bought in Venice. Milord had made a fortune by cheating the Ottomans and the little party were glad to deliver his profits and be free of the burden. Brother Peter especially was glad to see the back of the gold which he could only regard as the wages of sin, the profits from a massively dangerous gamble which only Milord had understood as he had played them all: Christians and Ottomans like pawns on a board.

Luca, Isolde, Ishraq, Freize and Brother Peter had said goodbye to Brother Jerome, breakfasted and met in the stable yard while the light was still cold and pearly. Isolde drew her cloak around her against the morning mist, and Luca reached towards her to lift the hood over her fair hair, in a gentle gesture that betrayed their intimacy.

'I can't believe our luck,' he said. 'That we should go on, and our roads still lie together. That Milord himself should order that we travel together. That we should be together for another morning, with another day ahead of us.'

'Every day is a gift for me too,' she said very quietly.

Behind them, Freize heaved a saddle onto the big horse that Brother Peter always rode. Neither Luca nor Isolde was aware of him, they could see only each other.

'We'll have to part one day soon,' Luca warned her. 'It's bound to happen. You have to go to your godfather's son, and I have to go wherever Milord commands. I don't know how I will face that day – I can't imagine it. I can't bring myself to imagine it.'

Isolde hesitated before asking the question that was becoming more and more important to her. Then she spoke so low that he had to bend his head to hear her whisper: 'Does that day have to come, Luca? Do you have to go on? Can't you come with me and win back my castle and lands? Won't you come with me, help me?'

He looked very grave and shook his head, his eyes on her face. 'You know how much I care for you – but I can't abandon my inquiry. I have to be obedient to my vows. I am a novice now, but I will swear. I am promised to God – my own parents agreed that I should go into the Church – and I cannot break my obedience to them or my oath to God. Milord took me from my monastery for this special mission, but I will return to it. In the meantime, I have sworn loyalty to the Order of Darkness and – you heard the other Inquirer – it is important work that we do. Perhaps the most important work that has ever been done.'

'You broke your vows once,' she reminded him.

As if it were a strange, erotic dream, he remembered the moonlit garden and the woman who had come in, masked and hooded, and given herself to him in silence, never saying her name, so that he did not know whom he had kissed, whom he had loved for that one magical night. Even now, days after that unearthly dawn when she had gone without speaking, he did not know who it had been, and Isolde told him that she, Ishraq and another woman had been outside the garden, and had sworn he would never know.

'I should not have sinned,' he said quietly. 'Whoever it was that night has a claim on me forever, as my first lover. But you told me the next day that I would never know her name. I would never know who came to me in the garden. It was not a betrothal in the real world but an isolated night of love, hardly to be remembered, never to be discussed. You told me yourself to never forget it, but never seek for the woman.'

'You will never know,' she confirmed. 'And we will not speak of it. But don't you see that you broke your vows that night? Whoever you were with, your vow of celibacy is broken. Does that not release you from your oath?'

He shook his head, but she pressed on: 'What if I were to win back my inheritance? Then we could have such a different life. Together. At my castle.' She was near to offering herself to him, and he watched as the colour rose from her neck to her chin to her cheekbones. 'I would be a rich women,' she whispered. 'I would be the Lady of Lucretili again, and you could be the new lord.'

'I broke my vows in a moment of sin, when I was alone

in the moonlight and drunk with desire for you; but that does not release me from them,' Luca said steadily. 'It makes me a bad novice, it makes me a failure, it makes me a sinner, but it does not set me free. And, even if I were free, you could not stoop to marry a man who was anything less than a lord or a prince. Isolde, beloved, I'm next to nothing! I am the son of a small farmer, tenant to a great lord, not even a landholder, and – worse than that – perhaps a changeling. I could be anyone's child, from anywhere. People said that I was faerie-born to my face, to my own parents. My own mother could not deny it, and now that they are both in slavery who will give me a name? Nobody knows who I am. In his anger, my own father denied me; he said I am a changeling!'

'Your father was enslaved against his will by the Ottomans!' Isolde exclaimed. 'He denied you in his anger. He is enslaved now, but I know you will free him. You will find and free your mother too. They will not deny you then. And nobody would call you faerie-born if you were by my side and you were the Lord of Lucretili.'

He was deeply tempted both by her and by the life she offered him. But he whispered a word of prayer and shook his head. 'You can't put a changeling bastard into the lord's seat at Lucretili,' he said steadily. 'It would shame you, Isolde of Lucretili. It would shame your father's memory: he was a great crusader lord. It would even shame me to be the cause of your disgrace. Nobody would ever forgive you for lowering your line and your great name, and I would never forgive myself.'

It was true; Isolde could not disagree. 'I know,' she said unhappily. 'I suppose I know. You are right, of course. But what are we to do? Are we simply to part when our roads go different ways? We've found each other now: are we just to leave each other as if it meant nothing? If we were born to be together, is that not more important than anything else?'

'Shall I get the other horses saddled?' Freize asked, cheerfully interrupting them. 'I have asked the kitchen to give us a saddlebag of food and something to drink. Only God Himself knows where we'll be at dinner time.'

Coming out of the inn with the heavy saddlebags, Ishraq laughed at him. 'At least we'll never starve, not with you planning the expedition, Freize.'

Isolde and Luca drew apart as Ishraq walked into the barn beside the stable where the horses' tack was kept, and fetched her horse's bridle. As she slung it over her shoulder, she saw something move behind the feed bins at the back of the barn. Something as small as a child; as quick as a child.

At once, in a moment, she was crouched into a fighter's pose, her knife pulled from her boot, her balancing hand extended, ready for trouble. 'Who's there?'

There was an urgent little scuffle, then a small door at the back of the barn swung open and banged shut, then silence. Freize, entering the barn to fetch the saddles, checked in the doorway and saw Ishraq straighten up from her fighter crouch. 'What is it?' he demanded. 'Did you see something?'

'I thought someone was there. Someone hiding.'

'Are they there now?'

'Gone, I think. Out through the door like a flash.' Ishraq tucked her dagger back into the scabbard in her boot, and went over to the back door and opened it. Outside was

24

a small paddock and an orchard, a few fat white geese nibbling at the grass. There was no one there.

'Have you seen something before?' she asked Freize, closing the door and coming into the tack room.

He nodded. 'All of this journey. I keep thinking I see someone or hear something.'

'But Freize, this was something strange. Something very small, no bigger than a bear cub. But moving as fast and as quietly as a cat.'

He nodded. 'The size of a child.'

He saw her shudder. 'A child couldn't have followed us from Venice,' she pointed out. 'We've ridden every day, and in open country. No child, not even a man, could have kept up with us and not been seen.'

'That I know,' Freize said levelly, his voice unnaturally steady.

'But you still think some creature is following us?' she asked very quietly.

He was silent.

'In Venice, there was a creature.' She spoke of it unwillingly. 'The alchemists said that they had created life. We saved it from the broken jar and put it in the water. Freize, do you think this is it? The creature of their making?'

'I've thought that,' he conceded.

She looked horrified. 'You think that it was the little creature in the glass vessel, that was as small as a lizard?'

He nodded, his face grim.

'But when we released it into the canal it was the size of a baby.'

'I know.'

'But now you think it is the size of a child?'

'Yes.'

'So it is growing quickly, impossibly so?'

He nodded.

'And, if it kept up with the horses, it is impossibly fast?'

Freize looked miserable.

'I thought it followed me in the water,' she said very quietly. 'I thought it kept up with a rowing boat, in the canal at Venice.'

'And now it keeps up with us on horseback,' Freize said. 'Day after day of travel.'

She was very pale. 'Have you told Luca about it?'

'No,' he admitted finally. 'Because I wasn't sure that I had anything to tell him. I thought perhaps I was imagining it. I hoped I was being a fool – jumping at shadows. Frightening myself with mysteries. I thought I'd turn a blind eye and it would just go away. But now you've seen it too.'

'I didn't really see it here. I only heard something.'

'At any rate, it's a real thing.'

Typically, Ishraq faced her fear. 'So what is it? Is it the lizard, grown to a child?'

'I've wondered about that,' Freize remarked. 'But then I thought of something else.'

'What? What do you mean, Freize? Are you talking in riddles now?'

'Never mind what it is. That's not really the question. The question is: why is it following us? If this is a mysterious Being, once as tiny as a lizard, now the size of a human child, why is it coming after us like a stray dog?'

Ishraq came a little closer and put her hand gently on

26

his solid chest. She could feel the rapid beating of his heart through the thin linen of his shirt, and knew that he was sharing her own superstitious dread. 'What do you think it wants of us?' she asked him, knowing he had no answers. 'And when will it turn and face us, and ask?'

~

They rode all day, following the old Roman road which ran due north, through little fields of wheat and rye, past gardens growing vegetables and fruit. Sometimes they left the road for a shortcut that a villager showed them, taking tracks that were little more than packmen's trails and drover routes, hard-beaten, single-file paths. There were a few dirty little farmhouses along the way, with their unglazed windows shuttered and their doors bolted.

They climbed higher and higher into woods that were vaultingly high and still at midday, not even birds singing in the green shade. There were no inns when they left the old road, so they were glad to stop at noon under the shade of the thick trees and eat the magnificent meal that Freize unpacked from the saddlebags and drink the acidic light wine.

It was late in the afternoon of the second day as their road wound down out of the hills towards a great expanse of river as wide as a smoothly moving lake – the Danube – and on the other side a handsome, bustling, stone-built quayside with a town wall and a gate. Without needing to say a word, the group changed the order of their little cavalcade: the women dropped back to ride together a little behind the men, their hoods pulled over their heads, completely hiding their hair, their eyes lowered to the ground, the very picture of obedient female docility. The ferryman came out of his house on their side and waved to acknowledge their progress, as they rode towards him.

'You wanting to go over to Mauthausen?' He nodded at the town on the opposite bank.

'Yes,' Freize said, getting down from his horse and pulling out his purse to pay the fee.

'You may not want to go,' the man warned them. 'They have a sickness, a dancing sickness.'

'A wise man would turn back here,' Freize agreed. He nodded to Luca to say that they had found the dancers and Luca swung down from his horse and stepped forward. 'How long have they been here?'

'Two days now,' the man said. 'Nothing seems to stop them. They got into town through the north gate and they'll have to leave that way, for I won't have them on my boat. They can't stop dancing; they'd overturn my boat on the water they're so mad. The gateman should never have let them in. They crept in quietly, that's their cunning. Now they dance round and around the square and who's going to have to pay to take them away? Us townsmen, that's who.'

'We have to cross,' Luca confirmed shortly.

Freize held the horses as the rest of the party dismounted. The ferry was a broad, flat-bottomed barge hooked at stern and prow onto a strong rope that looped across the river, mounted on great posts at each end. Freize led one horse after another on board and tied them to the hitching points in the stalls. The rest of the party came up the gangplank and the ferryman cast off.

The swift current of the river caught them and pulled

them in a looping course downstream. Luca, Freize, Brother Peter and the ferryman had to pull the craft along by going hand over hand on the rope which swung high above their heads, until they crossed the river to bump against the quay of the town.

Moored next to the ferry stage were barges from upstream and those that were beating their way back against the current, from Vienna, further east. The quayside was busy with ships' masters paying the toll to the custom house, and people loading and unloading goods, but every man was working in silence, each casting a glance over his shoulder towards the closed gate into the town. Everyone was hurried and anxious: there was no cheerful banter, no whistling, no songs to keep the time as a gang hauled on a pulley rope to unload a salt barge. It was as if there were plague in the town. All the bargees were in a hurry to leave, the toll collectors going through the cargo as fast as they could, and everyone waiting for the sound of an irresistible jig.

The big wooden gates of the town were closed, but, as the travellers' horses were unloaded, the quayside gateman opened one side to let them through. Everyone stopped work to watch them go into the town; Freize made a grimace at Luca: 'Seems like no one wants to go into the town but us,' he said.

'Of course,' Luca replied. 'But we have work to do here.'

'I know, I know,' said Freize unhappily, taking the reins of his horse, Rufino, and leading him through the gateway, followed by the others.

Inside the gate it looked like a normal, small, prosperous town. The streets were cobbled with big setts of local granite, running uphill to a central square where a stone obelisk in the centre served as a waymark, and the grand houses of the town were set square on three sides with the steps to a church with an old chapel behind it on the fourth side.

'Is there a good inn in this town?' Freize shouted at a man leading a cow before them to the square, his head down. 'Somewhere with an honest alewife, decent wine, and a good cook in the kitchen?'

'Not really,' the man said pessimistically. 'I wouldn't say she was a good cook. But you can try the Red Fish. In the market square, on your right.'

Freize nodded gloomily, as if this were just what he had expected. He led his horse up the cobbled street to the central square, where a sheaf of wheat hanging from a balcony showed that a dark doorway was the entrance to the bakery, and next door a drying bough of old holly was the sign for an inn. The others followed him.

It was obvious that things were badly wrong. The doors of the church which faced the square stood wide open and the travellers saw a family struggle with an elderly grey-haired man who was clawing his way out of the door as his son tried to drag him back inside the sacred space. In the square outside, a fiddler in a bright, tattered coat of motley colours was turning the pegs on a tuneless fiddle and nearly two dozen people were hopping and skipping from one foot to another. Some of them were dressed in their finest clothes, as if going to a harvest dance which had dragged on too long; some of them were in tatters, as if they had ripped their clothes dancing through brambles or pulling away from people trying to hold them back.

30

To Luca's dismay, he saw the distinctive headdresses and flying ribbons of other villages and towns, from far away, and guessed that the dancers were travelling from town to town, gathering numbers as they went. Some of them must have danced for days.

'What's going on here?' Freize asked the cow-herder, who was hurrying away, pulling his cow with a halter around her neck.

'They've run mad,' the man said solemnly. 'Started last Sunday, right after Vespers. Some woman came into town, chased by one of the woodcutters. As he was taking her to the priest, another woman came out of the church and just lifted her skirt clear of her boots and started to dance, then another joined her, and then half a dozen of them came in from the north with the fiddler and now they can't make them stop. Then the drummer gave them a beat, where's it going to end?'

'Whoa!' Freize shouted as a woman danced past, caught him by the hand and tried to pull him away. Freize took tight hold of Rufino's mane. 'Keep me steady!' he said in an undertone to the horse. 'You must excuse me, I don't dance,' he said politely to the woman.

Immediately, the cow-herder crossed himself, tugged at the halter and disappeared down the cobbled lanes to his house, hurrying to get away.

'I don't think she can hear you,' Luca said, fascinated, as the woman circled Freize, her handsome face set in a grimace of a smile, her eyes open but quite blind, pulling at his hand, at his collar, at the hem of his coat.

Freize gently fended her off, murmuring: 'No, Mistress, I really can't. I don't dance, ever. Forgive me.'

31

The woman seemed sightless, the pupils of her eyes so wide that it looked as if she had no eyes at all, just bottomless depths of blackness. Her face was stiff with a rigid, toothy smile and dried saliva was shiny on her cheek. She held Freize's hand and her feet kept moving, dancing on the spot as she tugged at him to follow her.

'I can't,' Freize said desperately, embracing his horse around its strong neck. 'I'm not the dancing kind.'

She was deaf to his words; all she could hear was the thud of the drum from the far side of the square. She jigged in time to the music, and then, to Freize's horror, the others came to join her, dancing in a line towards him, linking hand in hand in one of the old country dances, going one way with a kick, and then dancing back again, but always making progress, closer and closer to him. He looked at Luca.

'Sparrow,' he said. 'Save me. God knows what they want with me. But you know I am not the man for dancing. And this lady seems to have taken a mortal fancy to me.'

Luca led his own horse closer to Rufino so that he could walk alongside Freize. He put his arm around Freize's shoulders and gave him a hard shake. 'Come on,' he said. 'Let's get to the inn. Just ignore them. Keep hold of your horse. Don't let them grab you. Come on.'

Luca moved on, keeping a firm grip on Freize as the strange woman danced in front of them. Ishraq and Isolde put their horses shoulder to shoulder and walked before them, holding each other's hand. Brother Peter brought up the rear, his face grave, muttering a prayer, one hand holding his horse's reins, the other clenching his wooden crucifix.

The woman fell back to let the young men go as they reached the stable doors of the inn; but as the girls walked past her she grinned, a horrid grimace. 'Come and dance!' she said in a voice which croaked with exhaustion, so that it sounded like a curse. 'Come and dance, pretty girls! What girl doesn't love a dance?'

Both young women shrank back, and pulled their horses onward as the woman jigged beside them, and now once again she was joined by the other dancers, whirling around and waving their scraps of cloth, one of them rattling a gourd in time with the drum, someone tunelessly singing a dancing song. 'Come on! Come on! Come away!'

Luca ploughed forward, keeping his hand on Freize as the big stable gate swung open at their approach. The little party almost fell into the inn yard and the stable gate was banged shut and barred behind them.

'God save me,' Brother Peter said, crossing himself. He looked from the shaken young women to Freize's expression of petrified horror. 'God save all of us.'

'The town has run mad,' an older woman observed from the doorway of the inn. 'I take it you won't be staying.'

'We will be staying,' Luca declared, hiding his own shock. 'I am an Inquirer, sent by the Holy Father himself. I have come to discover what is happening here and, if I can, return the dancers to their normal lives, to restore them to Christian godly ways.'

'You'd much better leave,' the landlady declared. 'I'm warning you. First one then another catches the madness and goes off. You don't want the young ladies to run away dancing.'

33

'We won't,' Isolde said, but she was badly shaken. 'I would never go with such people. I would hate to dance like that. They looked as if they were ready to fall down in the streets from exhaustion.'

'They are,' the woman said, her voice harsh. 'And pull everyone else down with them.'

'We'll take rooms for tonight,' Luca said. 'And stable the horses. I have to know what is happening here. If God is willing, we might be able to learn all that we need to know and leave tomorrow.'

Freize suddenly recovered his wits. 'I'll see to the horses,' he said. 'But if you could do all the study you need, as fast as you can, so we can be away at dawn tomorrow, I would be a happy man. The faster your inquiry, the less likely one of us will catch this sickness. You know, she had tight hold of me, and was pulling me away!'

'I know,' Luca said grimly. 'For I had tight hold of you on the other side, and I was pulling you back.'

~

Luca made sure that the young women were sharing a room at the back of the house, overlooking a little herb garden and orchard with the stable yard beyond so they could not hear the beat of the drum in the town square. When they came down to join the men in the dining room at the front of the inn, and cracked open the shutters, they could see the dancers going continually round and round the square, dancing all the afternoon with their weary, shuffling stride, as if they could never stop. Only when the sun went down did they collapse onto the cobbles and onto the doorsteps of the houses, and moan for the pain in their feet and their exhaustion. One woman, in the bright clothes of one of the mountain regions, fainted, and her dance partner laid her on the stones and left her for dead, as if he had forgotten her.

Luca looked up from the papers that the visiting Inquirer had left with him. 'Nobody knows for sure what causes the dancing,' he said. 'In the south, they think it is the bite of the tarantula spider and they call the dance the Tarantella. But in other places it just seems to start and to stop without warning or reason.'

'We should ask the people why they have chosen to dance,' Brother Peter said.

'It's got a lot quieter now. We'll go and talk with them,' Luca said. He turned to Isolde and Ishraq. 'Please stay in this room and don't go out.'

Isolde nodded, and not even Ishraq insisted on her right to freedom. 'Will you take Freize with you?' she asked. 'Is it safe for him?'

'I'd like him with me,' Luca decided. 'But only if he is willing to come.'

'I'll come too,' Brother Peter volunteered. 'You may need me.'

Luca hesitated. 'I'd rather have you three in here, watching for us,' he said. 'If we get into any difficulty you can come and pull us away.'

Ishraq nodded. 'If you think you are going to dance raise your right hand and we'll come for you.'

Brother Peter took one look at the square, where only a couple were still on their feet, circling slowly, slumped with exhaustion in each other's arms. 'Very well,' he said. 'The dancers look as if they are resting, but I suppose they

35

could start again at any moment. You take care of yourself, Inquirer, and I will watch you from here. Don't step out of the square; don't go away from where I can see you from this window. And don't let them lay hold of you.'

Cautiously, Luca and Freize undid the bolts of the front door. The landlady stood behind them, ready to slam the door and bolt it again.

'I won't have them in the house,' she whispered. 'I'll serve them ale through the window and let them drop the money into a cup of vinegar. Same as when the plague comes through the valley. But I won't let them so much as touch me. If they take hold of you, they dance you away and you can't ever get back. Some ideas are like a plague. You must never entertain them.'

'Make sure that you let us in the moment that we knock,' Freize reminded her.

'I will,' she promised. 'But take my warning: and don't go out at all.' She turned to Freize. 'You especially. Now that they've laid hold of you once, they'll be looking out for you again. They'll want to claim you for their own. They'll think you are a dancer like them, one of theirs.'

'Indispensable. I have to go with my master – I am indispensable,' Freize explained, his face pale and frightened as he followed Luca into the quiet square.

~

The dancers were resting wherever they had fallen when the last dance had ended, some of them sprawled on the steps of houses, some leaning against the shutters of the closed shops at the edge of the square; others, too tired to move, slumped in little groups on the cobbles of the main

36

square, one or two leaning against the cool, worn stone of the old obelisk at the very centre of the town. Luca approached them and then knelt down beside one middle-aged woman who seemed to be all alone, the sole of her shoe flapping on her foot, her grey wool gown tattered at the hem.

'God bless you, Goodwife,' he said.

She opened her dazed eyes. 'And you.'

'You look weary.'

'I am near dead with exhaustion. Do you have something to drink?'

Luca nodded to Freize who pulled a leather flask of small ale from his belt and handed it over reluctantly. The woman took a sip and passed it back. Freize wiped the rim carefully and corked it again.

'Are you hungry?' Luca asked her.

She shook her head and lay back on the ground, cupped her hands under her face, rolled on her side, and appeared to go to sleep.

'Why are you doing this?' Luca persevered. 'Why this dancing?'

'I need to sleep now. We'll wake and dance again in a little while. I don't have the strength now – I am ready to die for tiredness. Let me sleep, boy.'

'Then stop dancing,' Luca suggested. 'I will take you into the inn and you can sleep in a bed. Think of that! A good dinner and a quiet night's rest!'

She looked at him over her hunched shoulder. 'I can't stop. I'm called to it. Aren't you?'

'No. Who called you? One of the other dancers? Did they lay hold of you?'

'Yes. Once they touched me, I was lost. But it was I who first ran after them. I wanted to dance and never stop till I died. And now, it seems, that's what I'm doing.'

'Don't you have a home?'

She shrugged. 'If you'd call it that. A young gentleman like you wouldn't stable your horse there; it's too poor for you. But it was good enough for me for years. Long, terrible years. I had a hungry childhood and miserable years growing up. Then my children left me and I have no help in my work and no dream of the future.'

'Can't you go back home? Don't you want to be with your family?'

She laughed as if he had made a merry jest. 'I'd rather dance to my death than go back there,' she said flatly.

'And all the others? Do they feel the same?'

'How would I know?' she said indifferently. 'Why would I care? I don't ask them, and they don't tell me. We don't talk – we just dance. I won't talk any more to you.' She wrapped her tattered cloak a little closer around her and closed her eyes.

Luca stood up and looked at Freize, who shrugged. The two of them walked to the side of the square where a man seemed to be pleading with his daughter to come away, while the dancers were resting. He had hold of her hands and was trying to pull her to her feet while she dug in her heels to keep her seat on the cold stones. He towered over her, a big brute of a man, and she was like the bent stem of a stubborn weed, resisting him.

'I won't go,' they heard her say.

'But your mother orders you to come, and your brothers want you home.'

'I can't stop dancing,' she said impatiently. 'You've seen me. I can't stop.'

'But you've stopped now.' Freize paused to reason with her. 'Why don't you try walking home now, while nobody is dancing and the fiddle is quiet? Your father here will help you. I'll help you. I'll set you on your road. We'll walk either side of you and keep you going.'

'I had to stop,' she said. 'I couldn't dance another step. I couldn't do anything but sit. But, as soon as I am rested, I'll start again.'

'Don't you want to stop?' Luca asked her incredulously.

'Sir, I swear she does, in her heart,' her father interrupted. 'She has everything to live for. A young man to marry, her work to do – we can't run the farm without her. And yet up she gets one morning and dances round the house, does nothing, though the cows need milking and the dairy needs cleaning and the eggs have to be fetched and the ox is lame so she has to pull the plough. But she'll do none of this. Dances all the day and half the night and then climbs out of the window and runs after the dancers.'

'She ran after them? They didn't take her? She sought them out? Why?'

The girl raised her head, her eyes were quite blank. 'Because I want to dance up a whirlwind,' she said. 'I don't care what it costs.'

The father shrugged his shoulders. 'She's run mad,' was his only answer. 'She was always a fool and now she has run mad.'

'Did you know of the dancers before you started dancing?' Luca asked the girl directly.

'The priest preached a sermon against them the very

39

day before!' the man exclaimed furiously. 'Said that they were a crew of sturdy beggars with runaway maids and worthless lads, led by a fiddler who tempted them into sin, coming our way, and that everyone was to shutter their windows and stop up their ears. Warned us that these were fools who did nothing but dance and drink while we have no time for anything but work. Every sensible person in the town takes the warning and closes their doors. But my foolish daughter doesn't do as she's told. Oh no! She knows better! She leans out of the window, looking for them, and, after they've gone by, up she gets and starts dancing. Runs after them, dancing all the way. Then I have to come chasing after them to find her here, in the middle of the village, dancing like a madwoman where everyone can see her, to my shame and hers. When I get her home, I shall beat her to within an inch of her life. I'll break her legs – that'll slow her down.'

Freize looked shocked. 'But, you old fool, why would she go home with you if she knows you're going to beat her?'

Luca knelt on the cobbles beside the girl. 'Would you stop dancing if you were not beaten at home?' he asked. 'If your life was easier?'

She raised her head and he could see that she was thin and tired, with a dark bruise fading from one eye as if someone had taken a fist to her about a week ago. 'I'll never stop dancing,' she said quietly. 'And I've always been beaten at home.'

'How can you do it?' Freize asked the man. 'How can you raise your hand to your own child? How can you use a little lass like this to pull a plough?'

The man shrugged at Freize's softness of heart. 'If I have

40

no ox, how else am I going to plough? If she is disobedient, she must be beaten. How else will she learn?'

Freize hesitated, as if he would speak with the girl again, but then as Luca moved away he followed him to a group of dancers whose ragged clothes and worn shoes showed that they had been dancing on the road for weeks. One of them, a young man, looked up from the stone step as Luca came towards him.

'Will you give us alms, sir?' he asked. 'We have no money for food.'

'Why don't you work for money?' Luca asked him.

'We can't work, we can only dance,' the man said. 'If you give us money, we'll dance away to the next village and leave you in peace.'

'Does every village pay you to leave?'

He laughed shortly. 'Of course – they're afraid of us. They're afraid that their children will run away with us.'

'Then is dancing your work? Do you do it for money? Are you really beggars?'

'No, truly we are dancers. I can't stop myself. I've had the priest drag me into the church and pour the holy water on my head, but I just danced down the aisle and out of the door. Then he saw there was nothing to do but get rid of me, out of his parish. He gave me some food and made me promise that I would go away and take the dancers with me. The people here will feed us and send us on our way, if not today then tomorrow. We're not wanted anywhere. They'll pay us to go. Won't you pay us to leave now?'

Luca shook his head. 'I want to know why you started dancing.'

The dancer rose, wincing at the pain of his blistered feet.

'If I lay my hands on you, you'll dance too,' he said. 'Or would you rather give me some money for food?'

Freize drew on all his stubborn courage and stepped forward. 'This is an Inquirer of the Order of Darkness reporting to the Holy Father himself,' he said quietly. 'You won't touch him, and he won't give you money.'

Mockingly, the youth stretched out his hand to the very centre of Luca's chest. He pointed his finger but did not touch Luca's thick woollen robe. 'If I touch him, he'll start dancing and not be able to stop,' he said. 'And you can report that to the Holy Father, with my compliments.'

Luca looked at him steadily, but did not step back. 'Don't threaten me,' he said gently, 'for I mean you no harm. I want to know what is making you and all these people dance, and if you can be cured and go back to your lives. I am here to help you if I can. Actually, I am ordered to help you if I can.'

The young man shrugged and abruptly sat down again. 'Nobody can help us; we're cursed,' he said. 'And if I touch you, the curse will fall on you.'

Luca was about to ask another question when a tentative patter on the drum made all the people around the square stir and look up.

'Better get inside,' Freize said nervously. 'Before they start up again.'

'Are you afraid that we will start dancing?' Luca asked him. 'Because someone clatters on a drum and scrapes a fiddle?'

'I don't know,' Freize said. 'And I don't want to find out. Come on, Sparrow. There's no point risking ourselves out here if they're starting again.'

Luca nodded, and turned towards the inn, when out of nowhere, a fiddler sprang up and blocked their way. He was a small figure in a multicoloured, ragged jacket, his fiddle under his chin, his bow laid on the strings. His gleaming smile was bright as he cocked a tattered hat and threw back his black cloak, drawing his bow across the strings with a warning wail of sound.

'Masters,' he said ingratiatingly. 'I can play you a pretty tune.'

'Come on!' Freize said, laying hold of Luca's arm and pulling him away, moving round the fiddler towards the inn door.

They were too late. The drum started to sound, urgent and impelling, a rapid staccato rhythm, and the fiddler burst into a tune so lively and so exciting that every exhausted dancer on the square sprang up, and started to whirl around.

'Quickly!' Freize yelled, truly frightened, as he felt his own toes tapping to the insistent beat and the tune seemed to enter his head as if he would hear it for the rest of his life. 'Come on!'

Luca and Freize linked arms to keep hold of each other and headed for the inn door. But now, gathered in a moment to the wild whirl of sound, there was a mass of dancers, in a line, forming a chain between them and the door, and in a second, one of them had got Luca by the hands and Freize by the waist and was spinning them off into a dance. Luca twisted his hands away and tried to push his way towards the inn while Freize thrust his dancing partner away from him and dived through the crowd towards Luca.

The inn door burst open and Isolde came out like a fighter from the sallyport of a castle, her head down, her hands over her ears, a long rope tied around her waist, Ishraq uncoiling it to let her sprint through the crowd towards Luca. Playfully, the dancers pulled on it, tossing her to one side and another, but still Isolde fought her way through them, struggling to get to Luca's side.

Freize and Luca could not keep themselves from being swept into the pattern of the dance. One eager grabbing hand after another snatched at them, held them, turned them until they were trapped in a circle of jostling, beaming dancers; but they grabbed onto each other's shoulders and tried to force their way towards Isolde as she battled towards them. Luca, feeling his feet wander underneath him, saw the blank brightness of the dancers' eyes and the sharp, predatory smiles, and felt that he was being absorbed by the music, by the beat of the dance, and by his own rising desire to join in. It was like being washed over and rolled around by the currents of a mighty river and he gripped Freize like a thrown rope as he felt himself being tugged away.

'Freize! I'm going!'

Freize grabbed hold of his friend, hauled him towards Isolde and the inn and suddenly yelled in his face: 'How many acres in a field five hundred feet long and seven hundred feet wide?'

'What?' Luca demanded, and even the dancers' feet checked as they turned and looked at Freize as they heard his extraordinary question.

'How many acres in a field five hundred feet long and seven hundred feet wide?' he shouted. 'In the new numbers.'

Luca blinked and as his mind went to the problem his feet stood still. 'Eight point zero three,' he said.

'Get Isolde!' Freize yelled and Luca, suddenly clear-headed, stretched his hands towards the girl and she grabbed him with all her strength. With Freize pushing him from behind, and Ishraq and Brother Peter heaving on the rope, they stumbled towards the door of the inn, the landlady flung it open for just a moment, and the three of them fell into the hall.

Isolde and Ishraq slammed the door and put their backs to it as Brother Peter shot the big bolt into place.

'The sacred Lord save me, I was moments from being lost,' Luca said, his face white, his breath coming fast. 'God bless you, Freize; if you hadn't held me, I would be out there now, dancing in a ring.'

Freize rubbed his sweating face with his linen shirt. 'God save us both,' he said. 'I have never known such a thing in my life. It is as if you lose your own will, you forget yourself.'

They could hear the beat of the drum and the insistent swirl of the tune through the closed door. Freize found his feet tapping to the music and got hold of Luca's arm. 'Let's get into the back room,' he said, 'away from the sound of that damned drum.'

Isolde got hold of Luca's other arm and together they stumbled into the public room that overlooked the stable yard and smelled of old ale and horse dung. A couple of old men looked up from their horn cups as the little party came in, then turned away.

'So education is no safeguard?' Isolde asked breathlessly.

'And being a man doesn't save you?' Ishraq prompted.

Luca, panting, shook his head. 'It goes past that,' he said. 'It goes past your mind and your pride, straight to your feet. Your thoughts have nothing to do with it. It's like you yourself have nothing to do with it. It's like hearing a song in your ear; you might not know the words, but you can't help yourself: it just gets into your ear and you sing it and it comes out in your voice, without your mind ever consenting. It's like being possessed.'

He turned to Freize. 'But what did you ask me? About the acreage of a field? Why ever did you ask me that?'

'I wanted you thinking like you always do,' Freize said. 'I wanted you in your right mind, your thinking mind, your usual track. I didn't even know if you would hear me; you were gone. But I thought if you made a calculation ...'

'Why, what did you ask him?' Ishraq demanded.

'I asked him the acreage of a field five hundred feet by seven hundred feet,' Freize said.

A slow grin spread across Luca's face. 'But why those numbers?'

'It's my father's field,' Freize said. 'We were hoping to sell it once. But nobody knew how big it was. We knew the length of the hedges, because we could pace them. But not how much land lay between them.'

Ishraq put her head on one side. 'If you multiply the length of the two hedges, you get the field area in square feet, and then you just have to know how many square feet in an acre.'

Freize looked at her with warm respect. 'There you go,' he said. 'That's the Moorish learning for you. But that's the other thing we didn't know.'

She laughed. 'What other thing?'

'How many – what did you call them? – square feet to an acre. Even if we could have worked out the paces, we still didn't know that.'

Luca laughed reluctantly, recovering from his fear. 'It's 43,560,' he said. 'It's 43,560 square feet to an acre, that's why you divide all your square feet by that number to get your acreage.'

'Well, I never knew that,' Isolde admitted. 'And I was educated to be a lord over great acres of land. I thought an acre was a team's plough day; I didn't realise you could measure it in feet. Freize is right, it's Moorish learning. We talk about acres at Lucretili, but it's just a guess; we only know that a farm is a hundred acres or a vineyard is twenty acres because everyone has always said so. Nobody actually measures it. And, of course, there is no need. Hardly anyone buys or sells land and, when they do, they know the land itself so they don't need the measurements. They just say the name of the field.'

Freize nodded. 'We were going to sell it to a stranger,' he said. 'To anyone else we would have just said we were selling the Green Field, next to the stream. Everyone knew what it was like. But he wanted to know how big it was.'

'The Greeks were the first to calculate it,' Ishraq told them. 'And then the skill was lost until the Arab philosophers translated their work. That's when I learned it, at the Moors' university in Spain. Where did you learn it, Luca?'

'I was taught how to calculate as part of my training in the Order of Darkness,' he said shortly. 'They kept me for months and taught me many things.'

'But what was it like outside?' Brother Peter interrupted. 'What did you think of the crowd, Inquirer? Could they be restored by setting them riddles, like Freize did to you? Is it a question of distracting them from their dancing? What shall we report?' He had his little writing desk ready, the flap open, the ink unstoppered. He waited until Luca and the others sat down beside him at the taproom table, and then drew a page towards him and dipped the nib of his quill. 'Tell me at once, while it is fresh in your minds. Did it look like a demonic possession?'

'I don't know,' Luca replied slowly. 'I suppose it must be; I don't know what to answer. Everyone is poor and desperate and everyone spoke of terrible homes; but they don't seem to have been poisoned, or bitten by a spider or anything that has made them run mad.' He looked at Freize. 'I didn't see any sign of insect bites on anyone? Nobody mentioned bites, not even a mad dog.'

Freize shook his head.

'They don't tell any one single story,' Luca went on. 'I spoke to three of them – their circumstances were all different, except for their day-to-day misery and their desire to dance. They seem not to care if they die dancing.'

'The first woman actually said that was what she wanted,' Freize pointed out. 'The lass said she wanted to dance up a whirlwind.'

'It's as if they are in a trance,' Luca said thoughtfully. 'Reminded me of the abbey.'

'Belladonna?' Isolde asked. 'But how would all of them eat the same poisoned herbs? They all come from different villages.'

'Something in the water perhaps?' Luca was puzzling away. 'If they come from villages all along the river? But, in that case, why not more people? Why not everyone?'

'Do they show any marks?' Brother Peter was writing rapidly. 'Marks of possession?'

Ishraq raised her eyebrows. 'You seem determined to find possession by demons. You believe in such a thing?'

'So would you if you had seen the things that I have seen,' Brother Peter said steadily. 'I have seen men possessed and I have seen demons exorcised. Just because you have not witnessed something does not mean that it has never happened.'

'Of course,' Isolde agreed. 'But equally it might not be there.'

'There were no marks,' Luca said thoughtfully. 'At least, I didn't see anything. Did you, Freize?'

'No signs in common at all except that they are all so tired they can hardly stand,' Freize pointed out. 'And their eyes are like fish.'

Brother Peter hesitated, his pen poised. He sighed at Freize who so often turned a phrase that was far from scholarly. 'Eyes like fish? What do you mean by that?'

'Oh no, he's right,' Luca said. 'Their eyes are dead: they have no intelligence or interest or sparkle.' Without being aware of his gaze, he nodded towards Ishraq's intent, thoughtful face. 'With some people, you can almost see what they are thinking by their eyes; you can almost see their mind working as their eyes gleam and darken when the thoughts cross them. But all the dancers' eyes are dead. Freize is right. They are people with eyes like fish.'

'You were like that, little Sparrow,' Freize confirmed.

'Your eyes went blank. Until I asked you to solve a problem, and then you came back to me.'

One of the old men in the corner, who had been listening to this, let out a crack of laughter. 'You're right, young'un!' he said disrespectfully to Luca. 'That's how they look the moment before they go. I lost my wife and my son in one afternoon when the dancers last came, and they looked at me with as much interest or love as if they were a pair of carp from the pond with string through their gills.'

'This is an Inquirer, from the Holy Father himself,' Freize corrected him. 'You call him "sir".'

'Call him what you like, makes no difference to me.' The old man was not at all rebuffed. 'But he has the right of it. You can tell the Pope that. You can tell him that from me.'

'Let him speak as he wants,' Luca prompted Freize, who was inclined to argue that the proper respect be shown to his master.

'Did your wife and son leave with these dancers who are in the town now? The same people?' Brother Peter asked the old man.

'No, with another lot,' he said. 'A different lot. They came through three years ago, just the same. They stayed two or three days and then we drove them out of town. But they took my son with them, the brightest boy in the town – everyone loved him. I was going to give him to the church for a clerk, he was so clever and able. And I heard later that he danced till his feet bled, the blisters went bad, and he took sick, and then there was no more dancing for him. They laid him on the floor of the church and bid him be at peace, but still he writhed about and waved his arms until he died.

50

'So they took him for nothing. I should think that they are the Devil's own; I should think they are possessed. You should tell the Holy Father that he must stop them. They steal our young men and women and dance them to death. The Holy Father should stop them.'

'Why do you think they dance?' Luca demanded.

The man shrugged. 'It's as if they all go mad for it, all at once. Why does anyone do anything foolish? Why do storks all come in springtime? They all act together without thinking.'

'Does Lord Vargarten do nothing to stop it?' Luca asked.

'He'd move them on if he knew they were here,' the old man said. 'But no one has dared to leave their house and go up to the castle to tell him. We've bolted ourselves into our homes and we just run from one house to another when the dancers go quiet or fall asleep. You should go and tell the lord that they are here again, frightening everyone, stealing children. You go and tell him if you're brave enough to cross the square and take the road to his castle. If the Pope ordered you to come here then God will keep you safe. Go and tell Lord Vargarten that the dancers are here again and we need his help. He should drive them out like the vermin they are.'

'Where is the lord's castle?'

'Just ten miles up the track going north. You can't miss it. Straight out of the north gate.'

Luca looked at Brother Peter. 'I'll go,' he said. 'I'll wait till the dancers are asleep tonight and then I'll set off before it's light.'

'I'll come with you,' Brother Peter said. 'We'll go to the

castle and see if he is going to move them on, or what he intends. I can send this report to Rome with one of his men. I take it that the dancers don't respond to prayer?'

'One of the men said that he had been taken right into the church and up to the altar and still danced away,' Luca said, as Brother Peter made notes. 'He said he had holy water actually on his head and yet kept on dancing. This is a stubborn sin. It's like a madness, but a madness that passes from one to another. A plague that you catch the moment you are touched.'

'I'll come with you too,' Freize said. 'We'll need to ride out of the stable gate and get through the square so quickly that they can't stop us. We'll do that better all three of us at once. Rufino can lead. We'll need to charge.'

'Will you be all right on your own?' Luca turned to Isolde and Ishraq. 'If we leave early in the morning, before sunrise, and get back before midday?'

'Of course we will.' Ishraq spoke for them both.

'Keep to your bedroom with your door locked. We won't be long.'

'We'll be safe,' Isolde assured him.

Ishraq nodded. 'I'll lock our door and guard it. And our bedroom faces the herb garden and orchard. We can't even hear the music when we're in there.'

'Block your ears if you have to,' Freize advised her. 'When you hear the drum start, it's the oddest of things. You just want to get up and dance. You think that no harm could come of it, and it's what you want to do. It feels like a good idea, like a merry thought. It feels like it is your own idea, nothing to do with all of them.'

'I don't think it's a merry thought,' Isolde said. 'I think

it's horrifying. It doesn't make me want to dance, it makes me want to hide under my pillow.'

'Keep your door locked till we come back,' Luca commanded. 'And we will be as quick as we can.' He glanced at Isolde and spoke as if to her alone: 'I will be as quick as I can,' he promised. 'I will not fail you.'

~

Before dawn, while a rain-hazy moon was setting, Luca woke his two companions. Despite the cold and his unease, he could not help but laugh when he saw Freize, who had forced two scraps of linen into his ears and tied up his head with a rag, looking like a man with toothache.

'They're not stirring yet,' Luca pointed out, cracking open one of the shutters of the inn's front windows and looking out at the quiet square and the exhausted dancers huddled in doorways. 'I think you're overprotected.'

'I'm taking no chances,' Freize said as he went out of the back door, carrying the horses' tack. He crossed the yard, the wet cobbles gleaming in the pale light of the dawn sky, and went into the stables. Something at the back of the barn moved quietly. 'There now,' Freize said, as if to himself. 'You here in this troubled town? Following us? Be still. Be quiet. Go your way. No need to pay any attention to me, and no need to follow us, either, what with the world ending and us always going to the worst places.'

He squinted into the gloom at the back of the barn and thought he saw a pale child, perhaps a boy, shrink back and disappear.

'Go your way and God bless you,' Freize said quietly,

shaking his head. 'As if we didn't have enough to worry about without you, you poor little thing.'

He waited in case there was any response and then he said again into the silence: 'I don't know who you are, nor *what* you are, to tell the truth. And if you are following me for gratitude because it was me that saved you from the alchemists' jar then you need not trouble yourself. All I want from you is that you go. Go well, go safely, but go. We have troubles of our own, and I can't care for you or keep you. And – no offence – if I wanted a little pet, I would have one less clammy.'

He finished this address into the silence of the barn and then led the horses out into the yard as Luca and Brother Peter came from the inn, took their horses and mounted up. Luca glanced up to the girls' bedroom window just visible over the tops of the orchard trees. Isolde's white face was looking down at him. He waved a hand to her and was glad to see a reassuring nod from Ishraq who was standing at her shoulder. Their bedroom door was bolted and they could close the shutters on their window; he thought that they would be safe while he rode to the castle, summoned help, and came back.

Luca, Brother Peter and Freize lined up their horses at the back wall of the yard, almost as if they were starting a race – the horses alert, slightly spurred on, but held back, shifting under a tightened rein. The stable lad and the landlady were at the double gates, and at a nod from Luca they opened them wide and the three horses went out at an explosive canter, shoulder to shoulder, across the town square without drawing rein. A few of the dancers started up out of their sleep, shouting and calling them back, but the horses were gone before they could circle them. Freize, clinging to Rufino's mane and glancing back, saw that the gates to the inn had been slammed shut.

'Let's hope we come back with an armed guard,' he remarked to Brother Peter. 'Let's hope this lord keeps a strong household.'

Brother Peter nodded, and the three of them rode under the arched gateway of the town where the sleepless porter told them to hurry and bring back help, and took the winding road north towards the castle as the sky slowly lightened and the sun came up.

~

The castle sentries were not alert in the early morning: theirs was a country at peace and although there were armed robbers and highwaymen working the roads, preying on vulnerable travellers, they would never dare to challenge the castle or the villages under the control of the Lord Vargarten. Luca, Freize and Brother Peter were at the castle gates before anyone shouted a challenge from the battlements, and a sleepy guard of four men tumbled out of the guardroom, opened the sentry grille and called to them to halt.

Freize rode forward and explained who they were. At once, the guard stepped back and lifted the great beam to open the gate, which creaked open, and the captain led them into the castle courtyard.

It was a pretty castle, a round tower with the square bulk of the hall beside it, around it a scatter of houses like a small village, all enclosed inside the great walls. At the centre of the courtyard was a deep well, and around it was an orchard of apple and pear trees, with hens scratching about in the grass, a cow with a calf grazing, and, in the pen behind the cottage, a rooting pig. As Freize, Luca and Brother Peter dismounted, a boy came yawning from the stables and took the reins of their horses and led them away.

The double door at the top of a flight of stone steps opened and Lord Vargarten descended slowly in his furred nightrobe, his wife following him with a cape thrown over her nightgown and her hair loose under her hood.

'Strangers, you are welcome,' Lord Vargarten said, no welcome in his gruff tones. 'However early.'

He broke off to look at Luca, as handsome a young man as had ever been seen in this part of the world, his face as clear and regular as one of the new statues that they were all making in Italy, his dark hair shining.

'Thank you, we apologise for the early hour,' said Luca. 'But there is grave trouble in Mauthausen.'

Lord Vargarten looked beyond him to the solid strength of Freize and the quiet presence of Brother Peter. 'What's the matter? And who are you, anyway?'

Luca came to the foot of the steps, speaking quietly and urgently. 'There are dancers in your town; they are growing in numbers, and becoming unruly, and it's getting serious.'

'And you are?'

'I am an Inquirer appointed by the Holy Father to discover the reason and meaning of these troubled times. This is my clerk, Brother Peter, and my friend and servant, Freize.'

'General factotum,' Freize said, bowing particularly to Lady Vargarten.

Lord Vargarten came down the rest of the steps, gave

56

his hand to Luca, and nodded to Freize and Brother Peter. 'How many dancers are there?' he asked briskly.

'About thirty, but they are growing in number all the time. They are deliberately picking people to dance with them and seem to want to pass on the disease. They are quite irresistible. They're begging, and threatening.'

'You've seen them yourself?'

'They tried to take hold of me. It was hard for me to break free. I couldn't have done it if my friends had not recalled me and pulled me to safety. The dancers are a real danger to your town and your tenants.'

The lord nodded. 'We've had this sort of trouble before. What do you suggest?'

'Certainly, they should be moved on. They say they will go if they are given food or money. But I would like to try some sort of Mass, encourage them to pray, wrestle with their souls, try to get them to stop dancing. I want to know what makes them dance. I need your help to hold them still and quiet while we speak to them. The town wants them moved out.'

'You want to cure them? You think you can?' Lady Vargarten asked angrily. She came down the steps and stood behind her husband, her dark eyes on Luca, her pale cheeks flushed red.

'If possible. Certainly, I'd like to understand what is happening.'

She shook her head. 'They stop only when the Devil has left them for dead. They start when He enters their soul. Nothing can stand against Him when He dances with them. No one can resist Him. They are weak and He has claimed his own.'

'You think it is possession?' Brother Peter asked her.

'My wife lost her sister to the dancers,' Lord Vargarten explained. 'Last time they came through.'

'She was a child!' she exclaimed passionately. 'And a man arrived with a flute which played a tune that no child could resist. Every child in the village went running after him, dancing where he danced, and they never came home again. My little sister was among them. Should such people be treated gently, should they be prayed over? Or should they be torn apart and left for dead?'

'Where did he lead them?' Freize asked.

'They said that a mountain opened up and they danced away to a secret land that he had promised them. Who knows where they went? Who knows who took them, or why? What would a man want with a dozen children? At any rate, we never saw any of them again, and we could not trace them though we sent out searches in every direction.'

Brother Peter crossed himself.

'A Mass or an exorcism is a waste of time,' she said passionately to Luca. 'There's only one thing you can do with the dancers—'

Lord Vargarten made a little gesture with his hand as if to silence her.

'What is that, in your opinion, your ladyship?' Luca asked.

'Drown them,' she said shortly. 'If the Devil has care of His own, they will swim away and then you are free of them.'

'But if they are innocent, just driven by some sort of madness, then they will be drowned in a state of sin, and their souls will be on my conscience,' Luca pointed out.

She shrugged. 'Madmen like that don't deserve to live. Why would you care? You can confess and clean your conscience as if you were a hangman who has drowned a witch, but at least they will be dead and gone. They are not people; they are a pestilence.'

She spoke nothing but what most people believed. Luca, with his own thoughts about justice and compassion, looked into her hard, beautiful face and kept silent.

'They are vile,' she went on. 'They are not like us. People who are not like us should not come near us. They should not be allowed to come near us. They destroy everything. It is better for all of us if they are just . . .'

'Just what?' Brother Peter asked quietly.

'Neco.'

Neco: it was the old Latin word meaning to bully someone to death. She said it as if she would avoid the blunt word 'killed', as if *neco* were a legal ruling which would make the dancers of Mauthausen disappear, and all of Lord Vargarten's lands a better place. As if people could simply vanish – melting into smoke and leaving no trace, as if they could be wiped out of the towns, burned out of the landscape.

'I'd better come with you to the town,' the lord said to Luca. 'We can drive them out. I won't have them on my lands.'

'We'd do better to return them to their homes,' Brother Peter remarked. 'If we drive them on, they'll just go to another town and their numbers will grow.'

'I don't care as long as it's not my town,' Lord Vargarten said grimly.

'But we have to care,' Luca told him bluntly. 'We have to

do what we can to cure these people of this madness. We have to be responsible for them. They are men and women just as we are.'

'No, they're not,' the lady argued. 'Don't you understand? They are like Jews; they are like Egyptians; they are like the infidel or strangers from another country. They're like Ottomans, Muslims. They live apart from us, and are different from us; they are *not* men and women like we are. They are different. We need not treat them as if they were people like us. If they are different they are our enemy.'

Lord Vargarten summoned the captain of his guard with a gesture and sent the man running to the guardroom. The castle bell began to toll and from the towers set in the walls, from the little cottages, and from the main body of the castle, men emerged, some of them untidy and dirty, some of them snatching a piece of bread to eat as they ran, some of them smart and ready for duty. They went to the guardroom beside the stable yard and stumbled into order. The captain of the armoury started to issue pikes and swords and the men lined up to receive their weapons, strapping on their leather jackets.

'Will you eat and drink while we wait for them to get ready?' Lord Vargarten offered. 'They won't be long, but they'll have to saddle the horses and finish issuing weapons.'

'Thank you,' Luca said, as Freize brightened visibly at the thought of breakfast.

'This way.'

The three men followed the lord and lady up the steps and into the castle.

They found themselves at once in a great hall, two storeys high with carved stone openings between the roof trusses where birds flew in and out and swallows came twisting in, looking for nesting sites against the huge dark beams. In the centre of the hall was a circular stone fireplace, as massive as a campfire, the logs still warm from the night before. Sleeping on the stone-flagged floor were half a dozen deerhounds and they lifted their pointed heads and stirred their tails in the dried rushes scattered on the floor, as the lord and lady walked by.

Lord Vargarten snapped orders at a groom of the servery who went first to the buttery, a large cupboard at the head of the hall behind the great table, and brought out cups of small ale, and then jogged out of the hall door and down the steps and across the castle green to the bakery to bring back hot bread rolls in a basket.

A kitchen boy emerged from an inner doorway with a tray of meats, and the three men seated themselves at the top table and ate a good breakfast with their hosts. As soon as he had finished, Lord Vargarten went to fetch his padded jacket and his helmet and see that his horse was saddled, while his lady sat in her chair, high-backed and as grand as a throne, and watched Luca eat.

'Drive them away,' she said privately to him. 'While you have the chance. You drive them into the river and they can drown like the worthless dogs they are. You would drown a dog with rabies, wouldn't you? Drown them.'

Luca suddenly found his food tasteless, got up from the table, bowed to the lady and went out into the morning sunshine of the castle yard.

Back in the town, Isolde and Ishraq had ventured down to the taproom that looked out over the stable yard. Now and then, someone slipped in from the square, tipped his hat to them and said that the dancers were resting, the drum and the haunting fiddle were silent, that actually it was safe if the young women wanted to walk out. The shops were open during this period of quiet, the priest was in his church, the town was trying to behave as if it were not under siege from madness, as if it were an ordinary morning.

'I'd like to attend Mass,' Isolde said. 'The church is just across the square.'

'Better stay inside,' Ishraq advised.

'You do right to stay here, at the back of the building,' another man interrupted. 'No point in taking risks. Do you go out to take the air when the plague wind blows? Not if you have any sense.'

There was a tap at the front door; the landlady peered through the spyhole and made a pleased remark, then slid the heavy bolts. She opened the door and a pedlar came in, easing the pack off his back. 'Where's the market today?' he asked. 'I came to show my goods here and found not

62

a stall in place, and nobody on the quayside. No one will even open their front door. Where is everybody?'

'There can be no market while the dancers are making merry in our town square,' the landlady said crossly. 'And they buy nothing and sell nothing and just turn the heads of everyone who hears them. Here are these young ladies, not even walking out, for fear of dancing. What d'you have to sell? And what can I get you to drink? Will you take something to eat?'

'I'll have a glass of ale and some breakfast,' the man said. He was a small man, no taller than Isolde, deeply tanned by the sun. He had one earlobe pierced with a silver ring like a sailor and his dark hair was tied at the nape of his neck in a ponytail. His face was lined like a man who smiles all the time. He leaned his pack, bulging with goods, against the legs of the common table and pulled up a stool.

'And are you ladies trapped in here?' he asked Isolde and Ishraq with a sympathetic smile. 'Besieged by merriment?'

'I wouldn't call it merry,' Ishraq replied. 'They dance like people in a dream, like people in a nightmare, not like people having fun.'

'You may be right,' he said. 'I've seen it once before in Italy. A young man took up his flute and went dancing off, his family ran after him and everywhere he went more people joined him.'

'What happened to him?' Isolde asked.

'He danced till he died, poor lad,' the pedlar said. 'They said he had been bitten by a tarantula spider; they named his dance the Tarantella after the spider. God help them and save them from themselves. Sometimes people can't stop themselves, you know. Sometimes a girl hears a jig and has to dance away.'

The landlady put a big pewter mug of ale before him and he nodded to her to put the cost on the slate behind the serving table. 'And God save all of us,' he continued, taking a deep drink. 'Have you come far? D'you have far to go? Shall you dance onward?'

'From Venice,' Isolde said.

'Ah, then I shall not trouble you with my poor things,' he said. 'You will have seen the finest of jewellery and lace in Venice. You will not condescend to look at my treasure box.'

'There were many pretty things in the city, of course,' Isolde said. Then, as curiosity got the better of her, she asked: 'But what do you carry?'

'Oh, nothing fit for you,' he said firmly. 'Nothing for a lady such as yourself.'

The landlady put some freshly baked bread and some cheese before him as he turned to Ishraq. 'But I confess, I have some silver earrings with the darkest of sapphires that would be beautiful on you, Lady.'

Ishraq smiled. 'You won't find a good customer in me. I have no money, and if I did I would not spend it on earrings. But dark sapphires? What are they?'

'Black star sapphires,' he said, lingering over the words. 'True black.'

'I've never seen such things,' she remarked. 'Are they really obsidian, that you are calling sapphires to mislead foolish girls? Do you take me for a foolish girl?'

He took a bite of bread and a pull of his ale and shook his head. 'No, I swear it. Star sapphires because they make a star shape when they sparkle, and black as night. Try them. You know that only a true gemstone can cut glass? Well, you could write your name on the windowpane with these.' He plunged his hand into the pack and felt around the side. 'Here,' he said, bringing out a tiny leather purse. 'I'd never seen such a thing in my life before I came across these, but it is true.'

Isolde watched, fascinated, as Ishraq opened the drawstrings and tipped the earrings into her cupped palm. They were beautifully worked, each shaped like a long stem of silver with hanging flowers, and the bud of each flower was black – darkest black – but sparkling like a diamond.

'Oh!' Ishraq breathed.

'Oh, indeed,' the pedlar replied. 'Try it yourself. I won't touch them while I am eating, for fear of getting butter on them.'

Ishraq took one of the earrings and drew a swift line on the windowpane. 'See?' he challenged her. 'Only a true gem will cut glass. They are black sapphires, and they could have been made for you.'

Ishraq hesitated, her eyes on the black stones.

'Mined for you and made for you,' he repeated. 'Dug for you from mines far away, in West Africa, brought for you by camel train to the Moors. Cut for you, and set by them into silver. You're the first woman I have showed them to, because nobody else could wear them. But they are the very colour of your eyes. They are yours. You should have them. Nobody but you should have them. Just try them on.'

'I'll put them in for you,' Isolde offered. She stood up and gathered her friend's thick dark hair away from her ears and hooked first one little silver spray and then the other in her earlobes. Then she stood back to admire the effect. 'He's right, they're perfect on you,' she said.

The pedlar smiled with pleasure at the sight of the beautiful brown-skinned girl with the black sapphires in her ears. He raised his mug and took a gulp of ale, then took up the second roll of bread. 'A dark beauty,' he murmured. 'As soon as I saw you, I knew that I had been carrying them all this while just for you.'

Ishraq glowed with pleasure. 'But we can't possibly be buying earrings,' she said quietly to Isolde. 'We're on a long journey and have to save our money. We will need funds to hire your godfather's son's army when we reach him.'

'How much are they?' Isolde boldly asked the pedlar. To Ishraq she whispered: 'We have the money that Luca's lord gave us, remember, to repay what we lost in Venice. We have the money that he paid us for the fools' gold.'

'But we traded your mother's rubies to buy the counterfeit coins!' Ishraq protested.

'So let's buy some black sapphires to put in their place!'

The pedlar named a sum that made the girls pause. Immediately, Ishraq offered exactly half. The pedlar laughed and sat back as the landlady brought him some dried apples and sweet biscuits. 'Ah, you know how to bargain!' he exclaimed with pleasure. 'You will take my sapphires from me, put them in your ears and never take them off again, I know. Have a glass of wine,' he said to both the young women. 'This may take some time. I cannot agree such a price, and you cannot refuse these sapphires. We're going to have to find a sum that suits us both.'

Ishraq touched the earrings as they lightly danced at her

66

neck. 'I do want them,' she confessed. 'But I am not going to be robbed.'

'No one is robbing you,' the pedlar said. 'Didn't I say the moment that I saw you that they were your very own? You are merely claiming what is yours and paying a fair price for them. Go and look in a mirror and see yourself in them. Tell me then that they were not cut to the very shape that would suit you best. Tell me that they do not dance on the curve of your neck. Tell me that they are not as dark and sparkling as your eyes. They are yours. I don't believe you will ever take them out.'

'There's a looking glass in my room, nailed to the wall,' the landlady advised her. 'You can go up and see yourself.'

Ishraq went to the door. 'We're not paying that price, so don't think it,' she warned him, smiling despite herself.

The pedlar winked at her and waved a slice of apple pierced on the blade of his knife. 'Beauty calls to beauty. You go and see,' he said, 'then tell me what you would pay for them, and I'll take a fair offer. You cannot say no – you know that you cannot say no.'

Ishraq shot a rueful, smiling glance at Isolde and left the room. They could hear the wooden stairs creak as she went slowly upwards, touching the slim silver strands with her fingertips, feeling them swing against her neck, knowing that they shone like her eyes.

'Do you have nothing pretty that you can show to me?' Isolde asked.

The pedlar crammed the biscuits into his mouth and pushed his plate to one side as if this were more important than food. 'I have only one thing,' he conceded. 'Only one thing that I would expect a noblewoman such as you to even deign to glance at. But I don't know that the size is right. Let me see your feet.'

Isolde rose up from behind the table and stood before him. Casually, he pushed a stool towards her with his booted foot, and she put up her shoe on it, for his inspection.

'I have a pair of shoes so beautiful that no woman could resist them. For that very reason, I have never yet showed them to any woman. I would not tempt her so. It would be a cruelty. Your feet would have to be exactly the right fit for them. It would not be fair to put them in front of you and then tell you that your feet were too big.'

'I don't have big feet,' Isolde protested.

'Or too broad.'

She slipped off her shoe to show him her bare foot. 'It's not broad,' she said.

'Or too bony, or with a flat arch, or bunions or chilblains.'

Isolde laughed. 'I don't have any of those. See!' She pointed her toe and showed him the high instep, the straight toes, the rosy, rounded heel.

'You have a dancer's foot,' he said. From outside the fiddle gave a little ripple of a chord to wake the dancers.

Isolde shuddered. 'This is not the place to talk about dancing. Show me the shoes, for I have to go upstairs away from the noise if they start playing again.'

'Ah, really, I should not. You will not be able to resist them.'

'I shall be the judge of that,' she ruled.

'They're leather,' he said, putting his hand deep into his

pack, but still keeping the shoes hidden. 'Beautiful, soft leather. Kidskin – you could have made gloves with this leather. I've never seen finer.'

'So let me try them!'

'And they are red,' he said. 'Scarlet. When you have them on, your little red toes will peep from underneath your gown as if they are laughing for joy at the beauty of your walk.'

She hesitated. 'Red shoes?'

'Red as a rose,' he said. 'Red as a poppy. I've never seen a pair like them. They need a beautiful foot; they need a beautiful woman. I wouldn't even show them to you if I didn't think that you were born for them.'

Eerily, the fiddle was playing a slow, lingering *chiarantana*, very unlike the noisy jig of yesterday. It was a beautiful, evocative sound that echoed sweetly in the square. It was the sort of song that makes a woman stand tall, toss her head, walk with her hips swinging, as if she knows a secret. Isolde shook her head, trying not to hear it. 'I must go. I promised that I would stay in my room, away from the music . . .'

'You should stay away from the music if you don't want to dance,' he agreed. 'Take a look at these before you go upstairs. I don't think you will be able to resist them.'

At last, he brought the shoes from his pack and put them on the stool before her as if he were presenting a work of art on a pedestal. Isolde stared at them. They were the most beautiful shoes she had ever seen in her life. They were small and slim-fitting, made of a leather – just as he had said – as soft as silk, as red as blood. At the front on the slightly pointed toe was a red buckle; at the back

69

was a small heel; a red silk ribbon ran through loops of leather to tie in a bow at the side. She knew without even trying them on that they would give her a little height and grace to her walk. They would flicker under the hem of her gown, she would delight in catching sight of them and when she could not see them she would revel in knowing that they were there, hidden but beautiful. She would feel the gentle stroke of the leather on her instep, the firm band across her toes. She touched them, and the leather was soft under her fingertips, like a glove, just as he had said.

'May I try them?' she asked longingly.

He gave a little laugh. 'I warn you, if you put them on, you won't be able to take them off again.'

'I will be captured?' she asked him, smiling.

'Completely.'

She laughed at that, and sat on the stool and slipped off her well-worn riding boots.

'I gave you fair warning,' he said, his voice as sweet as a lullaby, as if he were dancing with her in time to the music. 'You cannot resist them; you cannot take them off.'

Almost in answer, Isolde slid one foot and then another into the new red shoes. They fitted perfectly, not a pinch, not a rub; they fitted as if they had been measured and made for her. She took the silk ribbons and pulled them tight on each foot, tied a neat bow and saw how they drew the eye to her slim ankles. She stood up, and at once she took two steps, as if she were dancing. She felt the little lift that they gave to her height; she felt the elegance that comes from a small heel; she felt how they held her feet, so comfortable and

70

neat. They were cool on her toes; they were snug on her instep. She turned round, dipped a curtsey and laughed at herself. 'They are beautiful.'

'Comfortable for dancing?'

'I hardly know I have them on!'

She took a few dance steps. Another man, drinking his ale and eating his breakfast at the common table, said, 'Take care, young lady. Next, you'll be dancing away.'

'She has to dance in them – she is bound to dance in them.' The pedlar smiled. 'They are dancing shoes, after all.'

'They are perfect.' Isolde did a little turn on the spot, and the skirt of her gown flew out so that she could see the red toes, the pretty buckles on the toes. 'I must have them. How much are they?'

The pedlar had finished his breakfast. He drained his glass, slapped down a coin on the table, hefted his pack and headed for the door.

'Don't go!' Isolde called. 'I must pay you for these, and Ishraq wants the earrings. We have to agree a price. How much? I must have these.'

Suddenly, incomprehensibly, he ignored her. He was deaf to her calling; it was as if he had made the sale but did not want the money. Without a word, he unbolted the front door and opened it wide. The bright morning sunshine poured in with the haunting music of the dance, faster now, and with the drum pounding the time, echoing louder and louder in the wooden hall as if it were calling her. Foolishly, he left the door open to the music and to the insistent call of the dance.

'You can't go! I must have these!' Isolde repeated, raising

her voice to shout over the swirl of the music. 'I must have these!'

'Oh no, I think they have you,' he replied, and stepped out into the sunlight where the dancers were whirling round and around, where the drum was beating an irresistible rhythm and the fiddle was playing a dance tune that would make the dead rise up to dance, and then Isolde, wrongly, madly, held out the skirt of her gown with her new red shoes twinkling, and danced out after him.

At Lord Vargarten's castle, Luca found the men forming into squads in the yard. No one was very well equipped; no one was very well prepared. Servants and boys were milling around, bringing sharpened staves in the place of lances, and knives and wood-axes for men who had neither sword nor dagger.

'Yes, I know what you're thinking,' Lord Vargarten said, seeing Luca looking at the muddle of the muster. 'They're fools and villains. But the country has been at peace for years. I can't afford to keep an army at the ready. And a group of dancers will run away at the sight of us. I doubt there will be any actual fighting. But this lot can brawl and bully, anyway.'

'I don't want any fighting. I hoped that we would parley,' Luca said. 'I want to bring the dancers to a state of grace. I hoped that you would just hold them still, so that the priest can talk to them. I need to know what has inspired them. I need to see if they can be cured.'

'Ever done it before?' the lord asked him. 'Ever talked a band of dancers into quietness?'

'No,' Luca said. 'I am a new Inquirer. I'd never even seen dancers before yesterday. My clerk Brother Peter thinks they are possessed.'

The lord frowned, tipped his head on one side and looked at Luca as if he were a colt in the field, a yearling that might make a good horse, or could remain skinny and irresolute.

'Ever commanded men in battle? Seen any fighting?'

Luca shook his head. 'The Ottoman slavers raided my village when I was a boy, but I wasn't there.'

'Nobody would have fought them, anyway,' the lord commented shrewdly. 'I've yet to see a Christian army stand before the infidel. If the young Count Vlad can make his men do it, way over in Wallachia, he will be the very first. God bless him and make him brutal. Constantinople only held out for so long because it couldn't run away.'

'They took my father and my mother,' Luca said stiffly. 'I should have fought. If I had been there when they came, I think I would have fought them, for my mother's life. I hope I would not have let them go without doing anything.'

Lord Vargarten nodded, and dropped a hand on Luca's shoulder in rough sympathy. 'So it goes,' he said. 'But the

73

truth is that until today you have neither converted an enemy nor fought one?'

'I have seen some strange things and reported on them. Terrifying things.'

'But not a man of action.'

'No,' Luca admitted.

'Then take my word for it. It's easier to drive someone away than talk to them. Almost anything is easier than talking honestly and openly to someone,' Lord Vargarten said bluntly. 'My wife's view that we should drown them in the river is one that most people would share, and it's the quickest and simplest thing to do. And the end is certain and final – and, like most men, I like a final solution.'

'But you are the lord of these people,' Luca said earnestly. 'You have to do the right thing, not the certain thing.'

The lord laughed shortly. 'Where in the world have you come from? Where have you seen a man be a good lord against his own convenience and interest? Everyone does what is easiest and best for himself in this world, lords and beggars alike. Why should anyone do anything for anyone else?'

'Because you are rich,' Luca said simply. 'You have been educated. You have power. You have been blessed by God; you are like a shepherd with sheep. You have to lead them to safety. You owe them guidance in return for their service to you. Surely you want to be a good lord, not just a powerful one?'

Lord Vargarten laughed shortly. 'The people mean nothing to me, and most lords feel the same. They are like sheep, just as you say – the beasts that I shear for wool, the animals that I slaughter for meat. They are like the barley that I harvest for grain, or the earth that I plough. My tenants are my own, bought and sold with the land, and I keep them in their hovels as I keep my other beasts in the field or woods. When I die, my son will rule them, and my grandson will rule their grandsons. They are inherited with the fields, like ditches; they are my own, like my hounds.'

'No, you are wrong – times are changing,' Luca persisted. 'Since the Great Pestilence, people believe that they should be allowed to go where they want, and work as they wish. They want to work for themselves, and think for themselves and dream for themselves.'

'Fools,' Lord Vargarten said shortly. 'Why would anyone change anything to oblige them? I certainly won't.' He gestured at the guards who, though ragged and ill-equipped, were as ready as they were going to be. 'While I can command a hundred men, there will be no changes in my lands. And I will always command a hundred men for there will always be a hundred ready to serve me, for no pay, for nothing more than their dinner – if only because their fathers served my father and their grandfathers served my grandfather, for no pay and nothing but their dinner, and these are fools who can imagine nothing else. I am their lord – d'you understand? They follow me so that they don't have to think. They like a leader so that they don't have to think for themselves. And I make sure that nobody like you ever comes here with your ideas from the outside world and encourages them to think anything different from me.'

'You're wrong,' Luca said again, earnestly. 'People do want to think for themselves: there is the new learning, the new philosophies.'

The lord laughed harshly, hawked and spat on the ground. 'You're a dreamer,' he said. 'Some things are eternal. There is a master and a man; a man and his dog; these things will never change. Now, are you ready to ride with me and rid my town of these dancers?'

'No,' Luca said boldly. 'I have to insist. In the name of my holy Order and the Pope who commissioned me, I demand that you hold the dancers peacefully and let me speak with them. They must be given a choice to give up dancing before you drive them from the town.'

'Priest, you are making a simple job ten times more difficult,' the lord complained. 'And you said yourself, you know nothing about this. I can get the job done and finished by dinner time and only a score of fools dead and none of us hurt. Who cares for them?'

'I know,' Luca said with a smile. 'But I have a lord too, and He said that though two sparrows are sold for a farthing not one of them falls to the ground without Our Father knowing it.'

'Good God, what has that to do with anything?' his lordship demanded, irritated. 'Sparrows? Who cares about sparrows?'

'Christ the Redeemer cares about sparrows.'

'I swear by the saints that He does not! Is it Sunday? Am I in church? Did the bell ring for Terce and I missed it?'

Luca smiled. 'Lord Vargarten, I am bound to ask that you make a simple job more difficult and not drive these

76

poor people into the river, but let me try to persuade them to go to their homes. Let me see if God will show mercy and give them back their wits.'

'Mount up!' the lord bellowed to those of his men who had horses. To Luca he said, 'Come on then! See what you can do with these vermin before I whip them halfway to Vienna.'

The pedlar doubled back on himself, re-entered through the open doorway to the inn and ran up the deserted stairs to the girls' empty bedroom. He ignored the lumpy saddlebags, but opened the long box at the foot of the bed and pushed aside their gowns and capes to see if there was anything laid beneath them. He ignored the chink of coins in one of the bags, but when he saw a glint of steel he gave a little grunt of satisfaction, and unwrapped and drew out Isolde's father's broadsword from its hiding place. He could not mistake it – Isolde's brother had described it minutely to him: the ornate handle bolting the blade into the scabbard so that it could never be drawn without unlocking it with the missing key, the precious stones set deep.

'I must have it,' Isolde's brother, the new Lord Lucretili, had told him. 'I cannot claim the lordship without it.'

The pedlar drew it from the box, closed the lid, and slid it into his backpack. It stood tall above his head, so he thrust it lower, until the bottom of the scabbard knocked against the back of his legs. Then, still unseen, he went quietly down the stairs, slipped out of the open door, and was lost among the dancers.

The castle guard could hear the sound of music from the road outside the walled town before they even entered the gate. 'Close up,' the lord said. 'And, if any one of you starts hopping about, the man next to him is to give him the butt end of a pike in his belly, and then knock him out cold. Understand?'

'Aye,' came the grim reply as the men moved closer, shoulder to shoulder. Riding behind the guard, Luca, Freize and Brother Peter exchanged anxious looks.

'As long as *you* don't start dancing, then you and I are safe,' Freize said quietly to his horse, Rufino, who flicked a dark ear and seemed to agree. 'I will sit tight up here, and you keep your four feet steady on the ground.'

Lord Vargarten led the horsemen at speed, four abreast through the open gate, clattering loudly up the cobbled streets and into the market square. 'Get the fiddler,' he said to the man on his left. 'And you get the drummer,' he said to the man on his right. 'Silence the two of them, and we are safe.'

They were not quick enough; at the first rattle of hooves as the troop burst into the square, the fiddler tucked his instrument under his arm and ran as fast as he could out of the far end of the town square, disappearing between the houses. Two men bent low over their horses' necks and thundered after him, but then Luca heard them cursing and shouting as he had ducked down an alley, scaled the town wall and got clean away.

The drummer was not so quick; one horseman snatched him by the collar of his jacket and the other tore the drum from his neck, put a booted foot through it and threw it down to splinter on the ground. The dancers, circling and jigging, wavered and lost their rhythm without the insistent, pounding beat, but, even so, they did not stop dancing. It was as if they could still hear the beat in their heads, as if their feet must still obey the haunting tune, even though the drummer howled for mercy and the fiddler was out of sight.

'Herd them!' Lord Vargarten shouted at his men, using one hand to show them how to circle both sides of the square as if he were commanding his pack of hunting dogs. 'Quickly.'

The guard ran round the perimeter of the square, and then slowly came closer and closer. When they could link arms, they made a circle round the dancers and the dancers jigged and skipped closer and closer to each other until they were held, still dead-eyed and dancing, in the centre of the town square, completely encircled by Lord Vargarten's hard-faced men.

'I could touch you and make you a dancer.' A man put his hand before one of the guardsmen, who did not loosen his grip for a moment.

'I wish you luck with that,' came the dour reply. 'Ask my wife. I don't dance, I do nothing but stamp, and, if you lay one finger on me, I'll stamp on your head.'

'Let us go!' one of the women wailed as she was being crushed in the middle. 'We have to dance – you have to let us dance.'

His lordship glanced over at Luca. 'Time for your miracle, Priest. What have you got? Loaves and fishes? Walking on water? Raising a dead man? For I have captured your congregation and we are waiting for a magic trick. Save them and let us all go home in peace.'

Luca looked back at Brother Peter for help. 'Where's the priest from the church?' he asked.

The older man got down from his horse, handed the reins to a guardsman and came towards Luca, as he swung down from his saddle and handed his horse to Freize. 'Perhaps he will come out when he hears the music has stopped,' he said.

'We have to question them. We have to know why they are dancing,' Luca demanded urgently.

'You can try,' Brother Peter said. 'But look at them: they are beyond hearing us, I think.'

Luca took hold of one of the younger men by the shoulders. 'Where are you from?' he asked. 'Why are you dancing?'

The boy took hold of Luca's hand in return and smiled

blindly, without meaning; he danced around Luca as if he had not heard the words, bending under his arm, as if Luca were his partner.

'What is your name?' Luca demanded more urgently, holding him still again. 'The name of your father? Of your village? Tell me one true thing about yourself.'

The boy's rapid steps checked only for a moment. 'I am a dancer,' he said simply, and then he twisted from Luca's grip and danced away.

'Can we pray over them?' Luca demanded of his clerk. 'Shall we get Lord Vargarten to drive them into the church?'

'Better tell them that Lord Vargarten is going to drive them out of town and they could get hurt. Warn them.'

Luca jumped up onto the steps of the obelisk which stood at the centre of the square, so that everyone could see him. 'Good people,' he said.

'We are dancers!' a man cried out. 'We are not your people!'

'You must stop,' Luca said earnestly. 'You offend the sight of God and trouble the people of this town. You have danced yourselves ill and you have danced yourselves tired; you must stop and return to your homes and live in peace before you dance yourselves to death. Come with me now into the church and we will pray for peace, before this great lord – Lord Vargarten – drives you off his lands, onward and onward, and you will never be able to rest. Stop this, come with me to the church and pray for peace for your souls and ease for your feet. God will lift this curse from you. I will help you.'

'You are possessed by imps of Satan.' Brother Peter

supplemented Luca's appeal, his voice ringing out. 'Poor sinners, you don't know what you are doing nor how the Devil is working his way through you. Turn from him, stop dancing, and come to the church. You can be saved, you can be forgiven, you can be at peace.'

Slowly, one of the women ceased to jig up and down and walked unsteadily, as if she had forgotten how to put one foot before another, away from the dancers.

'Let her out,' Lord Vargarten commanded his men, who broke their circle and released her. Freize jumped down from his horse, hitched it to the wall, took her arm, and guided her towards the little church, and then stood back as the priest came timidly forward and took hold of her.

'Come!' Luca said anxiously to the others. 'You see, it can be done. That woman will go back to her ordinary life; she will be free of this madness. Step away from the dancers, come to the church, confess your sins, and be free.'

Another woman slipped from the circle, and a man followed her, both walking unsteadily as if they were drunkards.

'No!' shouted the youth who had danced with Luca. 'We can't stop. Nothing can stop us.'

'Knock him down,' Lord Vargarten said quietly.

'No!' Luca countermanded, but he was too late. A heavy mailed fist thumped into the young man's temple and he went down in a moment. Not one of his dancing partners went to help him; the jigging feet kicked dust into his face and nobody even noticed.

'Now listen to me!' Lord Vargarten raised his voice. 'All

of you. Enough of this. Go back to your homes. In a few minutes, I shall drive you from this town and all the way up the road until you are off my lands, and you can never come back again. You will be dancing, homeless beggars until you die of hunger on the road and the dogs will eat your bodies and your souls will dance in hell.'

Half a dozen people crossed themselves and ducked beneath the linked arms of the soldiers and hurried to the church, some with an odd skip in their stride as they fought the temptation to dance. But, in the centre of the ring of guardsmen, more than a dozen dancers still jigged on the spot, as if they could not stop their moving feet, and one of them raised the injured youth and danced with him though his head flopped to one side and blood oozed down his white face.

'*In nomine Patris et Filii et Spiritus Sancti!*' Luca implored them, raising his hand in a blessing. 'Devils, I command you to be gone!'

Still they kept dancing, white-faced, blank-eyed, with terrible, empty smiles on their faces, their heads cocked as if they could hear the rhythm of the broken drum or as if the runaway fiddler were still calling them.

'That's it,' Lord Vargarten decided. 'You've done all that you could, Priest. You've saved a few, be glad of that. I've got no more time to waste. Put them out of the gate.'

The men opened the circle and started to push the dancers towards the northern end of the square. Luca followed on foot. 'Gently!' he warned. 'Gently with them – they can't help themselves.'

The dancers skipped towards the north road, their weary feet slipping and sliding on the cobbles. Two of them

83

dragged the wounded youth along with them, his head lolling like a drunk, and someone started to sing a shanty, a haunting, catchy chant. Then they were all dancing in time again, their ragged heads bobbing, their strained eyes rolling as they staggered along, trying to keep in step with the insistent, demanding tune.

'Stop it!' Luca implored, following behind them. 'In the name of God, I forbid you from singing. Say your prayers instead. Say your prayers with me.'

Nobody joined him in prayer; they went onward, following a woman, her fair hair wildly tossed over her face as she snapped her fingers to the beat of the song and stepped out.

'Speed them up!' Lord Vargarten shouted at his guard. 'Let's get them out of here.'

The men closed up and started to push at the slower dancers as they entered the narrow streets. Now the noise of the song echoed off the buildings and above them people slammed shutters and cursed the dancers. Someone threw down kindling on their heads, another threw a bowl of slops. Luca, with Freize and Brother Peter at his side, walked behind Lord Vargarten's horse and the mounted guard as they pushed the dancers through the gateway and out of the town. The road ahead narrowed to a stone bridge across a swiftly flowing stream, and the armed men thrust the dancers on and on. At the bridge, like driven beasts, they hesitated, as if they were afraid to cross the stream and go north.

'Go on! Go on!' Luca shouted at Lord Vargarten, suddenly afraid that the man would follow his wife's hard-hearted advice, and throw the dancers over the low parapet and into the deep torrent that swirled under the bridge. 'Don't stop.'

'That one,' Lord Vargarten decided. He pointed at the young man that had called the dancers to keep dancing, before they had knocked him down. Two of the guardsmen pushed through the dancing crowd to get to him; they held him, his feet limp and his head lolling, as the lord rode up on his big black horse.

'Into the water,' his lordship ordered.

'No!' Luca shouted, but already the men had the half-conscious dancer balanced over the parapet on his back, his head dangling towards the river. Luca thrust his way through the other soldiers to grab the boy's feet. 'No! This isn't the way to deal with them. He was leaving town – he's going. He's already taken a hiding. We don't need to ...'

The young man regained consciousness, realised his danger, looked back up at Luca, and reached his hands towards him. 'Save me!' he said. 'Help me ...'

'Over,' Lord Vargarten said laconically, and the two guards simply tipped the boy's legs and let him go. They heard his yell as he fell, and then the splash and plume of water. His head bobbed up, his arms flailed wildly, the current took him, flung him against the stone stanchions of the bridge; they saw his hands grip unavailingly at the wall, and then his head bobbed beneath the water, came up once, his mouth gasping for air, and then he was gone.

Luca hesitated for a moment, leaning over the parapet as if he would dive into the stream after the young man and swim to his body, which they could see turning over and over in the current. Freize grabbed onto his jacket and hauled him back to safety. Luca furiously turned to Lord Vargarten. 'Why?' he yelled. 'Why would you do that?'

His lordship shrugged. 'So that others think twice before coming here again,' he said shortly. 'I warned you. It's easier to kill someone than change their mind with talk. Life is cheap and my time is precious. And, besides, I don't think of them as humans. Why would I argue with vermin? I just scotch them.' He nodded towards the dancers. 'Now, see how briskly they step out? How anxious they are to be gone?'

They were going faster, their steps speeding up, afraid of the soldiers; but even now, even in this moment of fear, they were unable to run – still they had to dance. Occasionally, prompted by their own inner rhythm, they would break away from the road, join hands, and jig round each other.

'Go on!' Luca shouted, wary of Lord Vargarten in case he gave another murderous order. 'Keep moving!' He had a sudden terrible awareness of his failure. He felt that all he was doing was persecuting these people, that he was no help to them at all and had learned nothing that might save other people in the future. He had meant to save them, but he was colluding in their terror.

The dancers were off the bridge now, stepping and twirling breathlessly up the stony track that led north. Ahead of them, scrambling out of a ditch, the fiddler stood up, keeping a wary eye on the guards, and they heard the scrape of his bow and the start of a tune. Luca shaded his eyes with his hand and watched them go. 'Will they just go on?' he asked desolately. 'On and on? And we can do nothing?'

'Till they drop dead of exhaustion, or someone else

chucks them in another river,' his lordship said hard-heartedly. 'You can't save people from their own stupidity.'

'I can't save people at all,' Luca said miserably.

'Who's the fiddler?' his lordship asked. 'You know, I think he's the rogue that came through last time. I swear he makes a living from leading and guiding beggars. If I catch him, I'll hang him on one of my own trees.'

'No more killing,' Luca pleaded. 'Let them go.'

The lord pulled up his horse and watched the dancers straggle down the road. 'Keep going!' he shouted. 'I can see you. Keep going and don't come back.'

Freize pulled at Luca's sleeve. 'There's something odd,' was all he said.

'What?'

'Something odd about that woman, the one at the front.'

'What?' Luca repeated irritably. 'And what does it matter now?'

'She had new shoes on,' Freize said. 'Nobody else has new shoes. Everyone we saw in the market square yesterday was in rags with worn shoes. Most of them were danced to pieces. Some of them had bleeding feet.'

They could barely see her; she was dancing up the road, her head bent, watching her feet, her loose blonde hair tumbling about her face. It was as if the feet were taking her away, almost against her will, and she was watching them go.

'I suppose so.' Luca could not be distracted from his guilt and grief about the young man that he had watched struck and then drowned, at the complete failure of his mission. He turned back, and Brother Peter put out a steadying hand.

87

'You could not have saved him,' he said quietly. 'Lord Vargarten is a most determined man. You got some dancers into the church and the others out of the town. You did the best that you could. You saved them.'

'I save no one,' Luca said shortly. 'I have no gift for it. And this is not the first time that I have understood nothing.' Grimly, he turned towards Mauthausen and started for the gate, not even looking to see that Brother Peter and Freize were following him. The town gateman, arms folded across his chest in the open gateway, was staring up the hill, watching the dancers go.

'I brought Lord Vargarten down on them and he is a murderer,' Luca berated himself. 'I led him to them. I thought I was saving them, but I brought their murderer straight to them. I asked them what they were doing, but they did not answer me and I made no inquiry. I still don't understand the dancing sickness and I let that boy die and the others be driven onward.' He swallowed bile. 'I let that boy be thrown into deep water when his skull was already split. I let him be killed.'

'Not at all, we saved about ten of them.' Brother Peter caught him up. 'And the rest will go free. Lord Vargarten won't chase them beyond his lands: all he wants is for them to move on. Now we'll go at once to the church and see how the saved ones are. When they make their confession, we will understand more. We will have to report to Milord if they can be recovered and returned to their normal lives. Nine sinners out of thirty lost souls. That's not bad. That is a victory for the risen Lord.'

'I did not save that boy,' Luca said bitterly. 'And in Venice I did not rescue my father. I let the boy go into the

88

river. I left my father in slavery. I don't even know where my mother is. Nine souls out of thirty doesn't seem like a victory to me.'

Lord Vargarten and his troop of guards followed behind Luca, Freize and Brother Peter, the lord high on his horse, the men swaggering like victors.

'You make sure you close the gate against the dancers if they come back,' Lord Vargarten commanded the gatekeeper. 'This gate and the quay gate are to be shut at sunset, and, if you see the dancers coming, you bolt it tight and send for me at once.'

'And what will you do?' Luca demanded.

'I'll ride down and put them to the sword,' Lord Vargarten said briskly. 'They won't get a second chance from me.'

Luca nodded and shrugged his shoulders and turned away, his head bowed at his failure.

'Good thing too,' the gateman assured them. 'They're devils, devils in human form. God knows what trouble and sorrow they have caused. And they took the landlady from the Red Fish, so who is going to brew ale now?'

'The landlady?' Freize asked. 'Did you say the landlady from the inn?'

'She had the door bolted shut, but some fool opened it and, when they got in, they danced with her, danced her round and round and out of the door, and left the inn wide open and the keys to the cellars for anyone to steal.'

'She's with them?'

'Oh yes, didn't you see her go by? And the fair-headed wench that was staying there?'

Freize whirled round and stared up the hill to where the last of the dancers were disappearing into the thick woods on the far side of the river. Without a word, he suddenly took off, running towards them, pushing through the guards, ignoring Lord Vargarten, deaf to Luca's startled yell, dashing like a desperate man through the slowly closing gate, back over the bridge to run after the dancers.

'Freize!' Luca shouted after him. 'What is it? Where are you going?'

'Go back to the inn!' Freize yelled over his shoulder. 'Look for Ishraq! That was Isolde! Isolde in the red shoes. If they've got Isolde, then Ishraq must be dead or captive. Find her!'

Luca took two rapid steps to follow him, but then realised that Freize was right. If Isolde was gone then Ishraq must be in terrible trouble. She would never have let Isolde go alone; she would never have opened the door to release her friend to the dancers. He turned on his heel and ran back to the inn. As soon as he entered the square, he saw that the worst had happened. The front door to the inn stood wide open, a man, slack-mouthed in amazement, lingered in the doorway. 'I never saw such a thing,' he said.

'What?' demanded Luca breathlessly. 'What did you see?'

'Mistress Schmidt, with her skirts kilted up, dancing like a girl; out of the door and away she went, and the bonny young woman with her, as if they were going for a Saturday dance at the threshing barn, as if they were happy to go.'

'How did the dancers get in?'

'That's the worst of it! They didn't get in; it was the women – the women themselves unbolted the door and ran out to them,' he said wonderingly. 'After spending all that time keeping themselves inside! Who knows what women think, eh? Aren't they mad as March hares? And now she's gone, who's going to make dinner?'

'And the other girl?' Luca shouted. 'The dark girl?'

The man shrugged. 'Did she go too?'

Luca swore under his breath and pushed past him into the taproom. It was quiet and still, cool after the hot sunshine outside. He looked into the back dining room and saw that no one was there – the candles smoking in the sunshine, the stools and settles empty – and then he tore up the stairs to the back bedroom on the first floor: the girls' room. It was horribly silent. Their travelling capes were flung on the floor, the box at the foot of the bed gaping open. Clearly, the room had been ransacked and they had been robbed. Luca tried the other rooms on the first floor, the room he and Freize and Brother Peter had shared – nothing, no one. He ran up the stairs again to the attic bedrooms and tapped lightly on the landlady's door. It swung open at his touch. Lying on the floor, as still as death, was Ishraq.

The dancers had a head start on Freize over the bridge and up the road, but they made only slow progress as every few steps they paused to dance with each other, or make a turn on their own. Freize, powering along with his long-legged stride and his pounding feet, got within hailing distance in minutes, but then thought he should hang back and see what was happening. He felt in his pocket and found his pieces of rag and again stuffed his ears and tied the cloth round his head. The haunting music of the fiddle was muffled and distorted. He could still hear it, but it was not so loud as to set his feet tapping and he could not distinguish a tune. He dropped back, and kept to the side of the road, ducking behind bushes and trees, hiding in the shadows as he watched the dancers.

It was Isolde dancing at the front of the procession, fresher and more energetic than the others. He could see her clearly now, and the bright new shoes that hammered the road and twirled around. The fiddler danced alongside her, and around her, as if to encourage the red shoes to patter along the stony way. Her head was bowed, as if she were watching the shoes, as if she could hardly believe that they were dancing of their own accord and she was being dragged along by them. Beside her, the landlady from the inn was already red with effort, breathlessly maintaining the pace, but yearning to stop. Now and then she paused in the middle of the road, one hand to her side as if she had a pain, gasping for air. To her, the bright tune of the fiddle and the rattle of the tambourine were like torture, forcing her onward and onward.

Freize's attention was taken by a movement on the opposite side of the road. He froze at once, and stared at the bushes and the saplings that were swaying as if someone were pushing through them. He was afraid it was one of

92

the dancers, doubled back to attack him, and he shrank away, deeper into the thick woodland which crowded the track. But then, where the undergrowth rustled, he saw a pale face, a big moon face, and someone no bigger than a boy, barefoot and half-dressed in a dirty linen shirt and a pair of breeches.

Freize recognised him at once. It was the Being that had followed them from Venice, the strange baby that Freize had glimpsed as he thrust it at Ishraq, the dwarf-child that she had released into the canal, that had trailed them on the road, that had haunted the stables. Now, as the creature turned his pale face towards Freize, the young man could see clearly on his broad forehead the letters of his name, inset into his skin like a brand, like an engraving of silver in a marble statue, the glistening fools' gold of Venice: *EMET.*

Freize shivered in fear as the dark eyes met his, and slowly a smile spread across the big face, a childish, trusting smile as a boy will smile at his hero. The Being raised his big, spade-like hand in a shy little gesture of acknowledgement, and waved.

Ahead, the dancers turned a corner and were lost from sight. Freize stepped out into the road, showed himself to the mooncalf gaze, spread out his hands to demonstrate that he had no weapon, no tricks. 'I mean you no harm,' he said slowly and loudly. 'But do not follow me.' He gestured to the road ahead, where the sound of the music was still pounding. 'These are people under a spell, taken by the Devil. They are not people that you should be with. So go. Go away, and God bless.'

He could not tell if the Being had understood him or

not; he just shrank back into the darkness of the wood. Freize felt that he had been unkind, as if he had pushed an animal to one side with an angry word. 'I wish you well!' he called to the moving shrubs. 'Go your way. But I have to go after Isolde. I have to rescue her. I am her squire, sworn to her service. I have no time for anyone or anything else.'

'Brother Peter!' Luca yelled down the stairs. 'Help me!'

He stepped towards the girl as he heard Brother Peter coming quickly up the stairs. 'Help me! Look at her! What should we do?'

Brother Peter arrived at the doorway and looked into the room. 'Lord have mercy on us, is she dead?'

'I don't know!' Luca said frantically. 'She's cold. She's really cold. But what is wrong with her? There's no sign of a wound. How could she die, like this? Alone? In a moment?' He fell to his knees beside her and cradled her in his arms. Her head lolled; her hand fell down and knocked on the floor; she was quite limp. 'Ishraq!' Luca breathed, patting her cheek. 'Ishraq, wake up!'

'Is she breathing?' Brother Peter asked. He crossed himself. 'Poor child. Poor child.'

Luca put his ear to Ishraq's nose. He could not hear her breath. 'No! What can we do? Christ help us! What can we do for her? She's so cold.'

'It may be that there is nothing that we can do now but pray for her soul. She is a lost soul, of course, an infidel. Poor child. Put her on the bed.'

'She's so cold.'

'Brother, it may be God's will.'

'No. No! Don't say that.'

The two men lifted Ishraq easily onto the bed and laid her on her back. She was as still and as cold as if she had died in her sleep in midwinter.

'What are those?' Luca noticed the earrings. 'I've not seen them before.'

'Can you feel her heart beating?'

Luca put his face against Ishraq's chest. Beneath the silk tunic he could feel that her body was cooling. He was conscious of the swell of her breast, of silence where her strong young heart should be steadily beating. 'I can't hear. I can't hear anything.'

Brother Peter put his fingertips gently on Ishraq's neck. 'There,' he said. 'I can feel it. I can feel a pulse. She's still alive – just. There's a pulse as soft and fluttery as that of a bird. She's barely with us.'

Luca looked up. 'Can we restore her?'

'We'd better get a physician, if this town has one. Or a midwife. Perhaps it is women's troubles, and nobody will know what to do.'

'But Ishraq's strong, she's healthy. She's never been ill before. You've seen her dive two storeys, from the top of a house into a cold river; you've seen her fire a bow. She wouldn't just faint away like this. It must be the dancers! Perhaps she tried to stop them taking Isolde.'

'Perhaps she is possessed,' Brother Peter said. 'Perhaps the Devil has stolen her soul, as he has stolen Isolde's feet. I'll go out and find Lord Vargarten. See if his lordship knows of a doctor.'

'I'll carry her down to her room,' Luca decided. 'Be quick, Brother. For God's sake, find a physician or a barber-surgeon or someone for her. She's so cold!'

The drummer had a tambourine in place of his broken drum, and the insistent beat and the occasional bell-like rattle as he waved it in the air led the dancers constantly onward, along the dirt track up into the hills and the woods, away from the town. The fiddler kept up a brisk tune and Isolde danced at the front, the red shoes pattering along, turning and sidestepping as if she were practising for a May Day dance with the girls at the Castle of Lucretili, and not in a daze of misery among a crowd of tattered beggars, dancing themselves into exhaustion.

The afternoon sun was high in the sky, a bright yellow-white burning disc, and the fiddler led them in and out of the dappled shade of the forest, sweat pouring down his own grim face, the drummer pounding away on the tambourine, keeping up the pace. Isolde was in a dream, incapable of knowing what she was doing, hearing only the irresistible calling of the joyful music, the inspiriting beat. Nothing could stop her, nothing could recall her to herself, she was entranced, beside herself, beyond herself, unconscious of the pain in her feet, insensate to the sweat and the heat, unaware of her own panting breath.

There was a final rattle of the zils of the tambourine and then they were stilled. In the sudden silence, Isolde looked up from her feet for the first time in hours, and saw to her surprise that she was in a wood, by a stream. She dropped to her knees and put her mouth down to the water, drinking thirstily and splashing her sweaty face and neck. Even now she did not know where she was or what she was doing. She looked around slowly, as if to confirm that she had no friends among the tattered, exhausted dancers. Her face was blank as if she expected no one, her blue eyes dark-ringed with exhaustion. Slowly, she sat back and stretched her feet towards the stream. Her ankles were swollen, her legs filthy with dirt from the road. Only the shoes were still bright and clean, red as blood. Isolde tried to undo the ribbons, so that she could paddle barefoot in the water, and found that her feet were so swollen and sweaty and the ribbons so knotted that she could not get them off at all. She shrugged as if it did not matter, and paddled her feet, red shoes and all, in the icy water. She did not notice as the leather shrank a little tighter still.

'Rest,' the fiddler commanded her. She turned her blank face up at him and shuffled back a little from the riverbank, and obediently curled up on the ground, head pillowed on her hands, lying on leaves as if she had not been raised to sleep on the finest linen behind a locked door.

Keeping deep in the cover of the trees, Freize could just see her, lying among the resting dancers as if she were nothing more than a beggar. He sank down out of sight, sitting against a tree to keep watch. He did not know how to get closer; he did not know if he could get her away from the dancers without alerting the fiddler or risking the drummer seeing him. But, on the other hand, he felt sure that he had to take the risk. This was the first rest they had taken all day and with every hour of dancing they were getting further and further away from the town and from help.

Freize had no idea where they were going and he feared some terrible destination – some mountain precipice or deep shaft where they would be danced down to their deaths. Lord Vargarten's wife had talked of the piper who had taken a band of dancing children into a rift in a mountain that had closed behind them. He was deeply afraid that the fiddler and the drummer would lead Isolde to the very edge of the world and they would all fall over into the abyss.

He needed to get her attention and then beckon her to separate herself from the dancers while they rested. Freize cautiously raised himself up to look around. Everyone seemed to be asleep; at last the fiddler had abandoned his watch and was spreadeagled on the ground, his arm round his fiddle, his bow across his chest. The drummer was seated by a tree, leaning back against the trunk, his head slumped. Everyone else was lying where they had collapsed, deaf and blind with exhaustion. This was probably the best chance to get Isolde away.

Freize pursed his lips and gave a low, clear whistle, the whistle he always gave to Rufino, Isolde must have heard it a hundred times. She heard it now. Even in her exhausted sleep she heard it, and it woke her. Isolde raised herself up, leaning on one hand and looking towards the shadows of the forest as she heard Freize's call, as familiar and beloved as a blackbird song. He stepped from the shelter of the tree and into a shaft of sunlight so that she could clearly see him. He raised his hand, he waved at her, smiling.

With a shiver of horror, he saw the blank face that she turned to him. She looked him over as if he were nothing to her, met his eyes as if he were a stranger and she was indifferent to him. She had, in her beautiful, expressionless face, the eyes of a fish, eyes empty of any recognition or affection or even intelligence. She looked at him with a long, blue, loveless stare as if he were a stranger to her, an ugly unknown stranger. Then she lay back down again as if she had seen no one, and fell asleep.

Freize shrank back into the shadows of the wood, back to his tree, and sat down again as his trembling legs would not support him. He realised that he was very afraid.

99

Luca carried the unconscious girl down one flight of stairs from the attic bedroom of the inn, and laid her on the bed in her sunny room. He chafed her hands, which were as cold as stone; he laid his head again at her breast to see if he could hear a heartbeat. Very quietly, very slowly, he heard a gentle thud, nothing like the strong, steady pulse of the young woman he knew, nothing like the vitality of the girl who would challenge anyone, who could not be contained, who would run from one end of the town to another, who would dive from a building into deep water rather than be imprisoned. It was not possible to imagine that she might not live. Luca remembered her steady gaze as she aimed the longbow, her tight hold of him when he was in despair.

He put his ear to her nose to hear her slow breath, and then sat beside her still body on the bed and whispered: 'Ishraq, for God's sake, come back to me.'

It felt like hours before the door swung open and Luca leaped to his feet in alarm to see a being in the doorway: Death itself. He was horrifically tall, with a high, black pointed hat on his head, and his face completely hidden by a white mask with an elongated nose like a white cone that left only black eyeholes for his searching eyes. His robes were as black as sable, flowing from his shoulders to the ground. Luca instinctively stepped between the terrifying figure and the silent girl. 'Stop!' he said. 'No closer!'

'It's the physician,' Brother Peter reassured him, coming into the room. 'He wears this mask with herbs in the nose so that he won't take the plague.'

'Take it off!' Luca said sharply. 'There's no plague here but a fainting girl, and she would faint again to see you dressed like that.'

100

Slowly, the physician took the beaky mask from his face and smiled at Luca's consternation. 'What caused her to fall?'

'We don't know. It might have been the dancers,' Brother Peter said. 'I felt a pulse. We think she is breathing.'

'She should be cupped,' the physician said, before he had even looked at her.

'No,' Luca said flatly, and when the physician turned his surprised gaze to him he continued: 'She's barely breathing, she hardly has a pulse, her heart is inaudible. Why would we drain her blood when she is fighting for her life?'

'To stimulate her,' the man said, as if it were obvious. 'To bring her to her senses. We could burn her, I suppose. We could put burning plasters on her hands and feet.'

'We're not going to hurt her in any way,' Luca ruled.

The physician looked at him pityingly. 'I see you have no learning in medicine,' he said. 'She is weak; we have to awaken her. How else will she come to life again without a shock?'

'I don't know. But we're not going to cut her or burn her or anything that would cause her pain.'

The physician looked at the older man. 'She will die if we leave her like this,' he observed. 'Obviously, she has to be wakened. How else can we wake her but by administering intense pain?'

'Brother Luca here has a gift – he often has an understanding,' Brother Peter said awkwardly. 'And this is a lady, gently raised; it would be terrible to hurt her. And who could lay hands on her, anyway?'

'We could get the midwife, who lays out the dead, to drag her out of bed and beat her?'

'No!' said Luca, losing his temper. 'Are you deaf? We'll do nothing to hurt her. I will not have her injured. I forbid it.'

The physician looked as if his repertoire of cures was running out. 'We could walk her?'

'How would we do that?' Luca asked.

'Drag her round and round the square, hire women two by two, one after another, to make her march until her feet remembered to walk again.'

Luca looked at him in despair. 'Do you have no physic? No herbs? Do you have no idea what has caused this, or how to cure her? Do we have nothing for her but pain or an ordeal? Do you know nothing but what you might do to a beast in the field, to torment it into obedience?'

There was a silence. The truth was that the physician had nothing to cure an illness, and almost no understanding of illness at all. The only doctors who had read the great Greek physicians were the Moors who had translated the manuscripts, and very few Christian doctors had defied the Church to read them. This man, in this little town, inherited his title of physician from his father who had mostly tended to the sick animals. He himself did nothing more than draw teeth and drain blood with the leeches that he gathered from the river and kept writhing in jars in his larder. Sometimes he cupped people, slicing into their veins and draining out their blood, hoping to rid them of fever; sometimes he fed them burning spices, hoping to warm them up. Only the strongest of his patients survived his treatment.

'We'll nurse her gently,' Luca ruled, feeling his sense of terror at his own ignorance. 'God is with us, and her. We'll treat her gently and she will come back to us. She loves life, and she loves Isolde. When we get Isolde back, she will recover to be with her. I won't have Ishraq tortured. I will trust her. I will trust her to come to her senses. We'll care for her till she wakes up.'

'It could be many years,' the physician warned him. 'I have heard of a woman who fell asleep like this. A deep sleep like death and she never ate nor drank nor aged. As you grow older and her friends grow older, she will just sleep, as she does now, sleep like a beautiful, untouched girl, and wake like an unfolding rose in time to see your old age and death, and know that she is alone in the world, and that you did not save her.'

'Then we will be here for her,' Luca swore. 'Older and tired, but ready to greet her, as if we love her, as if our love is untouched, even if we are dying of old age, as she wakes like an unfolding rose.'

Brother Peter looked as if he thought this was not a workable plan, and the physician exchanged a glance with him. The two men turned to the door together.

'He loves her?' the physician asked Brother Peter quietly. 'I thought you said he was a novice priest? But he's so much in love with her that he cannot think straight.'

Brother Peter spoke low, so that Luca could not hear. 'I had no idea. Indeed, I am sure that he has no idea. They are close – all four of them like comrades; but I had no idea that it had grown to a passion for him. Actually, I thought he favoured the other one. But – what would I know of these young people and their fancies? You heard him yourself – he speaks like a young man in love. This is a disaster! He's not free to love either of them, and she is an infidel. But yes, I think he loves her. I am afraid that he must.'

The long day was turning to evening, the sun was going down, but the dancers, who had been bobbing along for hours after their brief rest, showed no sign of slackening their steps. The fiddler's jig whined under the dark branches and the tambourine went pattering on as the dancers trailed wearily behind them. Isolde was still out in front, her feet keeping time, whirling around, following the fiddler, her pale face set and determined. No one was close enough to see that her dark blue eyes were filled with tears and her cheeks were stained, and no one in the wild, jigging crew would have cared. Far behind them, Freize worked his way up the darkening road, making sure that he kept out of sight, going from tree to tree, from shrub to shrub, watching Isolde and hoping that she would stumble and sit down, and that the dancers would go on without her. He could see that she was tiring, but she moved as if her feet were taking her against her will, as if she could not make herself stop.

The forest ahead was thinning; the narrow track that they were following ran into a clearing and the moon, a slim silver sickle, was rising over the darkness of the trees. The drummer gave a triumphant roll on the tambourine and the fiddler sawed a final chord. The dancers staggered off the road as if their legs were about to give way beneath them and most of them collapsed where they stood. Some of them had little flasks of small ale or wine; others had food. Nobody shared anything: it was as if they were each in their own solitary torment and could not help or care for each other. They could barely see each other.

Those who had cloaks rolled themselves up and lay down with only the tussocky grass for a pillow. Those who had nothing but rags huddled near each other for warmth, without a word of companionship. Nobody fetched wood; nobody made a fire; they turned to the night and to sleep as if they were animals, incapable of lighting a campfire or making a shelter, far from any sympathy or tenderness, far from helping and far from caring for each other.

From the darkness of the wooded side of the glade Freize watched, and saw that Isolde was not yet lying down or sleeping. She had brought nothing to eat – rushing out of the inn, dragged along by her shoes – and she had nothing to wrap herself in for warmth. But the landlady of the inn was edging towards the fiddler and his warm cloak. Isolde stood at the roadside, shifting from one foot to another, as if she could hear the music in her head, as if she still wanted to dance though her head was bowed with fatigue and, under the tangled veil of her hair, the tears were rolling down her cheeks.

As Freize watched her, hardly daring to hope that some longing for her home and her friends was quietly stirring inside her, she turned back down the road, the way that they had come, and started to walk towards him, not even knowing that he was there. She walked blindly, one foot slowly placed before the other, as if she were wading through invisible water that was pushing her back, making her way south, to the town.

'Come on,' Freize whispered. 'Come to me, come to me, and the moment you are near enough I will pull you into the wood and hide you from them.'

Isolde took one small step on her sore feet, and then another, steadily winding her way through the sleeping dancers who had dropped on the roadside or in the glade, slowly coming towards Freize, her face quite blank, her blank eyes sightless in the darkening shadows of the trees.

Freize kept in the gloom of the wood, waiting for her to come close, determined to take her hand as soon as she came near him and run with her, as fast as they could, back to the safety of Lord Vargarten's little town. But, as if sensing that he was losing one of the dancers, the fiddler raised himself up on one elbow and looked around. He saw Isolde making her slow way, then sat up and drew his bow across the strings in one enticing trickle of music. A few of the dozing heads came up, and someone laughed as Isolde turned as if she had been called, and danced back down the road to where the landlady and the fiddler shared his cape. She lay down beside them as if they were her chosen companions and only friends.

Freize waited patiently as, one after another, the dancers turned around on the hard ground, settled and finally went to sleep. They were restless sleepers; their feet twitching, they shifted uncomfortably from one side to another, shouting out in their dreams. As the moon rose over the tops of the dark trees and shone down on them, they slowly stilled, and the colour drained from the scene in the cold light. Freize shuddered and crossed himself; they looked like a village of paupers suddenly struck by plague, or a ragged army of dead men and women left to rot where they had fallen on the battlefield. He could not bear to think that the Lady of Lucretili was twitching in her sleep under a fiddler's cloak. He could not believe that he himself, who so hated adventure and discomfort, was hunkering down on the cold ground and waiting like a faithful squire in a fairy tale for his lady to recover from a deep enchantment.

Luca ate his dinner in Ishraq's room, seated on a little stool drawn up to the bed so that he could see at once if she stirred. The kitchen lad had fried some bacon and bought some bread from the town baker, but, with the landlady missing, there was no one who could cook anything better, and the taproom downstairs was silent and subdued, as if the drinkers were mourning the loss of the alewife.

There was the bang of the front door opening and a heavy tread on the stairs. Luca stood up and moved to the bed as if to protect Ishraq's deathlike sleep, as Lord Vargarten thrust open the door and came into the room.

'They told me your wench had fallen down like a dead woman,' he said. 'And that another girl was missing?'

'They're not wenches,' Luca said irritably. 'The missing one is the Lady of Lucretili, and this is her companion, Ishraq. They were travelling with us for safety.'

'Not so safe,' Lord Vargarten remarked cruelly.

'You need not remind me that I completely failed to protect them,' Luca said hotly. 'And the physician here has no idea what to do.'

Lord Vargarten looked down at the sleeping girl and was surprised. 'A beauty,' he remarked. 'Extraordinary. A Moorish girl?'

'Yes, but will she live?' Luca demanded.

The lord bent down and put his ear to Ishraq's nose. 'Hardly breathing,' he said. He put his hand to her cheek. 'Cold.'

'What do you think?'

'I think you'd better send for the priest to give her the last rites,' his lordship said bluntly. 'She won't last the night. She's cooling as she's lying here. Can't you see for yourself this is a dead girl? Pity. D'you know what caused it?'

'A man in the taproom said that the landlady admitted a pedlar, and when he went out he left the door wide open so that the dancers came in.'

'The dancers killed her?'

'Nobody knows for sure. Nobody actually saw them come in.'

'These are evil doings. We should've put them to the sword when we had them. I told you, Priest. Better dead than doubtful. Where's the pedlar?'

'Nobody saw him leave.'

The lord shook his head. 'Dark times. What will you report of this? What will you tell the Holy Father?'

Luca shrugged. 'What can I tell him, but that the dancers have come and gone and the Lady of Lucretili is missing and her friend is all but dead? And that I understand nothing, and am as helpless as a child.'

The lord nodded. 'Dark times,' he repeated. 'You'd better come back to the castle with me, for your own safety.'

'No, I can't leave Ishraq,' Luca said miserably. 'I won't leave her. Do you think we could carry her to the castle?'

'I'm not having this girl under my roof,' his lordship said bluntly. 'She's dying and we don't know the cause. You do nobody any good by making a vigil at her bedside. Leave her to die in peace, for God's sake. And anyway, what about t'other one?'

'I hope that my companion Freize will save the Lady of Lucretili. As soon as Ishraq—' Luca swallowed. He could not say the word 'dies'. 'As soon as I am free to leave here, I will go after her. Her ladyship was under my protection. I should never have left the two young women here alone.'

'You had no way of knowing that some fool would open the door. I'll leave two men in the market square; you can send them to me in case of need. I've posted guards on the town gate so that the dancers cannot return. If you see that pedlar again, throw him in the cellar and send for me. I'll come down and hang him.'

Numbly, his eyes not moving from Ishraq's pale face, Luca nodded.

His lordship slapped his shoulder. 'I'm doing the best I can for you,' he pointed out. 'The best would have been to hunt them down like vermin. But be of good heart,

Inquirer! If you ride about the world, looking for the signs of the end of times, you're bound to see some terrible things. You want to find them, after all. You're hoping for horrors. It's a sort of success.'

'I never thought I would sit by her deathbed,' Luca said shortly. 'This is one terrible sight I never thought I would see.'

'No,' his lordship conceded. 'And a beautiful girl.'

Luca looked up, suddenly animated. 'You should have known her. She was so much more than just beautiful. She was brave, she had tremendous courage and energy, and she loved the Lady Lucretili and would have laid down her life for her. She was as loyal as any comrade in arms. And she never shirked a challenge nor failed in anything she did.'

He broke off, remembering one night on a dark quayside when he had been most unhappy and she had come out into the darkness and challenged him to be a man, and fight his grief. He had listened to her when no one else could have reached him. 'She could fight with a sword,' he went on. 'She could shoot a bow. She spoke many languages, she was a scholar, and as hard-headed as a philosopher; but once I saw her go up a ladder at midnight to rescue a kitten stuck on a roof.'

He fell silent, as the words he wanted to say went quiet in his mouth. Then he spoke them: 'I love her,' he said quietly, and his own surprise at the words silenced him. 'I have loved her for all this time and never known it.'

'Bit late now,' his lordship said callously.

'Yes,' Luca agreed. 'I am a fool in this too.'

He was silent and the enormity of his confession filled the room.

'A man rarely knows his first love till he has lost her,' Lord Vargarten said, never having loved anyone. 'So God bless her, anyway. Are you sure you won't come to the castle for safety?'

Vehemently, Luca shook his head.

'Very well,' Lord Vargarten said indifferently. 'Good night.'

He left the room. Luca heard his heavy tread on the stairs, heard the outer door bang shut, and then silence. The room, the inn, the town was filled with silence. Somewhere, an owl hooted.

Luca touched his hand to Ishraq's cheek. She was even colder, as if her heart were slowly stopping and the warmth draining from her young body. Brother Peter came quietly into the room, followed by a priest carrying in a box the sacred oils for the last rites that are given only to a dying person.

'Is it time?' Brother Peter asked quietly, his eyes on the beautiful girl, so still and so cold on the bed.

'It's time,' Luca said, feeling his heart wrenched. 'But I don't think we should give her the last rites. She may not have wanted them.'

Brother Peter was profoundly shocked. 'We can't let her die unshriven.'

Luca raised his head. 'Brother, I don't really know what her faith was. I never saw her pray and I never heard her call on any god. I want to honour and respect her now, at her death, whatever her beliefs. I don't think we should give her the last rites without her asking for them. I think we should just pray for her.'

'Was she a heretic?' the priest asked, alarmed. 'She is dressed like a Mahometan.'

'She lived like a Christian woman in every way,' Brother Peter said, defending Ishraq now, despite his many criticisms of her in the past. 'She wore the leggings and robe as an act of modesty when we were riding. But she was raised in a Christian home and she said that her father was a Christian, though she did not name him. We owe her the proper observances.'

'I think she was a seeker after truth,' Luca said. 'I think she studied many texts. She was a philosopher. I don't know that she had a single faith.'

'Then we must pray for her soul,' the priest said firmly. 'For without a doubt she will go straight to hell. Everything that you say about her shows that she was born in sin and lived deep in sin.'

'She was always questioning,' Brother Peter said with a little smile.

'That's very bad, especially in a woman,' the priest said. 'That's sin.'

Luca could not contain a choke of laughter at the thought of what his funny, indomitable friend would say to that. 'Yes,' he said, giving up trying to explain that he thought Ishraq was not a sinner but a woman who was finding her own way in a world which was not generous to young women. The three men knelt beside the girl's bed and prayed until the room grew shadowy and night fell on the quiet town.

'And so, I will leave you,' the priest said, crossing himself. 'And may God have mercy upon her soul. She can be buried tomorrow. She'll have to be buried on the wrong side of the churchyard wall, outside sanctified ground, but we can say prayers over her grave.'

Luca nodded, not trusting his voice.

'I'll go to pray at the church,' Brother Peter said quietly. 'Will you eat something? Come with me?'

'I'll wait here. There must be some reason for this; there must be some explanation. I'll sit with her; perhaps I will be able to understand what has happened. I wish we knew . . . I wish we knew so much. We are like fools blundering about in darkness and now we have lost Ishraq. I'll stay here tonight. I don't want her to . . . to—' He broke off. Brother Peter realised that the young man could not say the words 'die alone'.

'Stay with her till the end,' Brother Peter agreed. 'I will pray for her soul.' He went quietly from the room.

In the dappled, moonlit forest, Freize waited until he was sure that the dancers were all asleep. Several times he started to creep towards them and then froze when one turned and cried out in their sleep, or another, chilled into wakefulness by the night dew, rose up and took a few steps of dance to warm up, and then lay down again.

He was about to take the risk of approaching Isolde

and trying to wake her, even though she was beside the landlady and the fiddler, when he saw something moving on the far side of the clearing. Something crept behind a tree, a bush moved, and then, crawling along the ground like a legless beast, he saw the strange Being worming his way silently across the open ground of the glade.

Freize stayed still and watched, wondering what the creature was doing, and if he would disturb the dancers, perhaps causing such a diversion that Freize could run in, pull Isolde to her feet, and get her away during the confusion. But, as the young man watched, he saw, with increasing fear, that Isolde seemed to be the goal of this stealthy progress. The Being was clearly snaking his way towards her, where she lay partly covered by the fiddler's cape, next to the sleeping bulk of the landlady.

Anxiously, Freize rose up, thinking that he should protect Isolde from this new danger, but then he thought that this might be a rescue attempt, and he should wait and see if it was successful. So far, the Being had wormed his way across the open ground unobserved, and was now creeping up on the sleeping trio.

The Being reached Isolde's side and reared up to his knees. In the uncertain light from the moon, he seemed taller than he had been just hours earlier and, as Freize watched, he put his hands under the sleeping girl's shoulders and knees. Drawing her away from the cape, he picked her up without any effort. Clearly, he was much stronger than any ordinary man for, holding the sleeping girl in his arms, he rose easily to his feet and started to take big, silent steps backwards across the clearing, his moon face watchfully turned towards the fiddler, his eyes on the sleeping dancers.

Isolde did not even stir as, without making a sound, the Being melted into the darkness of the forest. Unable to believe his luck, Freize watched as he carried the sleeping girl back to the little track that ran through the forest. 'He's done it!' Freize whispered to himself, quietly creeping through the woods after them. 'God bless him, for he has her safe. I could not have lifted her and carried her in silence, but the creature has done it.'

The Being had reached the track which led back to the village and – with the girl still sleeping in his arms – he turned and started to walk, not towards Freize and safety, but north, further and further away from Mauthausen.

'No, no, that won't do!' Freize muttered under his breath. 'You're going the wrong way, my friend!' He did not dare to shout aloud, and he did not dare to run down the bare road which was brilliantly lit by moonlight, so, keeping his eyes all the time on the Being and the girl he carried so easily in his arms, Freize ran through the woods, parallel to the track, keeping under the canopy of the trees, skirting the thin bushes, jumping fallen boughs, ducking under the lower branches, desperately trying to go faster so that he could intercept the Being and take Isolde from him.

As he ran, he racked his brains as to what he might do if the Being would not hand over the girl. He was bigger, still gaining height and strength at an unbelievable rate, and what he intended, Freize did not know. Was he a friend, saving Isolde, or an enemy capturing her and taking her into worse danger?

'The little lord should be here!' Freize exclaimed to himself. 'For here is a strange and terrible thing, this Being the very sort of thing he likes to see, a worthy topic for his inquiry, and we are a fair way to getting well acquainted. Indeed, to my mind, he's somewhat overfamiliar. There is my lady in his arms, and him not even introduced, let alone friendly.'

Freize struggled his way through the woods, stumbling on the rough ground, losing his footing in the darkness as clouds gathered over the moon. He realised that unless the Being slowed up or stopped of his own free will, Freize would never overtake, let alone challenge him. Freize's breath was coming in painful gasps as he stumbled onto the track behind the Being, who was taking long, easy strides down the shadowy road.

'Hi!' Freize tried to shout, but he was breathless and did not dare make a noise. He put his head down, and went at a panting run after them both.

The Being was travelling at remarkable speed – he did not seem to feel the stones under his big, bare feet, nor the weight of Isolde in his arms. Freize felt a rising sense of terrible panic. Clearly, the Being had not rescued Isolde at all, but captured her, and was taking her to some secret place, his own lair, and Freize was dropping behind a foot, a yard, at every step. Soon the monster and the sleeping girl would be far away on the moonlit road, and out of sight.

'Hi!' Freize panted. 'Wait up! You must wait!'

The Being turned his huge face and, with a chill of fear, Freize saw his recognition, and a slow smile spread across his face. The Being nodded with gruesome encouragement, as if inviting Freize to chase him, and then turned away and strode on, faster.

For the long hours of the night Luca knelt by the bed, seeing the slatted light from the shutters slowly move across the boards of the floor as the moon travelled across the night sky. Sometimes he held Ishraq's hand and felt for the faint, dying flutter of her pulse; he heard the chiming of the hours of the liturgy from the monastery outside the town. It reminded him of when he had been a boy and had to get up through the night every four hours to attend the church services. He thought that he would tell Ishraq about the coldness of the winter nights in the monastery and how Freize would sneak hot bread loaves that had been baked for the senior monks into his cold hands at choir practice, and then he realised that he would never tell Ishraq anything again.

He rose up once or twice and paced about the room, looking through the little horn window at the orchard below, at the stable yard beyond, at the jumble of roofs and the dark sky above them. He was desperately anxious about Isolde: where she was sleeping, and if she and Freize were even now safe together and hurrying back to the town. He was afraid that Isolde might arrive only in time to bury her dearest friend, a bitter ending to a lifelong love and adventure. He did not know how he was going to tell Isolde that Ishraq had died while she was gone; he did not know how he would speak of her without showing his sudden realisation that he loved her passionately. He thought that he had managed to fall in love with both girls, and declare himself to one, the act of a fool. To him, a novice priest, it was worse than folly, it was sin – a double sin.

He knelt at the side of Ishraq's bed and prayed for forgiveness for his own selfish and sinful confusion. But he kept returning to the thought that surely no young man could have known the two of them, travelled with them, laughed with them, challenged by their cleverness and courage, and not love them? Isolde, the beautiful lady of the castle like a heroine from a Romance, and Ishraq, a girl so powerful in her character and her decisions, so passionately real.

It grew colder towards dawn and Luca could feel the chill creeping from Ishraq's pale face, down her neck, into the core of her being. Her fingernails were turning blue, and he could no longer feel her faint pulse. He knew then that it could not be long, and he rested his forehead against her cold hand and prayed for the girl that he now knew he loved and for her immortal soul.

On the darkened road, stumbling all the time on the rough ground, Freize was falling further and further behind the strange creature and Isolde. As the sky slowly lightened and he realised that they had been hurrying along the road all night, he could see that Isolde was no longer being carried, but was at the Being's side, her hand grasped in his great palm, his other hand behind her back, pushing her forward. She seemed to be resisting him, as if her feet were dancing her away from him, and then he pulled her back.

Freize, horrified at the sight of Isolde being dragged against her will by a Being who now towered over her, drove himself onward, faster and faster but still he could not close the gap between them. Suddenly, from the road behind them, there was a skirl of sound. At once, the Being hesitated, and stopped, slowly turning his big head. Freize flung himself headlong into a bush at the side of the road, before the dark, staring eyes could see him, still following, and looked fearfully back down the road.

There was the fiddler, dancing along as fresh as a youth, and straggling out on the road a good half-mile behind him were the dancers, following the sound of the music as if against their own will, drawn by the haunting swirl of the fiddle, stumbling in the half-light of a cold dawn with the sliver of a white moon going down in the sky.

Freize had no doubt that the fiddler was following Isolde, trying to recapture her and win her back to the dancers. He looked up the road and saw her twisting and turning in the grip of the Being, as if she were trying to get away, and then, even more terribly, as if she were urging him to dance too, to dance as her partner. As he watched, one fist against his mouth to choke back his horrified shout, she took the Being's hand and turned under it, as pretty as a lady in a great hall, and then turned back the other way and curtseyed to it. The Being took both her hands as if they were going to skip together in a country dance; but, instead of dancing with her, he urged her quickly along the road, away from the fiddler and away from the dancers.

Trapped between the Being, whose desires and actions he did not understand, and the dancers led by the implacable fiddler, Freize shrank back deeper into the forest and tried to make his way towards Isolde through the trees, without breaking cover. Behind him he could hear the haunting sound of the music coming steadily closer, and slowly he felt his own feet failing him. He crammed his mufflers in his ears but they could not save him. He could hear the irresistible jig and now he was no longer running – his feet were pacing in time to the music. He knew it was only a matter of time before he started to dance and there would be no one to rescue Isolde, and no one to even witness that he himself was lost.

He tightened the cloth round his chin so that the plugs in his ears fitted more snugly, but he could still hear the penetrating melody of the fiddle and now the tambourine started a swift, insistent patter of sound that spoke of a world of people dancing for joy, the happiness of a circle dance, of a light hand on a young man's shoulder, of a man's gentle touch on a girl's waist, of the delight of moving as one. Freize's running steps stumbled as he started to pace in time to the music, and then helplessly, despite himself, he started to dance.

Some time at about five in the morning, as the dawn sky grew pale and silver, Ishraq stopped breathing. Luca had been dozing in the chair at the side of her bed and, though she only went from near-silent tiny breaths to complete silence, he immediately woke. 'Ishraq!' He scrambled to his knees beside the bed. 'Ishraq, don't go! Don't leave me!'

He put his ear to her nose: there was not even the tiniest whisper of a breath. He put his ear to her cool chest: there was no heartbeat. For a moment he was frozen by dread in the presence of death. Luca was a young man living in dangerous times – he had seen death many times before – but he had not lost a friend, a beautiful young woman at the very height of her youth and beauty, someone that he thought was certain to survive all sorts of dangers, someone he believed was destined for great things. He had seen her swim in a flood; he had seen her shoot an arrow from a longbow; he had seen her laugh for sheer joy; he had seen her face down an Ottoman slaver and smile without fear before a man with a handgun; but he had never thought he would see her die.

He gave a little inarticulate growl of pain and refusal.

'Don't go!' he said again, knowing that she could no longer hear him. 'Don't go! Don't go!'

He climbed on the bed beside her and put his arms round her, as if he would love her now, though he had never done so in life. He put his cheek to her cold cheek, he whispered in her ear, he slid his arm under her shoulders and pulled her towards him, wrapping himself round her as if he would be her lover despite death.

'Ishraq!' he whispered. 'Don't leave me.'

He felt the tiniest whisper of breath on his cheek almost like an answer; but he was holding her so tightly, he thought it might be his own passionate words.

Then he felt her move, slightly, hardly at all, it was only the recommencing of the rise and fall of her chest with a little breath. He checked himself at once, thinking that he had crushed the air out of her with his weight and that this was her dying breath, but then Luca felt the strangest and most beautiful sensation – he felt her inhale. He had moved her, pressing down on her frame, and forced her to take a tiny breath, and now she was taking another.

'Ishraq?' he whispered. 'Can you breathe? Love, my love, can you breathe?'

He was certain that she was a little less chill; her cheek against his was no longer icy, as if he had warmed her. He pulled back and looked down at her still face. Was there the slightest hint of colour in her face? Was there a tiny pulse at the base of her neck? Could it be that his body heat was somehow bringing life back into her lifeless, cold being?

Without knowing what he was doing, or what miracle was taking place, Luca spread himself on and around her, stretching on top of her so that they were belly to

122

belly and chest to chest and face to face. He pulled up the rough covers of the bed over them both so that they were cocooned together, hidden by the warm wool bedding. He was so close to her, so intent on her that now he found he was breathing in rhythm with her, breathing together, that he was forcing the breath in and out of her dying body, and, in his passionate longing that she should live, he dropped his mouth to hers, gathering her into the crook of his shoulder, rocking her slightly from side to side with each breath. He believed he could feel the rise and fall of her chest as she breathed his air, as his mouth met hers.

'Don't go,' he said in her cool ear. 'Don't leave me. I love you.'

He felt her quiver in response, a shudder that went all down her body, and he pulled back to see her dark eyelashes fluttering on her cheek as if she were trying to open her eyes, but was still held by sleep.

'I do,' he breathed. 'I love you. I never knew it till this night, but I love you with all my heart and soul. You are mine; you are my love. I am yours.'

He saw her lips move, as if she were trying to speak, like a swimmer choking in deep water. 'Take them out,' she croaked.

'What?'

Her whisper was no louder than a laboured breath. 'Take them out.'

He realised at once that she meant the earrings, and he carefully unhooked one and then another from her pierced ears. He thought that there might be some poison on the shaft and nuzzled into her neck to take the lobe of her right ear in his mouth, sucked a bitter taste and spat it on the floor, and then held her close so he could suck her left earlobe and spit. He knew it was to save her, but at the same time it was an act of intimacy that gave him a deep pulse of desire. He rubbed his mouth on the sheet of her bed as she gave a little sigh, as if some poison had been drawn from her. Her dark eyes opened and slowly she smiled at him.

'Kiss me.'

Though his mouth had already been on hers, and his body pressed against her, Luca felt overwhelmed with desire. 'Ishraq . . .'

'Kiss me.'

He rubbed his mouth clean of the poison and held her; he kissed her, feeling desire for her flood through him, and she felt her lust for life and her longing for Luca come together in a rising, unstoppable wave of pleasure.

'I love you,' he repeated. 'My God, Ishraq, I love you.'

Her dark eyes smiled, hazy with desire, back from the very threshold of death but still with a will as hard as rock: 'Never, ever say that to me again,' she said.

Freize felt as if his feet had mastered him. His scuffed brown riding boots were jigging along as if he were dancing for joy. Against his will they danced out of the safe cover of the bushes at the side of the road and into the middle of the track where the growing daylight exposed him to the dancers who were coming along behind him.

He heard an ironic cheer as they spotted him and then their breathless laughter as they saw he was dancing, dancing like them, with a sort of weary stagger and an irresistible hop every time the fiddler tore the tune out of the strings. The drummer kept them to time with the little tambourine: a steady, fast beat that nobody could resist.

They looked like a mad circus of wild people, trailing down the road with Freize at their head, followed by the fiddler and the drummer, who were swiftly gaining on him, then the landlady, labouring along with the other dancers from the town. In a few minutes, Freize knew they would catch up with him and then, he was certain, he would join them and never be able to get away. His determination to save Isolde would drain from him, he would be like them: without love, without loyalty, bound only to the dance. He would jig and reel and follow them wherever they went, to the next aghast town, to the next horrified village, to the next murderous lord, until he too was tipped over the parapet of a bridge, slammed with a metalled fist or simply left to die of thirst and exhaustion on a hard road outside a strange town, and Isolde would dance past him, unknowing.

Something in the triumphant skirl of the song alerted Isolde that the fiddler was victorious. She was still torn between dancing and running, keeping ahead of the straggling trailing dancers with the Being's hand pulling her forward, his big palm pushing her in the small of the back, forcing her onward, faster and faster, away from the dancers. But she turned and then she paused as she saw Freize.

The round face of the Being looked back too, and Freize saw Isolde say his name, and something else. Then the two of them stopped in their tracks, and turned towards him as if they would come back for him.

Freize wove across the road in a jaunty sidestep and then stopped and twirled. 'No! No! Go!' he said, as he realised that he could not break free from the dance. 'Go as fast as you can. Run! Save yourself, Isolde! Don't come back for me! You go on! You go on!'

They did not run. Isolde, white-faced, her feet still betraying her in the bright red shoes, urged the Being and they came back down the road towards him.

'Go! Go!' Freize shouted at her, and now it was like a race, the blonde girl with the strange giant of a companion, hurrying back to reach Freize, and, further down along the road, the whirling dancers, laughing as they closed on him. Freize himself danced as if he were wading through a mire, fighting to get away from the dancers towards Isolde.

She got to him first, reached out her hands and grabbed him. 'Freize! You're dancing!'

'I can't help myself. I was trying to come for you. You go now, you get away from them.'

'He's taking me from them.' She nodded upwards to the Being who towered above them and now took each of their hands. 'He'll help you too.'

Freize flinched at the damp chill of his grip, as if the Being had just come from the cold waters of the canal at Venice; but still his feet pounded the road to the rhythm of the drum.

126

'Where's he taking us?' he demanded, as he felt the Being take his hand in an overwhelming grip and start to drag him forward.

'Who cares? Away from them!' Isolde gasped.

The Being drew them on. Freize tried to make his wandering feet go straight forward, but he could not prevent a little hop every third pace. 'You've grown to a powerful height,' he said to the Being, gasping out the words.

The Being hauled them both onward and Freize felt his extraordinary strength.

'I think this fellow could carry us both if needs be,' he whispered to Isolde across the massive girth. 'But where is he taking us?'

'It doesn't matter, as long as we get away!' she panted. 'I know you can't stop dancing, but see if you can dance forwards.' She cried out as her wayward feet made a little drumming step on the spot. 'We have to hurry, we have to get away.'

Anxiously, she glanced over her shoulder. The fiddler and the drummer leading the dancers were only the length of a field behind them. 'Come on, Freize, we have to go faster.'

Freize scowled with concentration, trying to master his feet.

Isolde glanced behind again. 'They're slowing up – there's something's wrong with the drummer,' she said.

Freize broke into a couple of dance steps and felt the Being's arm come round his shoulders and scoop him onward. It was like being pushed by a big horse – the arm had the strength of three men. Freize stumbled under the weight of it.

Isolde gave a cry of delight. 'It's the landlady! Oh, she's wonderful. Look! She's laid hold of the drummer; she's stopping him playing.'

'Come on!' Freize said. 'This is our chance!' As the insistent pounding of the tambourine stopped for a moment, he found that he could break into a run and not dance on the spot. Isolde's feet in the red shoes went faster, and the Being gave a little grunt of encouragement.

Behind them, the fiddler burst into a wail of sound, but they pressed on, the distance between them and the fiddler widening all the time. They turned round a bend in the road and suddenly before them was a steep slope where the road curled and doubled back on itself, and at the bottom of the valley was a small walled village, a river all around it, and a bridge leading the road to the open, welcoming gates.

'If we can get help here . . .' Isolde panted.

'Come on,' said Freize.

Pushing forward, with their feet occasionally skipping to one side or another, they went down the steeply sloping road, sometimes cutting between one hairpin bend and another, stumbling on the stones and sliding towards the village. Isolde flinched as the thin soles of her dancing shoes tripped on the stony path; she would have fallen if the Being had not held her up.

'They're still coming,' she said breathlessly, looking back up the slope. High above them the scrape of the violin was matched with the drum of the tambourine. 'They've seen the village; they must know we're trying to get there. We have to get inside before they reach us.'

'Quick then,' Freize said, and the three of them raced

towards the bridge and to the gate of the village that was slowly but certainly closing against them.

'Open up!' Freize shouted. 'For the love of God!'

'Help us!' Isolde cried. 'Let us in!'

But there was no pity; someone inside was determinedly pushing the heavy double gates closed. They banged shut just as the trio staggered across the bridge, and then they could hear the dreadful sound of someone inside shooting the iron bolts.

In the little bedroom of the inn, Luca, in a dream of desire, heard Ishraq's words and their meaning shocked him like a dash of cold water in his face.

She repeated herself, a smile in her dark eyes as her eyelids fluttered and then closed again. 'Never say that again.'

He jerked back a little. 'You're alive?'

She blinked. 'I seem to be.'

'What happened?' He rolled to one side, but stayed close to her, propping his head on his hand, his other hand gently resting on her rising and falling diaphragm, as if he wanted to be sure that she continued to breathe. She did not push his hand away, but closed her eyes again and turned her face towards him, as if to draw comfort from his closeness.

He saw her inhale the scent of him as if he himself could give her life.

'It's like a dream that I can hardly remember. I was in the taproom with Isolde and a pedlar came in . . .' She broke off and struggled to sit up. 'Where is Isolde?'

'Freize is with her,' Luca reassured her, not daring to tell her the truth yet. 'Lie down. Rest. Go on.'

'The pedlar said he had some beautiful black sapphire earrings and Isolde wanted me to have them. I started to refuse, but when I saw them—' She drew a longing breath, he felt his hand rise and fall, and despite himself he stroked the soft warmth of her belly, the raised ridge of her ribs. 'They were really beautiful.'

He reached over to the table beside the bed where last night's candle and Brother Peter's rosary were beside the earrings in a little bowl. He brought the bowl so that she could see where he had put them. 'These?'

She looked at them wide-eyed, but did not touch them. 'Yes. Those. They said that I should try them on, and Isolde put them in for me. The landlady said that I might look in her glass, so I went upstairs to her bedroom.' She looked troubled. 'And then I can't remember. I think I fainted. I can't remember anything until now.' Unconsciously, her arm tightened round his muscled back. 'Until the moment that I woke.' She turned her face to him as if seeking his kiss. 'With you.'

'I think they may have been painted with some kind of poison,' Luca suggested. 'A sort of poison that froze, but did not kill. You recovered as soon as you told me to take them out of your ears, and I sucked your earlobes and the taste was bitter.'

She searched his face. 'You did that for me?'

'I would have swallowed the poison to save you. I would do anything for you.'

She nodded. They both noted that he did not repeat his words of love.

'There are all sorts of poisons,' she told him. 'The Arab doctors have some that can make the body completely still, as if turned to stone. Was it as if I was paralysed?'

'I thought you were dead. You were growing cold; you lost your pulses. You were not breathing. We prayed for your soul. The priest came to give you the last rites. Brother Peter is holding a vigil for you now in the chapel.'

'So, why didn't I die? How did you wake me?'

'I think the poison was freezing every part of you: your limbs first, then your breath. I think it was about to freeze your heart when I lay with you, and warmed you up, and breathed for you.'

They had moved closer to one another almost without realising and now they were all but mouth to mouth.

'How did you breathe for me?' she whispered.

'I didn't know what I was doing,' Luca explained very quietly. 'I am sorry – perhaps I should not have touched you. But I so longed for you to live, I can't tell you how much. I laid on you and put my mouth to your mouth, and when I breathed out, I felt as if you breathed in, so I kept on doing it.'

Her eyelashes flickered down. 'As if we were one.'

'Yes,' he said honestly.

'Breathing together. Breathing the same breath.'

'Yes.'

'Like lovers,' she pressed him.

131

He did not dare answer her.

She was silent, and he made a little move, as if to free her from his weight, from his touch. He felt torn by his powerful desire to hold her and never let her go, and his fear that she did not want him. He drew back a little and at once he felt her arm tighten behind his back. 'Don't go,' she said without a flicker of shame. 'You are warming me through. I feel as if you are bringing me back to life. Stay with me.'

'It's nearly dawn,' he said. 'I can't believe that you will see this day.'

'You saved me,' she said honestly. 'You sucked the poison; you held me and breathed for me. You brought me back to life when any other would have said I was dead.'

He flushed like a boy. 'I really think I did.'

'Then I am yours,' she said simply. 'I owe you my life.'

'I want you,' he said, hardly knowing what he was saying. 'I am yours, if you will have me.'

'Stay till the morning,' she said with sudden, open desire, bold as she was always bold, fearless and free of shame. 'Stay with me till sunrise, till full morning, Luca. Let's have this night together. Let's be together this night; let us live together for one night, this night that we have stolen from death.'

She turned her face towards him, as if she had come back from the very brink of death and left all ideas of how a young lady should behave in the grave. She gave him her mouth, and then opened the front of her shift and held his face against her cool skin to warm her all through. Tentatively, they moved together, shedding their clothes, touching and responding, moving like conscienceless animals seeking and giving pleasure. Luca was stripped naked, his strong body arching over her as she reached up and clung to him, and then when he held her and felt her shudder with pleasure he dropped his mouth to hers as if he would breathe for her once again, and they were mouth to mouth, body to body, completely entwined. But even when he knew that he loved her, that he had never loved another woman like this, he made sure never to say the words that she had forbidden.

Then they wrapped themselves up together in the warm rugs of her bed, and they both fell asleep.

His feet hammering the doorstep of the village gate as he jigged and pranced, Freize slapped on the great wooden timbers with his open hand. 'For God's sake, let us in!' he shouted. 'We are fleeing from the dancers, the dancers! We will help you guard your village against them. But you must help us. We are lost if you don't let us in!'

Isolde, looking over her shoulder, saw the fiddler and the drummer leading the dancers down the final corner of the winding path of the steep slope to the bridge. 'They're coming,' she panted. Despite herself her feet made a little jig on the spot. 'They're nearly at the bridge.'

'You're Christians!' came the shout from behind the gate. 'You're trying to trick us to open up!'

Freize exchanged an aghast look with Isolde. 'Of course we're Christians,' he said, completely bewildered. 'And we call on you in the name of Jesus to open the gate.'

'And what then?' came the bitter demand. 'Will you rape our women and tear our children from their arms?'

'In God's name!' Freize yelled. 'Do I look like a rapist? Or do I look like a poor man under a terrible spell, begging for refuge and help?'

'How do we know who is behind you?'

'You can see who is behind me!' Freize bellowed in frustration. 'A band of cursed dancers who spread the illness wherever they go, who are determined to catch me and this lady, to make us dance till we die. If you have any pity, let us in!'

'I dare not have pity. I dare not open the gate,' the voice came, but more uncertainly.

Freize collapsed on the stone doorstep. 'Then open it just a crack and let the lady in,' he begged. 'Leave me out here. I don't blame you, whatever your fears. They can take me if they will. But rescue the lady! She is Isolde, Lady of Lucretili, and I am her most faithful and most loving squire. I would die for her. Please. Let her in and I will lead the dancers away from you and away from this place, if you will only save her.'

There was silence. The Being, who had stood in complete silence while Freize went from yelling to pleading, now turned his big, round face to Freize and looked at him with limpid eyes. Slowly, he nodded, as if he had learned something very important.

'What?' Freize bellowed up at him, driven to anger by his fear for Isolde. 'What are you thinking? Why don't you just say?'

The Being stepped back from the gate and drew a breath. He spoke – for the first time Freize heard his voice. It was loud and sonorous, like a well-tuned bell. He spoke in a language that Freize did not understand at all.

'והיחיד האחד האל של בשמו השער את לפתוח.'

There was a stunned silence from behind the gate. The dancers were on the bridge now, twisting and leaping as they came closer. Freize could see the fiddler's knowing smile as they waltzed, the tambourine beating the enchanting, irresistible time. The dancers knew that Freize and Isolde were trapped between them and a barred gate, that the two of them would be snatched from the doorstep of safety as if they were helpless children.

'והיחיד האחד האל של בשמו השער את לפתוח.' The Being raised his voice, as if it were an old psalm loudly sung.

The tambourine started to sound more insistently as if announcing a triumph; the fiddler flourished his bow over the strings. Freize clawed his way up the gatepost into an upright position and felt his feet moving; turning towards the music, he saw Isolde straighten up; he saw the pretty red shoes start to turn away from the gate, her toes pointing as she shuffled slightly towards the dancers.

'I beg you!' he shouted.

The fiddler came to the head of the troupe; he pointed his bow at Isolde, and smiled, conscious of his power. He beckoned her to return to them at the very moment, quite without warning, the gate suddenly swung open, and the three of them fell inwards to safety before it banged shut.

Ishraq lay awake, took in the white walls of the limewashed little bedroom, the tiny window overlooking the orchard and the yard, heard the rippling song of the blackbird, high in the apple tree, and knew herself to be deeply happy. Luca's dark head was buried against her neck, and when she moved her head she felt his warm, soft hair against her cheek, and the scratch of the stubble of his chin against her naked shoulder. She was glad to hold this moment of peace; she closed her eyes briefly as if to dream that he was to be in her bed, in her arms, for the rest of their lives, that this was their first night of many, and that they would never be parted again. She inhaled the sweet male smell of him, and felt, all down her body at every point where they touched, the warmth of satisfied desire flickering into awareness once again.

Luca stirred, then lifted his head and smiled at her with such simple delight that she smiled back. 'You're alive,' was all he said.

She nodded. 'I think you saved me.'

'I'm glad. So glad.'

He pulled away from her, tucking the bedclothes back around her as if he feared her getting cold, finding his breeches, shouldering into his plain linen shirt, sitting on the bed to pull on his boots. He thought that not since his childhood had he had this sense of being blessed – paradoxically never before had he been in such a state of deep sin. He had promised himself to God and here he was: breaking his sacred vows. He had promised himself to the Order and to serve under the guidance of Milord and here he was: thinking of nothing but this girl. He had told Isolde, Ishraq's dearest friend, that he loved her, that she was his first love: and yet now he knew this was the love of his life. He thought that he should feel shame and remorse, but he could feel nothing but deep guilt-free joy.

He turned to smile at her and was surprised again at her unvarnished beauty, sitting up in the bed, her hands clasped round her knees, her dark hair tumbled over her naked creamy-brown shoulders. She radiated a sense of peace and a sensual shamelessness, as if their being together was an outcome completely natural and completely desirable. It was impossible for him to feel remorse when she was so beautifully carefree.

'My God, Ishraq, you are so beautiful.'

'I am reborn,' she replied. 'I feel as if you have brought me back to life and that every breath is precious to me. I feel as if this is the first sunrise of my life. I feel as if I am waking to a new world.'

'Everything is different,' he agreed. 'As if everything is new.'

She smiled at him. 'I suppose everything is different?'

'I must go and tell Brother Peter; he was desperately grieved for you,' said Luca, thinking that the world would press in on them all too quickly. 'And then we have to look for Isolde and Freize.'

The spell of guiltless sensuality was broken at once. She gave a little gasp. 'Isolde? What do you mean? Where is she? I thought she was safe, here, in the inn. Where is she? What's happened?'

Luca shook his head. 'It seems that she went outside. The pedlar left the door open. She and the landlady went with the dancers.'

Ishraq was horrified. 'Why didn't you go after her?'

Luca shook his head. 'Freize ran after them. I knew that if she was out there with them then you must be in danger. I came back to look for you.'

She paused at the thought of his vigil at her side, and their night together. 'Yes, I see. I see. But oh! You shouldn't have let her go.'

'How could I go after her, and leave you?'

She threw back the covers and slipped out to stand at the side of the bed. He gasped at her, so beautifully naked, her skin so smooth and golden, as lovely as a statue of a beautiful girl, one that the Greeks might have sculpted if they had marble the colour of dark honey, and warm as sunshine on silk.

Ishraq was unaware of his sudden rise of desire: she was thinking only of her friend. 'We must go after them now. We should have gone as soon as I woke.'

He could not stop himself; he went to hold her, and at his touch she suddenly went quiet, like a little bird will rest and be still. She paused for a moment as his arms came round her, her warm, naked body against him, as he burned up beneath his linen shirt.

'Are you really well enough to ride?' he whispered against her hair. 'Are you strong enough? Shouldn't I go without you and come back as soon as I have found them?'

She shook her dark head, pressing against him in a ready response. 'I must see her. We have to go after Isolde. Do you think that she spent the whole night out with them?'

'I hope that Freize caught up with them and got her away to safety,' he said, releasing her reluctantly. 'Perhaps he brought her back in the night, and they're here now?'

Ishraq tore herself away from him. 'Go and see,' she urged him, pulling on her pantaloons and throwing on her shift. 'And, if we need to go after her, I'm ready to leave at once.'

Freize and Isolde leaned their backs against the inside of the barred village gate, their breath coming in panting gasps, their feet gently pacing on the spot as they slowly ceased to dance. 'Thank you,' Freize said to the gateman. 'Thank you.'

The man looked surprised at Freize's speech. He stepped back from him, suddenly suspicious and fearful. 'Which of you speaks Hebrew?'

139

From beyond the gate they could hear the whirl of the fiddle and the beat of the tambourine. Isolde's feet started to move again, despite herself.

'Hebrew?' Freize repeated, putting an arm round her shoulders and taking hold of her, trying to force her to be still. 'Did you say Hebrew?'

The gatekeeper nodded.

'Those strange words? It wasn't us, it was the giant,' Isolde said, turning towards him; but the Being had gone.

'Didn't he come in the gate with us?' she asked Freize.

'We can't leave him outside,' Freize said, looking round. 'Did you see—' He broke off at the difficulty of describing the Being that he had seen as a little thing, more like a lizard than a child, and was now taller and stronger than a grown man. 'Did you see him – the other one that came in with us?'

'You two came in,' the gateman said. 'I was busy getting the gate barred again, against them outside. Who are they?'

'They're dancers,' Freize said. He had to raise his voice as the music outside was getting louder. 'Stop your ears and warn the village to close their windows and stay indoors. Everywhere they go, people join with them and can't stop themselves dancing.'

Even as he spoke, Freize's feet started moving again and he felt Isolde rise and dip under his restraining arm.

'I can't stop,' she muttered. 'Hold me, Freize, hold me down. I can't stand still.'

'Why, you're dancers yourselves!' the man said, looking at them with sudden hatred. 'As bad as they. And you tricked me into opening the gate. And you will bring the dancing curse in with you.'

140

'We're not,' Isolde swore to him, though her fidgeting feet told another story. 'I promise that we're not. At any rate, we don't want to be. They captured me yesterday and my friend Freize here came to get me away from them. We don't want to dance. We want to stop.'

'You stop then,' the man said flatly. 'Right this moment. Or I will turn you out of the gate to be with your own kind.'

Outside, the drummer started beating the time to a march. The gateman straightened his back like an old soldier, and fought to still his feet. 'Look,' he said. 'Look at me! I can feel it myself! You've brought danger to our door. We have enough trouble here, more than enough, without the dancing madness as well. You should be out there with them. You're no better than they are.'

'I swear I'm not a danger to you,' Isolde said, speaking rapidly and earnestly. 'I'm only dancing because of these shoes. I don't want them. I don't want dancing shoes. I'll take them off right now.'

Freize held the bars of the gate, forcing his feet to be still as the girl dropped to the stone cobbles and started to untie the ribbons around her ankles.

'They're knotted tight,' she said. 'Help me, Freize.'

The steady beat of the tambourine sounded through the thick wooden gate and then the skirl of the fiddle. Freize knelt before her and picked at the knotted ribbons. Despite themselves, Isolde and Freize swayed to the music though she was still seated and her feet were in his hands.

'I'm sounding the alarm,' the gatekeeper declared. 'And, when the watch comes, we're going to throw you out to them.'

'Hurry,' Isolde said to Freize.

He bent his head and picked with his strong fingernails

at the twisted knots. 'I'm going to have to cut them,' he said.

The gatekeeper put his hand to the clapper of the bell and the tocsin started to ring loudly, drowning out the noise of the tambourine and the fiddle. At once, people opened their shutters and looked anxiously to the gate; the men stumbled into the street, pulling on their boots and their jackets, wiping their mouths as they came from their breakfasts. A tall figure walked down the street behind them.

'Cut them! Cut them!' Isolde begged Freize, as her feet fidgeted in his hands. 'I don't want them. I wish I had never been such a fool as to put them on.'

Freize reached for his belt where he had a sharp dagger in its sheath, took it out and brought it to the ribbons. 'Keep still,' he said.

'I can't.' She turned to him, her face pale and sweating. 'I can't keep still. I am longing to get up and dance.'

'I know,' he said grimly. 'I can feel my feet itching to join in. Fight it, Isolde. Let me get these shoes off your feet. Think of something else. Tell me about Lucretili Castle – how big is the hall? How many people sit down to dinner? How many dishes did your father have at his table?'

'What's all this?' came a stern shout from the back of the crowd. A man in the dark robes of a rabbi, with a black hat trimmed with a yellow star on his head, came to the front of the crowd who parted to let him through.

Freize glanced up, and saw for the first time the distinguishing badge, saw the dark robes, and the people wearing their dark capes, all with a yellow star, and gave a gasp of horror. His face blanched with shock and he leaped to his feet to face them, his knife held before him, standing over

Isolde as if to defend her. 'Get back!' he shouted. 'Get back. We have come to you for help and refuge. We are under the protection of Lord Vargarten. You do not dare to touch us.'

'What?' Isolde demanded. She reached up and pulled the back of Freize's jacket. 'Put down your knife, Freize. Are you mad to draw a knife on these people? We want them to help us.'

'They're Jews!' He turned his frightened face towards her. 'Isolde! We've run into a Jewish village! God help us, for we have run from dancers and fallen among Jews. We shouldn't be in here. We'd be safer outside with the madmen than in here! They will kill us for sure.'

Ishraq, dressed in her travelling clothes of dark blue pantaloons and tunic with her long headscarf tied over her black hair and wound round her neck, was in the stable yard, feverishly tightening the buckles on her horse's bridle, as Luca pleaded with her.

'You're not well enough to ride. You can't go on your own.'

'I have to get the broadsword back. You go after Isolde and Freize, save them. I'll go after the pedlar and get the broadsword. I'll come back as soon as I can.'

'How can you be so sure that it was the pedlar who robbed you?'

'Any ordinary thief would have taken our gold. This is Giorgio's man – it's Giorgio all over, to send a criminal after his own sister to rob her of her father's sword. Of course it's the pedlar, and he will be going straight back to Lucretili Castle for his payment.'

'You can't ride on your own after him.'

She turned and leaned back against the horse's strong shoulder. 'Luca, I have to do this, just as you have to follow the dancers and understand their madness. The Lord of Lucretili himself put Isolde into my keeping; everything that I learned about fighting was so that I could keep the two of us safe. She has to take the sword to her godfather's son. When they came back from the crusades, Isolde's father and godfather exchanged their war swords and had them engraved with some message, each for the other. They bolted the blades into the scabbards as a sign of peace and gave each other the key. Isolde's father told her that after his death she must put them together and open them up and read the message on the blades. I cannot let the sword be lost or – even worse – taken to her brother. I have to get it. You must save her.'

'Brother Peter shall ride with you.'

'No, I'll be faster alone.'

'I won't let you go out like this, into danger!' he exclaimed.

She turned a hard face to him. 'I am not yours to command,' she said. 'It is not for you to let me go, or keep me here. Neither you, nor any man, has the right to tell me to stay or go.'

144

'You are mine, you are my ...' he broke off before he could say the forbidden word of 'lover'.

Steadfastly, she looked at him. 'You are promised to your God,' she said. 'You are the beloved of my dearest friend, who is as close to me as a sister. I don't claim you for my own. And I will never belong to anyone; and no man will ever command me.'

He nodded at her determination. 'I know ... I know. But ...'

'So bid me Godspeed, and you go and find Isolde and keep her safe.'

He bowed to her will and to his own desire to recapture Isolde from the dancers. 'All right, then. I'll go after her. I'll bring her back, and we will meet you here,' he promised.

She nodded and swung herself into the saddle. He could see how pale she was, her skin like cream on honey.

'Don't faint,' he ordered her, and saw her dauntless smile. 'I suppose I am allowed to say that?'

'You are.'

'And you know what I think, but will not say.'

'Never say it,' she said instantly. 'And this is not the time to think it either.'

He nodded, accepting that her devotion to Isolde came before anything. 'God speed,' he said and stepped back as her horse thundered out of the stable yard.

'There are dancers outside the gate!' the gatekeeper reported rapidly to the rabbi. 'And these two got in.' He gestured to Isolde, seated on the threshold stone, holding her bleeding feet, and Freize, white with fear, standing over her. 'They cried out in Hebrew; they asked for refuge in the name of the Lord so I let them in. But now I see they are dancers too, and Gentiles. Forgive me. I heard our language and I thought they were one of us: the Chosen.'

'You are Christian?' the rabbi asked Freize shortly.

'Yes,' Freize said. 'Under the protection of Lord Vargarten, travelling for the Holy Father himself.'

'We have to put you outside,' the rabbi said firmly. The ringing sound of the bell died away and now they could hear the tambourine and the fiddle outside the gate. Despite herself, Isolde's feet twitched and she leaned down and grabbed her toes to try to keep them still.

Freize swayed to the music, looking from the rabbi to the gatekeeper. 'You may not touch us and you may not touch her,' he said loudly. 'Keep back, or it will be the worse for you.'

'We don't want to dance,' Isolde said, looking up at the rabbi. 'It's these shoes that are making me dance. See, my friend has tried to rescue me – he will cut the ribbons, and when I get them off my feet I will be myself again. Please don't put me out there with them.'

The rabbi turned to the crowd. 'It's not an attack,' he reassured them. 'Not today, praise God. It's not a raid. God is merciful to us today. Go to your homes and close your doors and shutters so you don't hear the music. If anyone starts dancing, bring them to the synagogue at once. Guards, you stay with me. It is the dancing madness and, if we turn these people out to their companions and give them food, then they will dance away. But nobody is allowed to listen to the music.'

At once, the people turned away, hands over their ears, heads down, and hurried to their homes. Six men stayed with the rabbi and waited for his orders.

'Please,' said Freize. 'Don't turn us out. Just let me get the shoes off her feet and, as soon as the dancers are gone, we'll go. We want nothing to do with you. I warn you, our friends will come for this lady; she is the Lady of Lucretili, the god-daughter of Count Vlad the Second.'

There was a hiss of fear at the mention of the great man's name and the guards muttered among themselves. Freize had expected instant respect for the famous crusader count's name, but it only seemed to make things worse. He looked from one guard to another, trying to measure the threat they posed to Isolde.

'This is a good young woman, a Christian lady,' Freize assured them. 'You would be in terrible trouble if you handed her over to those outside. You would be destroyed if you did not help her and your village would be ruined if you hurt her or tried to convert her to your beliefs.

147

I promise you, nothing but trouble will come if you so much as touch her.'

'Nothing but terrible trouble comes to us, anyway,' the rabbi observed bitterly. 'We are always on the brink of ruin. If this lady is dancing, she has to be with the dancers, and this is not our fault. We will be in worse trouble if her friends come and find her here.'

The men behind him nodded. 'They'll say we stole her away,' one of them volunteered.

'I wouldn't let them say such a thing,' Isolde replied. 'I would say that you had saved me from the dancers. I will pay you a reward. I am asking you for help. Please don't put us outside.'

Freize shook his head at her. 'Don't,' he whispered. 'Don't even speak to them. Don't promise them a reward; they will take everything that you have. God knows what they will do to you if you are in their power. We have to get away from here.'

'We did fair business with the Jewish money changer in Venice?' she protested.

'Yes, in Venice! Where he was under the rule of law, watched all the time by the Doge's spies, living under a curfew. But here? In a village of Jews? Where they are free to do whatever they want? Why do you think that Christians are forbidden to even enter a Jewish village? God knows what they do. We are in terrible danger.'

'You hate us and fear us,' the rabbi said flatly. 'Why come to us for help?'

'Because I hate and fear the dancers more,' Freize admitted with incurable honesty. 'I call on you to help this lady.'

The rabbi looked uncertain. 'You can stay only until the dancers leave. We can't allow you to bring the dancing sickness down upon us.'

'That's all we ask for,' Freize said. 'Just let us wait here, in the gateway, until they are gone. Don't you come any closer to her; we'll just wait here. I'll cut the ribbons of her shoes now. I'll get the shoes off her feet.'

Freize held Isolde's foot with one hand, and put the blade of his knife under the ribbons that tied the shoes; but a rattle from the tambourine made her foot suddenly twitch, so that he sliced the delicate skin at her ankle. She cried out and the blood flowed from the cut, making everyone exclaim with horror at the bright red blood on the red shoes. 'Isolde! I am so sorry!' Freize exclaimed.

'You can't cut her here!' the rabbi exclaimed, even more frightened than Freize.

'I know you didn't mean to—' Isolde cried. 'He didn't mean to. It was me! I moved! But I can't keep still!'

Frantically, Freize grabbed at her feet, throwing his jacket down and wrapping it round her feet, trying to hide the flow of blood. 'Don't let them see it!' he exclaimed. 'Don't you know what they do with Christian blood?'

Isolde looked up at the rabbi, white-faced. 'He didn't mean to – it was my fault I couldn't keep still.'

'We can't have our threshold stained with Christian blood!' the rabbi said. 'They will come after us, every one of us, if they know your blood is on the gateway of our village. I am sorry, I am very sorry, but you have to go out. I cannot have a Christian bleeding in here. They will destroy us.'

'No!' Isolde begged him in rising panic, her hands clutching at her feet. 'You could not be so cruel! I will die if

149

I have to dance another day with them. You see the trouble that I am in. *You* do it! Have the men hold me still and cut the ribbons of my shoes! Cut the shoes off my feet!'

The rabbi looked from her frightened face to Freize, then he took a decision and waved one of the guards forward. 'Tobias, you do it,' he said. 'Hold her feet and Zacchariah, you cut the ribbons. In the name of God, make sure you don't cut her.'

'No!' Freize exclaimed in sudden fear. 'You may not touch her. I forbid it.'

But Isolde trusted the rabbi. 'You won't hurt me, will you?' she asked. 'The things they say about your people – they're not true?'

'Of course they're true,' Freize moaned. 'Who doesn't know what they do to Christian children? Who doesn't know that they crucify babies just as they did the Lord? Don't you know that they will lie to us and then skin us alive and use our skin for parchment?'

'They do that?' she whispered.

The rabbi's face was frozen with suppressed anger. 'Of course the things that they say about us are lies,' he said coldly. 'You would have to be a child or a fool to believe the slanders that are spread against us. We won't hurt you. We have never hurt anyone since the Crucifixion, and the Romans did that. But we don't want you here. We're not allowed to admit you. It is against the law, your own Christian law, for you to be here. I would far rather we put you outside the gate to join your comrades in their dance than have my men touch you.'

'They're not my comrades,' Isolde said quickly. 'Please don't abandon me to them.'

'Shall my men cut off your shoes? And then will you go

away?' the rabbi asked. 'If the shoes are cut off your feet, will you stop dancing, and when the dancers go onward will you leave? Is that your wish, Lady of Lucretili?'

'Yes,' she said. 'Yes.'

'Do you promise you will go?'

'Yes,' she said. 'I swear it.'

'And you swear on your Bible that you will not bear false witness against us and say that we stole you away to hurt you?'

She raised her bloodstained hand. 'I swear,' she said. 'I swear I will tell everyone that you took me in and saved me.'

Freize stood, his feet jigging on the spot to the loud rhythm of the dance, torn between his fear and his need to see the shoes off Isolde's bleeding feet. 'Take care!' he said, as one man knelt before her and took Isolde's leg in both his hands, trapping her foot between his knees, holding it so tightly that her frenzied movements were stilled. Another of the guards unsheathed his dagger. Freize, still convinced that Jews tortured Christians whenever they could capture them, rubbed sweat from his face, and danced first to one side and then the other, helpless to save her.

Isolde leaned back against the wall, weak with exhaustion as her body twitched and swayed to the music. The man with the dagger cut through the red silk ribbons of one shoe and tore them away, throwing them down on the ground. Then, with meticulous care, he cut off the ribbons on the other shoe. He sheathed his knife.

The rabbi exhaled, realising that he had been holding his breath in fear that they would hurt the young woman and bring down the anger of two great lords.

'Now get your shoes off, and we will give you a pair to walk in, and you can go.'

'I'm grateful,' Freize stammered. 'You have my thanks. And we will repay you as soon as we get safely home, I promise.'

Isolde nodded, and leaned down and pulled at the heel of the shoe on her right foot.

She tried again.

She turned to Freize, her eyes filled with tears. 'I can't get them off,' she said. 'My feet have swollen or something. Even with the ribbons gone, I still can't get them off at all.'

Ishraq held her horse by the reins while the ferry boat swayed and rocked as the boatman hauled them over the river. 'Did the pedlar come this way yesterday?' she asked the man.

'He did; around noon,' he said. 'Just as the dancers left town. I said to him: you could have walked around the town now that they're gone. I said: why leave now, now that the town is safe? Carrying a great big sword sticking out of his pack. Said he had traded it for shoes. I said, they must be very fine shoes.'

'Oh, did he!' Ishraq remarked to herself. 'Did he say where he was going?'

'He didn't,' the man replied. 'He headed on the old road

south.' They reached the quayside on the southern side of the river and before he could help her she was leading her horse up the ramp and urging him onto dry land.

'You'll want some help mounting into the saddle – that's a big horse for a young woman . . .' He broke off as he saw her step on the mounting block, swing into the saddle and gather up the reins.

'Thank you,' she said, and as he was about to reply the horse sprang forward and the young woman was gone.

She rode astride, sitting deep in the saddle, and urged her horse onward in a smooth, continuous canter down the track, straight as an arrow, that led south-west to Rome, the town of Enns before her. She guessed that the pedlar would take this road; the old Roman roads were still signposted with the old stone waymarks carved with Roman numerals now green with moss and lichen.

She thought he would be so confident that he had killed her, and destroyed Isolde, that he would have stopped to eat and sleep, and only set off again this morning. So when she came into the town of Enns she asked at both of the two big inns for him, and found, at the second, a stable lad who remembered that a man, with a broadsword thrust down the back of his pack, weary from walking, had stayed the night and hired a horse in the morning.

Ishraq grimaced at the news that her enemy was now mounted, but was glad to know that he had taken a leisurely breakfast and tipped well. He was on his way home, confident in his triumph. Clearly, he had no fears that he was being pursued and had ridden out only a few hours earlier. Ishraq thought of him entrancing Isolde so that she ran out to the dancers, and then taking the ferry, strolling down the road, and eating a hearty dinner, and felt anger burn hotly inside her.

She drank a mug of small ale and made herself eat some meat, though her stomach turned at the taste, and her head swam, reminding her that she had been near to death only the night before. She gritted her teeth. She knew that Isolde must have her father's sword to exercise his authority. She could not go to her godfather's son without it. Guarding Isolde and her authority was Ishraq's life's work.

'Are you tired?' the boy asked, looking at the sweating horse and the exhausted girl. 'Come far?'

'I'm tired,' she said honestly. 'But that pedlar is a thief, and I must get my things back from him. If he ever comes this way again, you should capture him, and call your lord and report him as a thief.'

Wide-eyed, the lad nodded. 'Will you rest?' he asked.

Ishraq handed him the cup, took hold of her stirrup and saddle and swung up onto her horse's back. 'Not till I have found him,' she said.

The lad was awed by her grim determination. 'What will you do to him?' he asked.

'I think I'll kill him,' she said quietly.

Luca and Brother Peter were riding side by side up the road through the forest, going north, past Lord Vargarten's castle and onward, following the path winding round the great trees that Isolde and Freize had danced along so wearily the night before. Each led a horse, for their missing friends. Brother Peter said nothing, but he thought it very likely that, even if Freize had got Isolde away from the dancers, a delicate lady would not be able to ride at all and that they would have to send for a litter.

'If only we could be certain that they came this way,' Luca said quietly. 'What if they left the path and went deep into the forest?'

'They won't have done that,' Brother Peter assured him. 'They have no food with them, and no weapons. They won't go into the forest; there are wolves and bears, wild boar, all sorts of dangers. A troupe like this is fearful; they go from town to town begging, always driven onward.'

'You're sure they're ahead?' Luca asked him.

'I'm certain,' Brother Peter said. 'This was the road they took out of town and we've seen no crossroads. They must be ahead of us, and they can't be very far. We ride much faster than they can dance.'

'When we first sight them, we'd better drop back and see what they're doing,' Luca said. 'Certainly, we need to keep away from the sound of the music. If we see Freize and Isolde among them, perhaps we'll be able to ride down on them, and catch them up.'

'We'll decide what to do when we see them,' Brother Peter ruled. 'But we can't risk losing you as well as her. We can't risk making a bad situation even worse.'

'How could it be worse?' Luca asked simply. 'Isolde is

lost to us, half out of her mind. Ishraq was near death and is now riding in the opposite direction. What could be worse?'

'If we lost you, an Inquirer on his first long journey out of Rome. If we failed to understand what the dancing means,' Brother Peter reminded him gently. 'Our companions are in danger, but the inquiry must go on. We have to know what is happening here. This could be far worse even than danger to the two young women, however dear they are. This could be the start of the end of the world. We have to understand what it means.'

Luca silenced his hot retort that the young women were more important than the inquiry, silenced his disloyal thought that he cared more about them than the end of the world.

'Whatever the distractions, we have to do our work,' Brother Peter said gently, with some idea of the turmoil in Luca's mind. 'I know they are both very precious to you – but this could be the end of days, a danger to everyone, to the whole Christian world, not just them.'

'They are very precious to me,' Luca confessed. 'Both of them. I cannot tell you—'

'You need not tell me.' The older man shrank from hearing that Luca was in love with one or both of the young women. 'You should confess when we are next at church, and consult Milord. He will advise you. But in the meantime you have to understand the dancing; the safety of the world might depend on it.'

Luca was about to answer when they came out of the shade of the wood and saw the road below them, winding down the side of the slope to a bridge at the bottom of the river valley. Around the gate were about twenty dancers, scattered, some lying in the road as if felled by exhaustion, some sitting at the edge of the water, soaking their bleeding feet in the river.

'There they are!' Luca exclaimed in an undertone. 'Resting before the gate of that village.'

'Can you see Isolde?' Brother Peter asked. 'Is she with them?'

They pulled their horses back into the shadow of the wood, dismounted, tied the four horses' reins to bushes and low branches, and picked their way carefully down the wooded slope, keeping under the cover of the trees.

'I can't see them,' Brother Peter said, cupping his hand over his eyes to shield them from the morning sun. 'Freize and Lady Isolde. I can see the drummer, I think, but I can't make out anyone else.'

'I can't see Isolde,' Luca exclaimed in a hushed whisper. 'Or Freize. Perhaps they have got away.'

'We would have met them coming back down the road,' Brother Peter pointed out. 'They must have got ahead of the dancers and gone into that little village and taken sanctuary there, in the church.'

'Yes, but I can't see a church tower,' Luca remarked. 'That's odd.'

The two men watched as the gateman appeared from the watchtower beside the gate. They heard snatches of the shouted demands of the dancers and the refusal of the gateman to release two runaway dancers.

'That must be them!' Luca said eagerly. 'Look, Brother Peter! Look!' They saw the rabbi appear over the top of the walls beside the gateman, as he climbed the steps to bargain with the fiddler. They saw his dark robes, and the unmistakable yellow star that all Jews were ordered to wear so that everyone knew of their shame.

'The Jewish star! That is a rabbi!' Brother Peter exclaimed. He crossed himself. 'They are in a Jewish settlement? God help them.'

Luca was equally shocked. He turned to Brother Peter. 'We must get them out at once.'

Brother Peter looked very grave. 'It is against the law to even speak to Jews, forbidden to enter their towns.'

'We'll have to speak to them, if they have Isolde and Freize.'

'Surely they wouldn't have gone inside willingly,' Brother Peter said doubtfully. 'Jews kidnap Christian babies – at any rate, kidnaps are reported again and again. I have been present at two inquiries into Jewish crimes and both times I have seen the mark of Cain on these people, and the terrible guilt that they carry for the death of Our Lord.'

'Isolde might have asked for sanctuary? We dealt with a Jewish money changer in Venice and he treated us fairly. After all, Brother, you know well enough that the trade of Christendom would collapse without them!'

'The more shame to us,' Brother Peter said steadily. 'A Christian is forbidden to lend money at a usurious rate, so any man who wants money, vast sums of money, has to go to the Jews. God forgive them. I have no doubt that our rulers will see sense and ban moneylending, drive them out, drive them right away.'

'To go where?' Luca demanded. 'For aren't they exiles without a homeland?'

Brother Peter shrugged. 'They killed Our Lord,' he said.

'It is written that they will always be exiles, that they will always be in pain. Until the end of days.'

'There's no sense in talking of this,' Luca said impatiently. 'Who knows what the truth is? Look, Brother, you stay here and keep watch and I will ride and fetch Lord Vargarten. If the village stays barred to the dancers, and protects Isolde and Freize, Lord Vargarten can drive the dancers onward and release the two of them. Isolde is safe if the Jews will keep her till the dancers are gone.'

Brother Peter's face was grim. 'Oh, the Jews will keep her now that they have her. There's no doubt in my mind. They will force her to marry some man and make her convert to Judaism, and then they will try to get her with child. They'd want a boy born from the Lady of Lucretili. Such a child would inherit her lands and the title. Think of what that would mean to them – to capture Lucretili Castle for Israel!'

Luca was as shocked by Brother Peter's cold hatred as his prediction. He swung into the saddle. 'I'll leave the spare horses with you. I'll be as fast as I can. Whatever the truth of this, whether our enemies are dancers or Jews, Isolde is in terrible danger and we need help to save her.'

159

In the Jewish village, the shutters were barred on every house, every door locked. The gateman, standing on the gate tower with his fingers stuck in his ears, shouted down to the dancers below: 'Stop the music and we will give you food.'

At once, the tambourine rattled with a shimmer of brassy zils and the fiddle ended the tune with a triumphant chord. Inside the gate, Freize slumped on the ground beside Isolde, as if his legs had been cut from under him, and Isolde's feet in the red bloodstained shoes were suddenly stilled, the red ribbons scattered around her like trails of blood. She leaned forward and clasped her calves as the muscles went into rigid cramps.

There was an eerie silence. Outside the village walls, the dancers dropped to the ground with exhaustion. Those who had any food unwrapped their meagre supplies of bread and cheese, watched hungrily by the others. Some of them stumbled down the steep banks of the river to the water's edge and drank, bending their heads down and gulping thirstily. Some of them splashed their faces; a very few stripped off their shirts and washed in the cold water. The drummer confidently leaned back against the village gate, as if it were the entrance to his own hometown, stretched out his legs with an air of satisfaction, and dozed, his tambourine resting on his chest. The fiddler found a patch of soft grass and laid on his back, his face turned to the sun. Nobody could be in any doubt that the dancers were resting, waiting for their breakfast, only so that they would be ready to start again. The silence was nothing more than a temporary truce.

On the inner side of the door Freize knelt at Isolde's feet, desperately pulling at the shoes. They were so tightly fitted that he could not get them off. 'How did you ever get them on?' he asked, pulling at them and twisting her foot.

'They just slipped on,' she said desperately. 'Easily, without a moment's difficulty. They should come off easily.'

It was impossible for him to get a grip on the slick leather. On the foot where he had cut her ankle, the blood was still flowing and the shoe was wet and slippery. His hands were damp with nervous sweat. Now her shoes and her feet were smeared with blood and, though he pulled and pulled at them, he could not tear the shoes off.

'I'm so afraid of hurting you,' he said.

'Pull them off!' Isolde demanded. She was panicking now, her voice high and frightened. 'I don't care if it hurts. If they start playing again and the shoes start dancing, it will hurt me far more then, Freize – it will be the death of me.'

Freize scrabbled at the back of her foot, trying to get his fingers between the shoe and her heel, but there was no gap, and he could see the redness of her skin where his fingernails had raked her.

'Pull them off!' she said again.

'Looks like you'll have to cut them off,' the rabbi observed. 'While she is still.'

'Yes!' Isolde exclaimed. 'Cut the shoes off.'

Freize looked from his dagger to the red shoes. 'I can't,' he said. 'I can't do it without hurting you. I daren't. My knife isn't sharp enough to cut through this leather without sawing at it, and then I'll cut into your feet.'

Isolde looked stricken. Any open wound was likely to

go bad, and a bad wound was fatal. Often, the poultices of the wise women and the treatments of the physicians only made things worse. Someone with a stab wound, or even just a scratch, could die in terrible pain, with no other injury, the wound swollen and stinking, the patient mad with infection.

'I really can't,' Freize said. 'Isolde, I dare not do it. I might cut your heel off. I don't dare.'

The rabbi shook his head at a guard who had put his hand to his dagger. 'We can't do it,' he said simply to Freize. 'If the knife slips and we cut her then Lord Vargarten will never believe that we weren't torturing her.'

'I will tell him that you were helping me!' Isolde exclaimed. 'I give you my word.'

The rabbi looked at her with pity in his dark face. 'You might be dead,' he said frankly. 'If we cut you deeply and we can't staunch the bleeding, you will die. And then Lord Vargarten will destroy this village and kill every one of us. Nobody would believe that we had not murdered you. You people say that we bleed Christian babies to death for our own amusement. Who is ever going to believe that we were trying to help you?'

'Isolde, everyone knows that these people sacrifice Christians,' Freize whispered to her. 'And it's certain that they kidnap Christian babies. These are not Jews like the moneylender in Venice who was living in a city alongside Christians, bound by our laws. They are living here according to their own religion; they hate us, and we hate them.'

'We have put ourselves in danger just by admitting you inside our gates,' the rabbi went on. 'We are supposed

162

to live here without contact with Christians, except for serving them or lending them money. There are dozens of laws about when we may or may not see you. You are breaking these laws just by being here – we broke them when we opened the gate – but it is us who will be punished if anyone finds you here.'

Freize tore at his hair. 'What are we to do? What?'

'Perhaps we can persuade the dancers to go away,' the rabbi said, nodding his head towards the barred gate. 'When they are gone, we can put you on the road again, even if she is still in the shoes, and you can find your friends and they can help you.'

'Won't we hurry after the dancers if we are still dancing?' Isolde asked.

The rabbi shrugged. 'Perhaps. I don't know.'

Isolde put her hand on Freize's arm. 'I have to get these shoes off,' she said passionately. 'I can't go out there with them on. They will make me dance, and I will run after the dancers, I know I will. I have to get them off.'

Outside the gate, the tambourine rattled as the drummer stirred in his sleep. Isolde gave a little moan of fear. 'Do you have a shoemaker in this village?' she asked the rabbi. 'Could he unpick the leather, get the uppers off the soles, tear them apart and get these shoes off me?'

'He can look at them,' the rabbi offered. 'But we won't do anything which causes you injury.'

'Do you eat Christian blood or not?' Freize demanded directly, his own fear driving him to ask. 'Is it true that you bleed Christians to make your Passover bread?'

The rabbi turned his head from the question. His contempt and disdain were clear. He ignored Freize and instead he asked Isolde: 'Did you just hear the tambourine? Did that slight sound, that little rustle, make you want to dance?'

Shamed, Isolde nodded her head. 'But please don't put me out with the dancers,' she pleaded. 'I have so much to do. I have to get back to my friend. I have to get back to my home and win it from my brother. I was born to be the Lady of Lucretili: it was my father's wish that I should look after our people. I have to get back to my lands. I can't just die here on the road because of a stupid moment of vanity when I saw a pair of shoes and wanted them.'

The rabbi nodded to one of the guards, who went running up the main street. Isolde watched him go, seeing how the houses leaned against one another as if in mutual support, odd buildings, unlike anything she had seen before. There was a building rather like an inn but blank-walled – with no windows on the street. It had beautiful paintings on the outside walls and the doors stood open as if inviting everyone to come inside.

It was a small village just like any other, the main cobbled street leading from the gate to the central square, the greater merchants' houses with their double doors high and wide enough to admit wagons into the ground floors where they stored their goods, the smaller houses leaning on the back walls behind them. She would not have known it was a Jewish settlement except for the absence of a church tower constantly chiming out the hours of the liturgy, and the remarkable cleanliness of the place. The ditch down the centre of the little street ran with a clean stream of water and there were no animals roaming through the village, no pigs rooting in the rubbish heaps in the alleys, no chained dogs barking in backyards. Again, her gaze went to the building with no windows – that must be their church, their synagogue, where they performed their mysterious infidel rites. Isolde shuddered.

The cobbler and the baker with food for the dancers came down the street together. The baker carried a basket over his arm filled with yesterday's bread, a couple of cheeses and some smoked fish. Someone had added two bottles of wine and a jug of small ale. The rabbi glanced at the basket. 'Lower it with a rope over the wall,' he said to the gateman. 'Tell them they must take it and be gone, or we will come out and drive them away.'

'They will know that we don't have weapons,' the gateman said quietly. 'They will know that we can be attacked and have nothing to defend ourselves with, we're not even allowed to fight in our own defence. They will know that we are *always* attacked and we are *always* defenceless.'

'Tell them they have to move on – we have nothing for them here. This is all they will get.'

The gateman nodded and took the basket. They heard him go up the stone stairs to the top of the wall and shout down at the dancers.

The cobbler knelt before Isolde and took her restless foot in his hand. 'Lady, this is no ordinary shoe,' he said, after a moment. 'There's no stitching that I can unpick. It's been made out of one piece of leather and pleated very tight around your foot. I was expecting a seam that I could unstitch, but these are unlike anything I have ever seen. Did someone sew them on to you? I can't see how else they were made and fitted so tightly. I can't see how they will ever come off.'

'No one sewed them on. I did not allow that, I would not,' Isolde gasped. She was crying now, tears running down her face. 'I just tried them on because they were so pretty, and the leather was so soft.'

The cobbler shook his head. 'I can't understand why they're not worn through, and then we could have torn them off. But I can't unstitch them,' he said. 'And they're so tight-fitted that I can't cut them off without cutting your feet. I might lame you for life. You might never dance again.' He looked up at the rabbi. 'We'd have to hold her down,' he said. 'Or tie her to my workbench to keep her still. And then she still might be injured. I don't dare to do it. Forgive me, I am sorry, but I will not do it.'

Ishraq rode down the straight Roman road, through the woods and across the plain, headed south-west. The sun was hot on her back and she knew it would get hotter later. She imagined that the pedlar, calmly confident that he had got clean away, unaware of her behind him, following his tracks, would stop in the shade of a tree at midday to rest. She thought that if she came upon him then, she might steal the broadsword and his horse and get away before he woke.

She pulled her horse to a halt under the shelter of a tree

at the side of a stream and considered what she should do. She dismounted and let the horse drink, feeling her rage harden into an icy determination. She realised that she did not want to simply steal the sword and get away from him, she felt a cold fury that she knew was pushing her on to violence. She wanted him to feel the pain and the terror that he had wished on Isolde, and she wanted him to take back to Giorgio another message that the young women could defend themselves. Ishraq – an experienced trained fighter – let the rage wash through her and leave her. She knew she would be more accurate, and more deadly, if she were calm.

She could see that the forest around her was thinning and opening out into empty pastureland ahead, the road running straight across the plain. When she came out of the shelter of the woods she would be clearly visible on the empty road if the pedlar should glance back. She had her knife in her boot where she always carried it, and the belt of her pantaloons was a knotted silken cord that could be used to strangle a man; but apart from these she carried no weapon.

She waited patiently for her horse to slake his thirst, and then she patted him on the neck, encouraged him to climb the bank out of the water and hitched his reins to the tree. She unwound her long headscarf, her hijab, from her head and neck and ripped a small swatch from the end. She took the dagger from her boot and made four holes, one at each corner. She had a rope tied to the saddle for tethering her horse and she sawed the knot from the end and stripped two long threads from it, as long as her outspread arms. On one she made a loop to go over her middle finger; on the other she tied a little knot, and she threaded each one through the holes in the ends of the square of cloth, tying them tightly to make a sling with the cords on either side.

She left the horse and scrambled back down the bank of the stream. The stream bed was rocky with water-rounded pebbles. Ishraq picked out half a dozen of them and tucked them in the fold of her pantaloons at her waist. She picked up one and put it in the sling, testing it for weight. She whirled the sling one way and another in a smooth figure of eight motion then she released the knotted string and the sling flew open, flinging the stone across the stream. Ishraq narrowed her eyes to judge the range and accuracy of her throw, heard the sharp crack as the stone ripped into the bark of a tree. She smiled: it was a killer's smile, merciless.

'Do it!' Isolde begged the cobbler, stretching out her feet towards him. 'I can hold my feet without moving, now that the dancers are eating. I can hold still as you cut the shoes. If you cut me by accident, I will not blame you. I would let no one punish you for helping me. I give you my word.'

The rabbi rounded on her. 'You cannot promise. You have made your word meaningless. You heard your servant ask me to my face if we kidnap Christian children and crucify them at Easter for our own amusement? He asked me if we really draw Christian blood to make matzo bread? You probably think that we poison wells, that we caused the *Peste*? You expect us to trust you, when we know that you and all Christians despise us? What does the word of a Gentile mean to a Jew? If you promise us that we are safe why should we ever believe you?'

Freize gulped. 'It's just what I've heard,' he said apologetically. 'Everyone says it. And I have to protect this lady.'

'Who protects our women? Our children? Every Church feast, men ride out here and break down the gates or scale the walls and attack us in our own houses and synagogue. They destroy whatever they don't understand; they break into storerooms and take away our food; they steal our belongings, our furniture out of our houses. They ride their stinking horses into our synagogue and laugh when they piss on the floor. Our wives and daughters—' He broke off. 'If they find them, they rape them,' he said shortly. 'The women and girls have hiding places; they run as soon as they hear the alarm bell. Our men take a terrible beating; often someone dies of his injuries. They kidnap our little boys and baptise them as Christians, then throw them back at us, shamed.

'And how often does this happen? I'll tell you. Every Easter when they work themselves into a frenzy about the death of Jesus, that they blame on us. At Christmas when they are drunk and the best way to celebrate the birth of your God is to burn down a Jew's house. After haymaking when they want some sport; always at midsummer after the harvest is in and they know that our barns are full.

169

We have to endure this every year, several times a year, without fail. It is the same in every Jewish village across all of Christendom! And then you ask us to take a terrible risk for you!'

Isolde was horrified. 'But why? Why do people do this to you?'

'Because we are Jewish,' the rabbi said simply. 'Because they blame us for all the sins of the world. Because they are violent, drunken men. Because they want to.'

'But Lord Vargarten . . .'

'We are under his protection!' the rabbi shouted. 'Don't you understand? All this happens under his lordship's tender care. It is his men who attack us; it is his markets that cheat us. He gives them permission. We pay our taxes and we give him a special payment every year, to keep us safe. But he says that, after all, we did crucify his Lord, and that we have been chosen to suffer and men must have their sport. He lets the attacks happen; he makes sure they don't go on for more than a few days and that they are not more than a few times a year. But he allows them. They are his way of keeping his men loyal, his way of keeping us poor and afraid. He allows his men to play with us as if we were a chained bear to be torn down by his dogs for sport.'

'Can't you fortify the village?' Freize asked. 'Hold out?'

'Hold out for what? Who do you think would ride to our rescue?' the rabbi demanded irritably. 'Don't you know that we are hated by everyone? The nearest Jewish village is a hundred miles away and they suffer just as we do. All across the German states, all across the Russias, all across Christendom it is the same. Small Jewish settlements,

170

sometimes no more than a few houses, sometimes a walled area inside a town, always in danger, always threatened. A hundred years ago we were respected for our learning and protected by the emperor, but not now. Now we are envied for our learning and no one protects us. It is against the law for us to own a weapon. We are not allowed to defend ourselves. We can enter a Christian house only as a servant; we cannot bar the door against a Gentile. All we can do is pray for a quiet year, hide our goods and our children when the Christians come, and pray that this will not last forever.'

Freize's ready compassion overcame his fear. 'This is terrible,' he said. 'Do they really take the little boys?'

'They take anyone they can find. They take the boys, baptise them and sell them as servants in the town – they say this will win them eternal life; they take the girls and rape them so they give birth to Christian bastards.'

'I'm sorry,' Freize said, shuffling his feet in the dust. 'I am very sorry.'

'When will it end?' Isolde asked.

The rabbi's smile was twisted with bitterness. 'We say "*La-shanah haba'ah bi-Yerushalayim*: Next year, Jerusalem."' He looked down at her white, tear-stained face. 'I see your fear now, but this is what every Jewish woman feels every day. There is not a woman in this village who has not tasted fear like yours, who has not cried as you are weeping now. So, though I am sorry for you, we cannot take a knife to you. Truly, we dare not. We can do no more for you than put you outside the gates when the dancers are gone.'

'I said that I would bear witness for you!' Isolde reminded him.

171

'They would say that we raped you,' the rabbi said bluntly, ignoring Freize's exclamation of horror. 'And that we had driven you mad. When you are hated, as we are hated, nobody can even hear a true word about you. They become deaf. It is how they keep up their hatred. They can hear any lie, but not a simple truth.'

'I am so sorry,' Isolde said helplessly. 'I am so sorry for you and your people. I did not know. I did not understand.'

For a moment he looked at her, his dark eyes narrowed. 'Oh really? Are you saying that you didn't know?' he pressed her. 'Are you sure? But your friend here knew. He knows all the things that people say against us, don't you?'

Freize bent his head, nodded.

'And, if your father was a lord, he must have agreed to protect Jewish moneylenders and Jewish traders on his lands. You must have seen them? He must have made them pay for their protection. He must have let his men loose on them now and then, to remind them to pay.'

Isolde blushed a deep red in shame. 'He was a true crusader, he did not make war on his own village,' she said quietly. 'He fought in the Holy Land.'

'Then he must have killed Moors, and he worked Jews to death,' the rabbi told her. 'And you knew. You are the same as all Christians. You all know. You all always know. But you try not to think about it. And when we cry out for help you try not to hear. And when someone asks you what happened to a Jewish family who are missing from their shop, or a Jewish writer whose books are no longer on sale, or a trader who is no longer at his shop, you say that you did not know, that you were not sure, that you could not be certain. You say that you are good neighbours, but you did not notice. You buy our treasures at a good price; you move into our houses. You don't ask where the owners have gone. You say that it is within the law. You say that you are sorry, but what could you have done? You say that you cannot be blamed for crimes that are done in your name, to the glory of your God. You say you didn't know. But not knowing is a choice that you make, it is as bad as doing.'

'In my part of the world . . .' Freize started.

'Your part of the world is the same as anywhere in the world.' The rabbi swept over his objection. 'We are hated all over the world for no reason that makes any sense. You have to make up reasons. And they still make no sense. But it means that when the Jews are taken, you can say that you didn't know, but it probably had to be done.'

Isolde acknowledged that he was right. 'I am sorry,' she said. 'I am very sorry. I did know. I chose not to know.'

'We endure,' he said bravely. 'We pray that it never gets any worse for us, the People, than it is today. We pray that the day never comes when someone, a new madman, speaks against the Jews and everyone listens, and many act, and everyone else says that they did not know. By coming here, you have put us into great danger. By staying, you continue to endanger us. If you truly have pity on us, then you will go.'

Isolde turned to Freize, her eyes filled with tears, her bloodstained feet twitching in the red shoes. 'He's right. We have to go out to the dancers,' she said. 'We can't stay here.'

Luca rode as hard as he dared down the twisting track, through the dark woods, back to Lord Vargarten's castle. He pulled up his horse before the gateway and shouted: 'I need to get a message to his lordship. The dancers are threatening the Jewish village. He has to send help.'

'Why would he help the Jews?' one of the guards asked. 'Let them dance away with the other madmen.'

The other muttered an obscenity and the two of them laughed together.

'I'll speak to him myself,' Luca decided, not trusting them. 'Open the gate.'

As he rode into the castle garth, Lord Vargarten himself came out of the great hall and down the stone steps. His wife stood in the doorway of the hall and looked down on Luca with her cold gaze.

'You again,' she said, without a word of welcome.

'I've come for help,' Luca said shortly, swinging down from his horse and greeting his lordship. 'The dancers have stolen the Lady of Lucretili and she and my comrade Freize have found sanctuary in the Jewish village, but the dancers have all but set siege to them. We have to go and move them on again.'

'You should have put them all to the sword when you first had them,' her ladyship said flatly from the top of the stone stairs. 'Then you would not be troubled now.'

'We should have done,' his lordship agreed.

'I could not allow it,' Luca said. 'It would be against everything that I believe in. But this is different now – it's worse. My lord, we have to go to the aid of the Lady of Lucretili.'

'She's breaking the law if she's in the Jews' village,' his lordship said. 'And I will punish them for kidnapping her. They will pay for it.'

'She was running from the dancers,' Luca said desperately. 'What else could she do? They have probably saved her life.'

Lord Vargarten shook his head in disapproval. 'It's worse to be with Jews than with dancers,' he said. 'The dancers are mad, but the Jews are the enemy of the world, beyond the mercy of God.'

'I beg you,' Luca urged him. 'I serve the Order of Darkness. I am commanded to seek the help of the lords spiritual and temporal in my work to discover the causes of the end of days. The lords are commanded to help me.'

'But you're not discovering the causes of the end of days,' her ladyship pointed out. 'You're trying to rescue your travelling companion from a situation she should never have got herself into. Why should we lift a finger to help you? Why should my lord risk himself and his men for a woman who has chosen to go dancing, and has danced off to the Jews? She went off with vile people, as bad as animals, and now finds herself among vile people, as bad as vermin.'

Luca looked up at her, trying to control his rage at her words. 'My lord told me that you lost your own sister to the dancers. Can you not pity Lady Isolde? Do you not want to see her come safe home? Don't you know that she would ride out for you, if she were in her castle and you were missing?'

'I would never go to a Jewish village,' she said disdainfully. 'No dance would lead me there. I believe in the purity of my family, of my people.' She turned to her husband. 'Of course, it shall be as you wish. If you think you should ride out for the second time, once again showing mercy to madmen, and go on to save this woman who has run from her friends to the Jews.'

He looked grim. 'Certainly, I feel less merciful now.'

'I beg you,' Luca said again. He could hear his voice tremble and he knew himself to be at the edge of despair.

His lordship's answer was to bellow towards the guardhouse, and the muster bell was rung. 'We'll take the horsemen only,' Lord Vargarten said. 'That should be enough, and we'll be quicker.' His squire came running down the steps with his padded jacket and his helmet. His groom brought his horse from the stable.

'You have no armour at all?' Lord Vargarten asked Luca.

'I am an Inquirer of the Church,' Luca exclaimed. 'Of course I have no armour.'

'Then someone will probably knock your head off with a rock,' Lord Vargarten said cheerfully. 'You'd better ride behind me. Stay close. Borrow a leather jacket. Will you at least take a sword? A mace?'

Luca shook his head.

'Pray for another miracle then,' his lordship said.

'Though God knows He didn't choose to be so helpful last time.'

Ishraq never took her eyes from the unrolling road before her, watching always the distant horizon, as far as she could see, never wavering in her attention. She was rewarded when only an hour out of Enns she saw the pedlar a mile or two ahead of her. She could not be mistaken, for though his pack was now hidden in a saddlebag, on the side of his horse, she could clearly see the broadsword strapped on his back, the carved hilt above his head giving him a strange, hunched profile, dark against the cloudy white dust of the old road.

The pedlar, on his ambling horse, sat heavily in the saddle, thinking of his dinner in the inn at the next town, and of his likely reward from Giorgio, the new Lord of Lucretili. He was pleased with the success of his mission, singing a folk song of his childhood quietly to himself, so he did not at first hear the sound of distant hoofbeats behind him, coming up fast. When he heard the sudden thunder and looked around, alarmed, it was too late. Ishraq was in a cloud of dust, bent low over her horse's neck, urging him on at a flat-out gallop, swinging her sling so that it was a whirling blur as she rode down on the pedlar.

She released a stone and it struck him hard on the back of his head; he slumped over his horse's neck, stunned, as his horse shied. Ishraq wheeled round, turning her horse on its hind legs and reining it in as she gathered in the sling. The pedlar struggled back into his saddle, looking up, his face dazed, as Ishraq loaded her sling with another stone, stood high in her stirrups, whirled it, and released it, straight into his horrified face. He went head over heels backwards off the horse and lay where he fell, slumped face down on the ground, perfectly still. Isolde rode up to him, jumped down, took the knife from her boot, and put her foot hard on his back. He did not protest, or stir.

She thought that the stone had cracked his skull and he was dead, as she carefully drew the precious broadsword from where he had strapped it to his back. Only when she had it safe did she turn him over with the toe of her boot, keeping her knife in her hand ready for a counter-attack.

As soon as she saw his face, she knew that he was alive. He was limp, his face grey, one bleeding bruise on his neck below his ear, another ugly wound swelling rapidly on his cheekbone. Ishraq put the knife to his throat and bent her head to listen if he was breathing. He was conscious, panting like a dog with the shock. She turned from him to her horse, strapping the broadsword to her saddle. She looped the reins of both horses to a roadside bush, and then took his water bottle from his pack and poured the contents in his face.

The pedlar, suddenly deluged with water, choked and squirmed on the ground, put his hand to the terrible wound on his face and blinked up at her. 'The dead infidel,' he said bleakly as if she were a dark ghost come back to haunt him.

'The dead infidel,' she agreed.

Outside the gates of the Jews' village, the drummer finished his meal, crammed a bread roll in the pocket of his motley jacket for later, and stroked the skin of the tambourine with his dirty finger. He tapped it, as if to hear the resonance, then flicked a fingernail against the zils.

Isolde beckoned to Freize and he helped her to her bleeding feet. They held each other tightly as they made little involuntary dance steps in response to the gentle rattle of the tambourine. She bit her lips into a narrow line of determination. 'Open the gate,' she said to the rabbi. 'I will not be the cause of your misfortune. I will leave.'

'It will be the death of her,' Freize said over her bobbing head to the rabbi. 'I'll go out to them, if you'll just keep her.'

She shook her head, her eyes on the gateman. 'Please,' she said. 'Open up. Open up before I change my mind.'

'Wait,' the rabbi ordered. 'We have a guest in the village, he might cut the shoes off for you.'

'Who is he?' Freize asked, suspicious and fearful all at

once, weaving like a drunkard. 'And why would he take the risk if you will not?'

The rabbi looked anxious. 'He's not a Jew,' he said. 'And he does not live in this country. He is not a servant of Lord Vargarten, he belongs ... elsewhere. He carries his own sword, and he is practised. He is accustomed to danger. He will not stay here. He is leaving today.'

'Who is he?' Freize asked. He was even more suspicious.

'He's an Ottoman,' the rabbi said quietly. 'A trader, I believe.'

Freize gave a muted exclamation of rage. 'An enemy! A heretic! As bad as a Jew, God knows. And what's he doing here? An enemy of the country?'

'Travelling,' the rabbi said evasively.

'A pedlar?' Isolde asked, her pale face going even whiter.

'No, no, a great man. A wealthy man, he travels with a servant and a guard and six horses. But he carries a great sword. He might be willing; he might have the skill to cut off the shoes. And if you swore that you would tell everyone that it was not us ... And not even mention him?'

'Please,' Isolde begged. 'Please send to him, and ask.'

'Isolde.' Freize knelt before her, and drew her down beside him, holding her hands tightly in his own. Even kneeling, they were both constantly moving, as her feet, folded beneath her, still tried to dance, and he swayed from one side to another on his knees. 'Isolde! Think! You don't know who this man is. He is a heretic and godforsaken. He may have no skill; he is the enemy of our religion and the enemy of our people. Your father rode out on crusade against people like him. We don't dare let him draw his sword on you.'

180

Her face was twisted with pain. 'I know, I know it. But at least let's see him and ask him if it can be done.'

The gateman was on the tower again, shouting down at the dancers. 'You've eaten your fill. Now go.'

The fiddler got to his feet, tucked the fiddle under his arm. He looked up with an insolent smile. 'You have two dancers inside the town,' he said. 'One of them is a lady and worth a king's fortune in ransom. Send them out to us, or we will play a pretty tune and all your young people will come out and dance with us.'

'Don't play!' the gateman said quickly. 'Those two are not yours for the taking. They've stopped dancing. They're resting and walking around, quite themselves. You've lost them. Now move on.'

'Show them to us,' the fiddler suggested. He drew his bow across the fiddle and there was a long, inviting glissade of sound. 'Send them out so we can see them, walking and resting and being quite themselves.'

'They're resting, I tell you,' the gateman said irritably. He glanced down at the rabbi, who nodded that the gateman should continue to argue with the dancers. 'But you must go on. Go on, or we will get word to Lord Vargarten and tell him that we are troubled by you, and he will send his soldiers.'

'We're no trouble to anybody.' The drummer got to his feet and joined the fiddler. 'It's not us who bear the mark of Cain; it's not us who crucified the precious Lord. You take care who you name as troublemakers. Aren't you the troublemakers since the world began? Send for Lord Vargarten and see what his soldiers will do to you! Far worse than anything they would do to us. We are just dancers, mad for a moment; but you are damned forever.'

181

The rabbi slowly mounted the steps again and stood beside the gatekeeper on the wall, looking down at the dancers who were already on their feet, some of them jigging, some of them walking around in aimless circles, awaiting the hard command to go onward.

'We are the People,' the rabbi admitted. 'And I have a purse of silver, which we can ill afford, for you to go away. Will you take it and go, or shall we send to Lord Vargarten and say that – miserable Jews though we are – we are troubled by dancers? Do you not think that he will come with his soldiers? Do you not think that he likes to have us in his lands, lending money, trading goods, connecting merchants and craftsmen, working across all of the Holy Roman Empire, trusted and reliable where no one else can be trusted? Do you not think he needs a people whose word is their bond and who pay their debts when his Church and his own family cheats and fleeces everyone, constantly? Yes, he will come to help us against you, if only to make sure that we pay our taxes this year. Do you not think that we are his sheep that only he shears, that he does not want the flock troubled by any wolves but himself?'

The drummer shifted uneasily. 'Send out the two dancers you have kidnapped from us, give us the money and we will go,' he offered.

'They are cured of dancing,' the rabbi replied. 'They won't come out.'

'Swear it!' the fiddler said with acute malice. 'If you speak the truth then show me. Swear it on your god or on your scrolls or on your bread, or whatever heathen thing you have, and show the two of them to us, and we will go on our way.'

182

The rabbi looked down to where Isolde was kneeling on the cobblestone pavement by the gate. Wordlessly, she looked up at him while holding her bleeding feet tight in her bloodstained hands. Still her feet danced, even when there was no music but only the whisper of the tambourine, casually shaken. The rabbi knew that as soon as the gate was open and she heard the music she would have to dance, and it would be the death of her.

'I will get the purse of silver – it will take me some time to collect coins from our people – and then I will swear,' the rabbi said, buying time. He looked away from the gate, towards the village square. One of the guards was running ahead of the Ottoman trader, leading him down the cobbled street to the gate.

The stranger walked like a prince, dressed completely in black. He wore a turban with a glossy black feather pinned in place with a diamond of black, a black cape around his shoulders, a black waistcoat blazing with black diamonds, black pantaloons and black leather boots. In his hand, sheathed in a black scabbard, which glittered with more diamonds, he carried a scimitar, curved like the crescent moon, and his tanned face was smiling.

The wounded pedlar trembled as he lay beneath Ishraq's boot, her knife to his neck. 'Will you give me time to say my prayers? I know you're an infidel, but even you must understand prayers. I have to confess my sins – I have to pray.'

She let him wait for her answer – she could smell the acrid scent of his terror. 'I'll give you more than that: I'll give you your life if you answer my questions.'

A little gleam of cunning came into his hazy eyes. 'And spare me?'

'If you are honest. Remember that I know Lucretili and Giorgio, probably better than you do. Don't lie to me, for I swear if you do, I will cut your throat without a moment's remorse.'

He gulped. 'I'm thirsty, and I have a terrible pain.'

'Yes,' she said without any sympathy. 'You're lucky to feel pain. If the stone had been one inch higher, you would have lost your eye and died. So to my questions: Who sent you to us?'

'The lady's brother Giorgio. He said I was to kill her or destroy her and get the broadsword.'

'Why did he want the broadsword?'

'For the authority. It's the lord's sword – he always had it mounted up before him when he sat in judgement. Nobody will obey a fool like Giorgio without it.'

'Did Giorgio say anything about a message that it carries?'

'No.' The pedlar shook his head and then moaned with pain and held his head still.

'D'you know why it is bolted into the scabbard?'

'I swear I don't know. I just had to get the broadsword.'

'Why did you attack me?'

184

'Everyone knows you would die to save her. Everyone knows you are her trained and dangerous bodyguard. He told me to kill you first and then get rid of her.'

She nodded, she could feel her anger like a fever. She took a breath and banked it down. 'Where did you get the poison for the earrings?'

'Giorgio gave it to me. I had poisoned rings and a necklace as well.'

She took a little breath to contain her hatred of him and his master. 'Why send her out to the dancers? Wouldn't it have been easier to poison her? Why did you do that? And how did you do it?'

She saw at once that his thudding head was clearing; she had reminded him of his power. She held the blade of her knife gently against his cheek and thought that she could plunge it into the pulse point. 'If she went away with the dancers then no one would come looking for me,' he said. 'I didn't calculate that you would recover. I am surprised at it. That's a powerful poison.'

She nodded. 'How did you send her out?'

'I have a gift,' he said, his voice softer, persuasive. 'Like lulling a child to sleep. I can talk like this, gently, softly, and I can make someone do whatever I wish. Whatever I wish, little lady. I can put the thought into their head as if it were their very own. Why, even you might be glad to hear me speak gently to you. Who else speaks gently to you? You might be tired, your eyelids might be heavy, you hear what I am saying and you just want to sleep. If I were to count from five to one, you would be asleep by the time I got to two. It's just a little thing I can do – you would like it.'

He put his hand to where his cheekbone was throbbing,

but his eyes were sharp above the darkening bruise. 'Because you are weary and you have ridden a long way, and you were sick when you set out,' he whispered. 'So of course you are very sleepy. I'll start to count now,' he said gently. 'Five ... four ... three ... two ...'

But Ishraq's gaze was steady on him; her hand holding the knife did not soften; certainly, her eyelids did not droop. 'And you are a dead man when you get to one,' she told him, her voice as gentle as his.

Isolde rose unsteadily to her feet, and dipped and swayed in a dancing movement. Freize took her hand and together they faced the stranger as he came down the street, his hand on the hilt of his great scimitar, his dark blue eyes unwaveringly fixed on her.

'Wait a moment,' Freize said quietly in her ear. 'Isn't this the Ottoman slave trader? The one that is the sworn enemy of Luca's lord? The one who told Luca how to find his father in slavery?'

'Radu Bey?' Isolde asked. Despite herself, her feet moved a little as if they would dance, even without music.

'That's the one,' Freize said drily. 'And Ishraq was his secret friend, though he was Milord's sworn enemy.'

186

'I never met him,' she said, as she eyed the man coming towards them, light on his feet in his black leather riding boots. 'I only saw him from the inn windows. Are you sure it's him?'

'There can't be too many like him,' Freize remarked. 'I would swear it is the same man. He's said to be a great commander of the Ottoman army, a Christian by birth, second in command to the sultan. So what's he doing here, in this village?'

The stranger stopped before them and made a little bow, a mere nod of his head, then turned to the rabbi and put his hand on his heart and made an obeisance.

'Are you Radu Bey?' Freize said bluntly. 'For I think we have already met.'

The stranger turned to him and took in the stocky truculence of the young man, the dirt on his clothes and the exhaustion in his face.

'We've met,' he said shortly. 'But you were then in better times.'

'Oh,' said Freize. 'I've had all sorts of times since then. You wouldn't believe it if I told you. But I think perhaps you have too. When we met, you were a slave trader on a great slaving galley with maps and knowledge of the stars and a wicked ship with a great spike in the prow. You dined with my master, Luca, and I think you crept into our house at midnight and pinned your badge on the heart of his lord to show him that you could have killed him while he slept. Am I right?'

Radu Bey inclined his head in assent, smiling slightly.

'A threat,' Freize said. 'To Luca's lord.'

'Say more a jest, a family joke.'

'So what d'you call yourself now?' Freize demanded.

'Still a trader,' Radu Bey said, with a smile to Isolde that almost seemed to ask her to forgive such a transparent lie. 'And I was never a slave trader – I was not slave trading when you saw me. I was travelling on my own galley.'

'As I remember, it wasn't rowed by free men,' Freize said sharply.

'No,' Radu Bey replied. 'My crew were slaves, of course. I have no great interest in the freedom of infidels.'

'And are you a Jew now?' Freize asked rudely.

'Freize!' Isolde exclaimed.

'I was born a Christian, but I converted. I am now a Muslim. I honour the Jewish faith, as anyone must who loves scholarship. We are all People of the Book.'

'You must forgive us both,' Isolde interrupted. 'We have been in danger and very afraid. We are in terrible trouble now. I was going to ask you a great favour.'

Radu Bey bowed his head. 'I am bound to help a lady who seeks my help,' he said formally. 'What may I do for you?' he asked as if he could not see the constant shifting of her feet, and the red shoes stained a deeper red with her blood.

'I want you to cut off my shoes,' she told him. 'We can't get them off. I have to be rid of them. They're making me dance, and nobody here dares to do it. Can you cut me free?'

'Without hurting her?' Freize added.

Radu Bey looked doubtful. 'My scimitar is so sharp that you could shave with it,' he said. 'But to cut your shoes from your feet without injury? It would be easier by far to hack your feet from your legs and leave you with stumps.

That would prevent you dancing, my lady! Would you risk that?'

Isolde took a deep breath and sat down on the cobbled threshold, rested her back against the gate, stretched out her legs and showed him her ceaselessly twitching feet. 'Cut the shoes,' she said. 'Try. And if you can't do it: cut my feet off.'

He hesitated, as if she had surprised him. 'You really want me to cut off your feet?' he asked. 'This is a poor joke.'

'Cut the shoes,' she said. 'If you can. But if you have to take off my feet at the ankle, then do that.'

'The pain would be unbearable,' he cautioned her, and was surprised at the unflinching reply.

'I understand that.'

'And you would bleed badly – you might bleed to death.'

'I am willing to take the risk. And you must bear witness that these Jewish people did not encourage me. If I die, you must put me outside their gates so they are not blamed.'

He blinked at her uncompromising courage. 'You will be a cripple,' he warned her. 'You will lose your beauty and your grace. Nobody would have a footless woman for his wife.'

'I am unlucky, it seems.'

He exchanged one look with the stunned rabbi. 'What can a young woman want more than her feet?'

'I want to hobble back to my home and defeat my false brother and win back my castle,' she said grimly. 'I want my rights more than I want dancing feet.'

She saw in his face a sudden respect. 'You would lose your feet if you could defeat your brother?'

'Yes.'

He gave a short laugh. 'You know, I think I will do it; for my brother is my enemy too, and I know that I would pay with my feet to defeat him. But, be warned, if I make a mistake by a hair's breadth, I might kill you.'

'I will die if I go on dancing,' she told him. 'I would rather die than run after the dancers and dance till I starve to death, in shame.'

'You have a very high opinion of your honour and your rights,' he observed.

She did not lower her gaze with maidenly modesty. She met his eyes like an equal. 'I do.'

He measured her determination and he smiled at her. 'I admire your courage,' he said quietly. 'I admire your pride. And, because of that, I will do what I can.'

'Here,' said Freize. 'Wait a minute. Remember, you can't hurt her.'

Radu Bey threw him a careless, smiling glance. 'You heard her,' he said. 'You heard the Christian lady. She said cut off the shoes and if I can't – then cut off her feet. I'll do that.'

He turned to the rabbi. 'I'll need a couple of logs of wood to raise her feet,' he said. 'So that I can swing the blade. And get the blacksmith to boil up some pitch. If I miss the shoes and slice her feet then we'll have to dip the wounds in pitch to seal them.'

Freize choked on his horror. 'She cannot be hurt. I swear you may not hurt her.'

'Oh, it will be a killing pain,' Radu Bey assured him. 'Do you think she has the courage?'

Freize looked down at Isolde who was grey-faced against the grey wood of the gate. 'She has all the courage in the world, but she cannot be crippled,' he said. 'You had better be sure that you can cut the shoes. If you are thinking of taking her feet off at the ankles, you must stop right now.'

'I'll do the best I can,' Radu Bey said, and Freize shuddered to see his dark smile. 'You'll have to trust me.'

Freize dropped to his knees beside Isolde. 'For pity's sake, let me tie your feet together and carry you away from here,' he begged her. 'Don't let this barbarian touch you. Don't let him draw his sword. Don't you see he is laughing at us? Don't you think it is a plot between him and these terrible people, so that you are crippled for life and they cannot be blamed – they can say that you asked for it?'

Her lips were as white as her pale face. 'I do ask for it,' she said, and she shuddered as if she were chilled to death already. 'I do ask for it.'

Ishraq had the pedlar kneeling on the hard ground, his hands behind his back, tied to his ankles with the rope from her saddle. It was an agonising position, and the bruise on his cheek was bleeding and throbbing with pain. 'You poisoned me and sent my friend Isolde out to her death; you tell me why I should not kill you?' she asked reasonably.

'I beg of you,' he said. 'I meant only to drug you to sleep and send her ladyship out for the afternoon. She has probably returned already.'

Ishraq did not believe him for a moment. 'Will you go back to Giorgio without the sword?'

'I have nowhere else to go; he is my master. I did not want to do this – he commands me.'

'Tell him that if he comes against us again, we will turn in our tracks and come after him. Remind him that his sister and I are stronger and braver than he, and that we will not hesitate to shed family blood if we have to. Tell him that we are going east, to make a new life for ourselves. We have all but forgotten Lucretili. He can keep the castle; he can keep the lands. We just want to live in peace.'

He frowned. He could not be sure whether or not he should believe her. She certainly did not look like a woman who had accepted defeat. 'I'll tell him,' he said. 'But he won't believe me. Will you send the broadsword as a sign that you give him the lordship?'

'I will,' Ishraq said. 'But first we have to get it unlocked. We have to put it with Count Vlad's matching broadsword. When we've done that, we will return it to Lucretili. I swear to you, the sword will come back to Lucretili. That's why we're going east. To find the new Wallachian count and match swords together.'

'I will tell him,' he promised. 'I swear I will tell him all this.'

'Convince him,' she urged. 'You don't want to meet me again, and I will remember you, even if it is years from now.'

'Of course, of course. I will never come for you again, I will persuade him to leave the two of you alone.'

She nodded.

'So we have an agreement?' he proposed. 'You let me go now, I tell him that you are going into exile, and you send back the broadsword.'

She hid her smile. 'I might bring it myself,' she said so lightly that he did not hear the threat.

She got to her feet and went to his horse and untied the fastenings on his saddlebags. There were little purses of jewellery, scraps of lace, ribbons and carved ivory toys. There were Isolde's riding boots.

'You stole these?' Ishraq turned with them in her hand. 'Her own boots?'

'To prove to Giorgio she was in dancing shoes,' he said.

Ishraq brought out a pair of red shoes. 'And these?'

'In case the others did not fit tightly.'

'You made her think they would force her to dance,' she said wonderingly. 'I've seen a snake charmed out of its box and dancing. You did that to her.'

He nodded and then stilled himself as his head swam. 'If you've seen it done then you know – it can be done to anyone who is ready to believe.'

'Why did you not do it to us both?'

He looked resentfully at her. 'They told me you were not easily persuaded.'

She laughed shortly. 'But what made the other dancers leave their homes? The ones we saw with the fiddler? Someone like you? Making mischief?'

'No, they do it to themselves – they convince themselves,' he said. 'They hear of dancers and they long for escape from their own lives. You'll have heard that someone

193

heartbroken can lie down and die, die without a mark on them? They wish it on themselves. All I did with Lady Isolde was wish it on her.'

'It's in their own minds?' Ishraq asked, thinking what Luca would want to know.

'Like miracles and seeing angels,' he said sourly. 'Everyone knows you can do that for wishing. Like seeing monsters when you're drunk.'

Ishraq tipped out his pack, kicked the things around on the ground, not touching them with her hands, ignoring his squawks of protest. She tucked Isolde's riding boots back into his saddlebags, but tipped out his purse of coins and threw it in an arc, as far as she could, the purse turning in the air, spilling coins as it fell.

'Infidel! Lady! Why rob me as well as injure me?'

'Because anyone rescuing you will stop to pick up the gold,' she explained. 'I expect you will scuffle around in the dust for the money as soon as you are freed. I don't want you following me again.'

'I would not,' he protested. 'I hope to never see you again.'

'You should hope it,' she said. 'You should make sure of it. For if we meet again it will be the last errand you run for Giorgio. I have been merciful this time – you won't get a second chance.'

'I know it, I know it,' he said. 'We have an agreement. And you will untie me?'

'No,' she said. 'I'll leave you as you are. You'll get out of your bonds in an hour or so, I should think, or someone will come by tonight or tomorrow. But I will say farewell to you here, and remind you to never come after Isolde, or me, ever again.'

'You can't leave me here! Wounded? And tied up?'

She smiled without humour, her eyes cold, her face hard. 'As you wish, of course. If you prefer, I can just kill you.'

'No! No! Gracious lady. But you would loosen the ropes?'

As her answer she swung into the saddle of his horse, and took the reins of her own to lead him.

'My horse!' he moaned.

'Why don't you will yourself free?' she suggested. 'Five, four, three, two, one!' She laughed at his angry face. 'Goodbye, Poisoner.'

Freize and Isolde waited in frightened silence as the blacksmith came down the street with a smoking bucket of boiling pitch. The dark stench of it smelled of the winds of hell. The Ottoman swordsman stood beside them in silence, nodding his head thoughtfully as if rehearsing something in his mind. Someone had brought a stool for Isolde to sit on, and two sturdy logs of wood which they placed under each of her legs. One of the guards helped her to sit on the stool as Freize stood, appalled, beside her. The guards positioned the logs under each calf, her ankles sticking out to give the Ottoman a clear sweep.

'Please. Tell him no,' Freize muttered.

Isolde shook her head. He could see her teeth were clenched, biting her lower lip. She was very pale.

'Hold her shoulders still in case she faints,' Radu Bey ordered. Freize stood behind her and put his hands on Isolde's shoulders. He could feel a constant slight tremble running through her, like a trapped animal that shivers on every breath.

'No,' said Radu Bey shortly. 'Not like that. You need to hold her so tightly that she can't move at all. Kneel down behind her. Get a good grip of her.' He looked at Freize's grey face and grim expression, and nearly laughed out loud. 'Wrap your arms round her and hold her tight as a lover,' he recommended. 'I promise, you don't want her to shy away and me to miss my stroke.'

Freize obeyed him and felt Isolde shaking all over as she leaned back against him. He put one arm round her shoulders and across her chest, and one arm round her waist. He could feel the rapid pulse making her whole body vibrate as she panted with fear.

'You and you,' Radu Bey said, pointing his sheathed scimitar at two of the guards. 'Hold her legs still. She must not move so much as a hair's breadth.'

The rabbi looked at the three men holding Isolde. Radu Bey spoke: 'You consent?' he asked. 'You are sure you want to risk this? You want these men to hold you down while I unsheathe my sword?'

'I consent,' she said. Her voice was a breathless thread of sound.

'Even that I take my scimitar to you?' Radu Bey showed her the wicked curving blade, reached forward and plucked

196

a hair from her head, dropped it and slashed through it. They all saw the hair sliced in two: the scimitar was as sharp as a barber's blade.

'I consent,' she repeated, her voice hoarse.

The rabbi nodded at the guards and each one straddled one of her legs, gripping her knees with their calves, holding her twitching feet in their strong hands at the ankles, keeping her as still as they could. They ducked their heads and closed their eyes so they did not see the Ottoman with his vicious sword; no one could have seen him and not flinched.

'If I miss my aim and cut off her foot, any part of her foot, you kick away the log of wood and plunge the stump into the bucket of pitch at once,' Radu Bey commanded the men. 'Don't wait for a second. It must be done at once, or she will bleed to death and die of the shock.'

Grimly, they nodded. Isolde felt their grip on her ankles tighten like a vice.

Freize wrapped around her, his arms around her body, her head jammed against his neck. He felt that time had stood still and that he was trapped in a terrible nightmare. His head was swirling as he tightened his grip. 'Tell him no!' he whispered to Isolde. 'For God's sake, tell him no.'

He felt her head tremble in denial and then he looked up as Radu Bey held the scimitar high over his head.

Freize thought he would cry out, forbid the Ottoman to take the risk. But the man moved too fast, without warning. All at once there was a sudden whistle of noise, like someone slashing through silk, and in a blur of movement the dark-robed man whirled on the spot, his blade high as if cutting down an opponent, and brought it down once, spun around again in a full circle like a dervish,

197

and slashed down again like a cracking whip, moving too fast to see. Isolde screamed aloud and Freize felt her go limp in his arms as she fainted. He gripped her tightly, but could not bring himself to look down at her feet, expecting to see her legs horribly mutilated, her feet sliced off on the cobblestones, and the guards thrusting the bleeding stumps into boiling pitch.

But, when he did look, the two men holding her feet were falling backwards, their faces incredulous; her bloodstained feet were naked, the pleated soles limp on the cobbles, the uppers peeling away clean, as a cut ribbon. Isolde was coming round, blinking her eyes and looking down fearfully at her feet, freed from the red shoes at last.

Freize gave a hoarse sob of relief, and buried his face in her icy neck; but Isolde made no sound. She reached down and felt the soles of her feet, fingering them all over, as if she could not believe that they were not skinned to the bone by the merciless blade. She held her toes as if she would count them, then looked up at Radu Bey. She was dazzled, she could not see him – he was a threatening silhouette against the brightness of the morning sun.

'Get me up,' she said to Freize. She never took her eyes from the Ottoman lord as she struggled up and stood gingerly barefoot. 'I owe you a great debt; you have saved my life.'

Cleaning his sword on a piece of black silk, he glanced at her and nodded. 'You're unhurt?' he confirmed. 'Not even grazed?'

'I did not believe it could be done,' she said breathlessly.

'Then you were brave indeed to hold still,' he said. 'Quite surprising in a woman.'

Her white face flushed red. 'I am the Lady of Lucretili,' she said with a sudden rush of pride. 'I am not a frightened slave.'

He nodded. 'I know of your father,' he said. 'You are his daughter indeed. He was a brave man.'

'You knew he was a crusader?' she asked tentatively, wondering if perhaps his father had met the Lord of Lucretili in battle. 'Were your people his enemy?'

'My father was a Christian. Your father and mine fought side by side,' Radu Bey said. 'My father loved him like a brother. He told me that your father came on crusade thinking to destroy everything; but, like a few others, he had the eyes to see and the ears to hear, and he married an Arab princess, and took her back home to his castle in Italy to be his lady and her sons to be his heirs.'

Isolde's hand on Freize's arm tightened its grip. 'No. That's not true. He did no such thing. He already had a wife – my mother.'

The Ottoman lord slid his scimitar back into its jewelled sheath. 'Yes,' he told her. 'He converted to Islam, and he took an Islamic wife. Ask anyone. She was his second wife – she knew of the first; she was content with the arrangement which is not unusual for us. It was agreed and done by our laws.'

Isolde choked for breath. 'This is a lie! The Arab woman came to our castle as a guest; she had no son. Her only child was a girl – she is my friend and companion. You lie when you say the woman was my father's wife. That is a lie. Take it back.'

'Lady Isolde, this lord just saved your life,' the rabbi interposed. 'And he is our honoured guest.'

She glared at him, her dark blue eyes burning. 'It doesn't buy him the right to lie about my father. My father was a crusader! He answered the call of the Holy Father! He went to recapture Jerusalem from the infidel. He would not have converted. He would never have imperilled his soul. He would never have brought an infidel wife home to our castle; he would never have put a half-Arab bastard into his chair.'

Freize heard her voice grate and knew that she was near to breaking down. But Radu Bey raised an eyebrow. 'I see your gratitude does not last too long,' he remarked. 'I see your pride has a dark side of contempt.'

'I just meant that my father would never have been unfaithful to my mother,' her voice was shaking. 'Our family honour is pure.'

'I am sure he rode out as a crusader and came home again looking quite unchanged,' he said. 'And perhaps he did not tell you – who must have been a baby in your mother's womb when he left – all that happened.'

'He was faithful to God. He was true to my mother,' Isolde insisted.

Radu Bey nodded. 'As you wish,' he said indifferently. 'Fidelity and truth are hard to measure, especially for us, the children of great men. And who knows what god any man serves?' He turned away from her to the rabbi, as if he understood that she was near to breaking down. 'I must go,' he said. 'I won't endanger you by staying any longer.'

'I thank you for this.' The rabbi gestured to the shoes, limp and bloody in the dust. 'We all thank you. I thank God that you were here. We owe you a debt that we will not forget.'

The lord nodded with a gleam of a smile, as his horse was brought down the narrow street, his groom and his servants mounted and riding behind it.

'You're going?' Isolde exclaimed. 'Now?'

He bowed to her and turned away. Without any apparent sign passing between the horse and rider, the horse bent one knee to the ground as Radu Bey took hold of the pommel of the beautifully embroidered black saddle and vaulted up onto the animal's back in one smooth movement. The horse stepped up to its full height. Radu Bey bowed again to Isolde from his high saddle and looked past her to Freize. 'Who was it that you came in with?' he demanded.

Freize jumped. 'When we came into the village?'

'Don't play the fool,' Radu Bey advised. 'Whoever it was that spoke Hebrew. You two certainly don't.'

'I don't know,' Freize said honestly. 'I don't understand it. He helped us get away from the dancers, and he called on the gateman to let us in. Then he disappeared.'

'And where did he come from?'

'Perhaps Venice?' Freize said cautiously. 'But I can't tell you what sort of thing he was. I didn't bring him. I didn't want him. Twice, I told him to leave us. I think he just followed us.'

Radu Bey frowned as if thinking deeply. Then he nodded at the rabbi, his servants saluting the older man. 'I think you may have a protector,' he told them. 'I think these foolish Christians may have accidentally brought in your saviour. Perhaps he will protect you. Until I return . . . until we return in force.'

'Radu Bey . . .' Isolde stammered.

He pulled his big black horse to a halt though it sidled on the tight rein. 'My lady?' he replied.

Isolde limped on tender feet so that she stood at his big horse's flank, looking up at him. 'I thank you very much,' she said. 'I know that I owe my life to you. It is a debt I will not forget. Forgive me – for what I said to you just now. I was very troubled by what you said about my father.'

His dark smile warmed his face. 'Troubled?' He laughed. 'Never in my life have I seen a woman in more trouble than you, with your bloodstained feet, wishing for your brother's death,' he remarked. 'Nor one better made to face trouble with courage.' He bent down to her. 'Release that courage, and you will need no one's help. If I were you, I would go home now and face your brother without any help. God knows you are woman enough to fight your own battles.'

'I cannot,' she said. 'I have to get help against my brother.'

'And where are you going for help?'

'The Prince of Wallachia.'

He nodded slowly, as if she were telling him something of great significance. 'Ah, the good Count Vlad. Do you know him at all?'

'No, he is the son of my godfather; our fathers exchanged swords as a sign of their friendship, so I have his father's crusader sword as he has mine. He is bound to help me if I call on his aid.'

Radu Bey frowned. 'I don't admire your choice of ally,' he said shortly. 'I would warn you against him. He and I have been enemies for a long time. He chose his path and I chose mine and I think that his way has led him into terrible darkness.'

'There is no one else that I can call on,' she hesitated as she looked up at him, as if she wished she might ask him for help once again.

He shrugged. 'May your god guide you, as mine blesses me.'

She pressed a little closer and put her hand on his horse's silky neck, looking up at him. 'You bless me,' she said. 'You saved my life today and I owe you a debt forever.'

'I hope that I never regret it,' he replied coolly.

She raised her face to him. 'Do you regret it now?'

Reluctantly, as if he could not resist her, he bent down and pushed back her tumbled fair hair from her flushed cheek. 'Not now, I don't,' he said. 'I am glad to see a woman like you stand on her own feet.'

She flushed at his touch but she did not move away. 'You must come to me, when I have won back my castle,' she whispered. 'I will repay you for what you have done for me today.'

His face was grim. 'Believe me, we will come,' he said. 'All the way to Rome. But I doubt you will welcome me then.'

He gestured to the gateman to fling open the gates, holding his horse back on a hard rein till the opening was wide. Before the dancers outside realised what was happening, he had galloped through them, his servants close behind him, and was gone at a gallop, heading east. The gates slammed shut behind him and the gateman dropped the heavy bar.

Inside the village, they all stood frozen, listening until the thunder of the hooves on the track had faded away, and Radu Bey was gone.

Hidden at the edge of the woods as the sun slowly rose to midday height in the sky, Brother Peter saw horsemen suddenly burst through the gates and gallop away from the Jews' village, but they were too distant, and gone too fast, for him to see the standard of the peacock feather against the black silk.

A little later he heard the sound of horses cantering again, but this time they were coming at speed from the south, and riding towards the Jewish village; and then he saw them as they burst from the wood at the top of the valley and scrambled down the road, hardly checking their speed, down the hill towards the little stone bridge where some of the dancers were sitting on the parapet, others on the bank kicking their feet in the cold water of the river, some of them leisurely finishing their meal, and waiting for their purse of silver.

The dancers at the gates heard the noise too, and the drummer rattled the tambourine to sound the alarm. In one fluid movement, the fiddler leaped to his feet and dashed away, around the tall perimeter wall of the village and out of sight.

Alarmed, the dancers struggled to their feet, but now

the drummer was gone too, over the parapet of the bridge onto the riverbank below, running downstream. There was no one to tell them what to do. A couple of them pounded on the gates of the village, begging to be let in; two others, paddling in the river, simply left their tattered shoes on the bank and splashed away upstream, struggled to the river edge, and ran away, stumbling and clawing, up the valley, through rocks and stunted trees where the horses could not easily follow, and got away into the woods. The rest, the landlady of the inn among them, pressed themselves back against the stone wall of the village and waited fearfully as the troop rode towards them. Lord Vargarten was at their head, his sword drawn, his visor down, his eyes glaring through the dark slit.

'Are you ready to abandon this May-game and walk to your homes?' he demanded coldly. 'For I will have no mercy this time.'

The landlady stepped forward, hobbling on her bruised feet. 'Your lordship, I am ready to go home,' she said. 'As best I can. I can't walk for pain, but I'll never go dancing again.'

'Get going then,' he said without sympathy.

She glanced at Luca, who saw the dark blue bruises on her bare feet above her worn-out shoes. 'Surely she can ride behind one of the men,' he muttered to Lord Vargarten. 'We gain nothing by losing her on the way.'

'If we gain her death, we are one fool less,' his lordship said grimly. He raised his voice. 'Start walking,' he ordered her. 'All of you, start walking back to your homes and pray that I forget this folly when I meet you again.'

Most of them bowed their heads, and set off on the

long trail back to their homes, but one man stood and did a little jigging dance step. Even in this moment of danger, he could only dance. At once, one of the men of the troop spurred his horse forward, without waiting for an order, and swung his terrible axe. It was the work of a moment. There was a cry and a sudden thick gout of blood, and the dancer lay in the dust of the road, his face half sliced, his brains spilling out of his skull.

The troop cheered and shouted bawdy oaths. They felt for their own swords and axes, their horses shifting and pawing the ground, as if they wanted to charge, like a hunt that has been blooded and smells more prey.

Luca, one hand holding his horse still, pushed his fist into his mouth and stifled the rising vomit.

'Anyone else want to dance with me?' the lord yelled. 'For this is the dance we're doing today! Take your partners for a dance with death. Anyone want to partner with my sword? Have a little jig with a naked blade?'

The dancers' eyes were glazed with shock. They turned and started to straggle back up the road over the hill leading back to Mauthausen. Some of them were so fearful of Lord Vargarten's merciless temper that they tried to run, a horrible, shambling stagger, glancing over their shoulders as if they feared that the troop would ride after them and cut them down. Lord Vargarten reined in his horse, pushed back his visor, and watched them leave, his expression as hard as his helmet.

Luca spat bile in the dust of the road.

His lordship glanced over. 'Never seen a man beheaded before, Priest?'

Luca shook his head.

His lordship laughed. 'Well, you have now. And next, perhaps you will see a village burned to the ground.'

'The village? But they have done nothing! They may have saved the Lady Isolde. She could be inside! Lord Vargarten, we cannot ...'

Lord Vargarten winked at Luca. 'I rule my lands by terror,' he said quietly. 'That's why my tenants pay my fees, my rent, and my fines. That's why this village pays me a tax every year, and every other fee that I demand. I don't need to know anything about their religion: what they think. I don't need to know anything about them: what they believe and how they live. I know what I think, and I know what I believe about them. I have no interest in the truth or anything else. All they need to know is that I can destroy them because I wish it, and nobody will stop me.'

'The emperor? Are not all Jews under his personal protection?'

'He knows how it is. He trusts me to keep the country at peace – he doesn't care how I do it. We all need the Jews to lend us money, to send money to distant towns, to trade. Why, my own sister needed money in Paris and I sent it from here, in this very village! You would think it impossible, but they did it. I sent her a note from this rabbi here and she took it to a Jew in Paris and he gave her the money. In gold, accurate to the last grain. How can such a thing be? Hundreds of miles and hundreds of nobles, on the promise of a name scribbled on a piece of paper sealed with their sign of a six-pointed star. What is that if not some sort of black magic? How do they do that if not by some satanic brotherhood? Nobody but the Jews can lend money across hundreds of miles; nobody but them can be trusted to pay. Thank God that it is His will that we keep them in subjection. Thank God that we are commanded to keep them down.'

'No,' Luca said emphatically. 'It is not God's will. The Church is very clear: they are not to be attacked. They are sinners, I agree, and the trade of moneylending is despicable; but it is not for us to punish them. God will decide their fate.'

'I will help Him.' Lord Vargarten laughed, his voice thick. He turned to the gateman, high on the tower beside the gate, looking anxiously down at them.

'Your lordship is welcome to our poor village,' he said, his voice a nervous thread. 'Most welcome. What can we do for you?'

'You can open the gates!' Lord Vargarten shouted.

'Your men?'

'They'll stay outside for now.'

There was a low murmur from the Vargarten men as if they had been looking forward to galloping down the main street; but the lord did not even turn his head to them.

'I'll open them,' the gateman promised and ducked down behind the wall. They could hear him struggling with the great beam which barred the gates shut, and then one of the gates swung open wide enough to admit only one horseman, as if he hoped to slam it shut after his lordship.

'Fool,' Lord Vargarten said. He rode into the village with Luca following close behind him.

Brother Peter waited for the dancers to limp past him, back along the road to Mauthausen, and then mounted his horse. Riding slowly, trying to look unconcerned but painfully conscious of the stares of the Vargarten men, he set his horse to walk down the road, leading the other two horses. The soldiers watched him come, recognising him as the old priest who had failed to bring the dancers to their senses.

'Let me through,' Brother Peter said steadily to the first of the men. 'I wish to see Lord Vargarten. My brother in Christ, Brother Luca, an Inquirer of a Holy Order, is with him.'

The troop drew their horses to one side to let Brother Peter pass. 'Tell him to send us out some dinner,' one of the men said in an undertone. 'Tell them we are thirsty.'

The captain of the troop rapped on the wooden panels of the gates and shouted: 'Gateman!'

At once, the gatekeeper slid back a panel and glared through a grille. 'A visitor for his lordship,' the captain said.

The gateman, seeing Brother Peter riding determinedly towards him, scowled and opened the gate for him. Brother

Peter, shrinking from the gaze of the Jewish man as if it carried a pestilence, rode towards Lord Vargarten and Luca.

Ishraq rode at a canter on the smooth track, only slowing to a walk when the ground was rough. By the afternoon, she had crossed the River Danube and was on the quay of Mauthausen, before the barred quay gate.

'Why's the gate shut?' she demanded of the gateman.

'Lord Vargarten's orders, in case the dancers return,' he replied.

'They might return?'

'He went out after them this morning, with his mounted guard,' the man said. 'They've joined with the Jews as one wickedness loves another. His lordship will kill them all, as he would knock down a wasp nest, or burn out a brood of rats.'

'But the Lady of Lucreili is not with the dancers,' Ishraq demanded. 'Surely she has returned with her friends?'

'Not her. She danced off with them to the Jews. You'll not see her again.'

'Let me in!' Ishraq said shortly and led both horses through the town to the stable yard of the inn. The stableman was lounging in the yard.

'Take my horse and see that it is rubbed down and turned out to grass,' Ishraq said shortly, handing over the reins.

'The mistress has come home exhausted, and gone to bed. Tired out by dancing,' he told her.

'And the young lady?'

'Still with the dancers, or run off with the Jews now,' he said, relishing the scandal. 'But his lordship will destroy them all, for sure.' He took the reins of her horse, but did not interrupt his story. 'They're as bad as each other: Jews and dancers. Both strange, both unruly, both unknown, both responsible for plague and hunger and danger, though who knows how?' He glanced at Ishraq's dark face. 'Infidels,' he said. 'Other.'

Ishraq turned away from his insults, mounted the horse she had stolen from the pedlar and rode out of the stable yard, through the north gate and as fast as she could down the road. When she went past the lane that led to Lord Vargarten's castle, she could see the tracks of many horses on the mud of the road, and when it turned a corner and she came out from the trees she could see the road winding down the steep slope to the river, the bridge, and the village with the mounted soldiers waiting before it.

She set her horse down the slope, and rode past the men without a glance at them though they loudly remarked on her Arab dress and on the great crusader sword in the sheath at her saddle. 'Admit me,' she said imperiously to the gateman, who swung open the gate without hesitation.

As soon as she was through, she saw Luca, and Brother

Peter, dismounted from their horses, talking earnestly to Lord Vargarten who sat at his ease, high on his horse, above them.

'You're safe!' Luca exclaimed.

'Yes,' she said shortly, as if it were of no importance. 'Where is Isolde?'

'Safe too. God be praised, these people gave her refuge,' Luca answered. He turned to the rabbi. 'This is our travelling companion, Ishraq, the friend of the Lady of Lucretili.'

'You will want to see her,' the rabbi guessed. 'She's in my house. She is quite unhurt. She insisted on coming into our village and promised we would not be punished for giving her refuge. You can go straight in.' He gestured to a house which stood adjoining the synagogue, in the middle of the square, facing the gate. 'She has been perfectly safe,' he said to Lord Vargarten. 'She will tell you herself. We rescued her from the dancers and we have not touched her. She came into the village at her own request. She begged for entry.'

'Christians and Jews have to live apart,' Lord Vargarten ruled. 'It's the law. You've broken the law. You'll be fined.'

The rabbi bowed his head. 'Your lordship knows that Christians come and go here and everywhere, as they wish. How can we stop them? We're not allowed to bar a door to them.'

'I'll find her,' Ishraq said. She jumped down from her horse, handed Brother Peter her reins, threw a quick smile at Luca and went to the house where the door stood open, tapped on it and went inside.

She blinked as her eyes became accustomed to the

212

shadowy room. At first glance she could see that it was not a Christian room, but Ishraq had seen the beautifully ornate interiors of the Moorish houses of Spain and it did not frighten her. Unlike Christian houses there was no little icon on the wall, nor a candle before a crucifix. Instead there was a sideboard with some silver cups and a silver plate marked with symbols around the rim, and a beautiful, many-branched candelabra with pure white wax candles unlit.

Isolde was seated on a stool before the cold fireplace, her feet in a bowl of water, a woman kneeling before her, sponging the bruises and scrapes on her battered feet. She looked up as she heard the door open and the relief on her face shone as she recognised Ishraq.

'Ishraq!' she said. 'My love. Thank God it's you.'

'Sister,' Ishraq replied. She took two swift steps across the room and wrapped Isolde in her arms, kissing her head and stroking her blonde hair. 'I was afraid I would never see you again.'

Eagerly, Isolde pulled Ishraq down so that their two heads, one very dark and one very fair, were level. 'And you? Are you quite safe? Luca said that the pedlar put you to sleep, but that you had gone after him?'

Ishraq paused for a moment, thinking of the night of unconsciousness, and the dark swim out of death, thought of waking with Luca's arms around her, waking to lovemaking and wanting to never let him go, then the breakneck ride after the pedlar, the stone to his face, and holding him down on the road with her heel in his back.

'So much to tell you! The earrings were poisoned, and I fell unconscious on the landlady's floor. I didn't come

213

round till morning, and found you were gone. That was terrible. The pedlar stole your broadsword so Luca went after you, and I went after the thief and got it back. Are your feet all right? Are you very hurt?'

'Just bruised, just scratched. It was as if I was mad; but I'm in my right mind now.'

'What happened?'

'It was the shoes . . .'

The woman kneeling at her feet moved the bowl to one side and started to pat Isolde's feet dry. 'This lady has soaked my feet with some herbs,' Isolde said. 'She has been very kind.'

'I have your riding boots in the saddlebags,' Ishraq said. 'I'll get them.'

She went out into the brightness of the village street and at once sensed a change in the air. The street was deserted, the shutters all barred, every door locked. Only the door to the rabbi's house behind her was still open, and, as she looked uneasily round, that closed quietly behind her and she heard the lock click.

She went to the horses and found Freize waiting with them. 'Freize,' she said, and there was love in her voice. 'I am so glad you are safe. I am so glad you went after her. I am so glad that you were with her. I knew she would be safe if she was with you.'

His eyes were warm on her, but he looked anxious. 'I don't know if we're that safe now,' he said quietly. 'It's gone very quiet here, and his lordship keeps saying that they must be punished for saving us. They won't listen to me. Is she able to ride? We should leave.'

'What's happening?' she whispered, undoing the leather

straps on the bag and pulling Isolde's boots from the bundle.

'Lord Vargarten is walking down the street, talking with the rabbi. Demanding to know what happened with us and the dancers. Whatever the rabbi answers, Lord Vargarten says that he has broken some rule or other and that the village has to pay for it. I've tried to tell him that they gave us sanctuary here, that we would be dead without them, but he won't hear me, he won't even listen to Luca. Now he's called for them to set up a table in the square and to serve him dinner and pay him money. Luca is arguing, but the lord is beyond reason.'

Freize looked baffled and furious. 'I know they're Jews,' he muttered. 'I understand that they cannot be treated like Christians. But they saved our lives. They saved us from the dancers and they helped get the shoes off Isolde's feet. It's wrong that they should be punished.'

'Is that why all the doors are bolted?'

He nodded. 'All the girls and women vanished the minute Vargarten came in the gate. They know what's going to happen and they just melted away. Looks as if they don't think a dinner and a tax will be enough for the lord and his men. Looks like they're expecting worse.'

'Then we'd better go.' Ishraq's first thought was of Isolde.

'Yes,' Freize said bluntly. 'We can't stop Lord Vargarten's men doing whatever they want to this poor village, and we're better out of this. Luca is talking with him now, trying to agree a fair price for their fine, but his lordship has sent for wine and is drinking. I doubt he'll listen to reason.'

Freize hesitated.

'What?' Ishraq asked. 'What is it?'

'D'you remember the Being?' he asked her. 'The funny little thing? That came from the alchemists' jar? The thing that we never quite saw?'

She nodded as if she did not want to say its name. 'Yes. I remember it, though I only glimpsed it when it came after us on the road. Have you seen it again?'

'He followed me as I followed Isolde,' he whispered rapidly, anxious to tell her. 'He was in the shape of a youth then. All along the road he followed me, as I followed the dancers, growing all the time until he was taller, as tall as me then overtopping me by a head. Growing stronger too. Strong like a horse.'

She shook her head. 'Freize, this isn't possible.'

'I know it isn't; but I saw it. I was watching Isolde as she slept among them, on the ground like a poor woman, and he crept up on them, when they were sleeping, and lifted her up like she was a child. It was him who got her away – it wasn't me. I was helpless, and then I started dancing myself, so I was no better than any of them. I would be off with them now, but he got hold of me. He had Isolde in one arm and me in the other. He saved us both. Truly he did, Ishraq.'

'He saved you?' she queried. 'But how?'

'Ishraq, he was grown. Much taller and stronger than me. He wasn't a youth any more. God knows he wasn't a lizard. He got hold of both of us, his arm round Isolde's waist, hand in mine, dragged us to this place, the only place that we might be safe. They had the gates bolted shut, they wouldn't open, but the Being shouted some strange words.'

216

'What words?'

He shrugged. 'Foreign words. Magic words. I don't know. Perhaps a password? Their words, Hebrew words, they said. But they opened the gates the moment they heard them and we fell inside and then he disappeared.'

'Disappeared?'

'Slipped away,' he said. 'We were in a bad state: I was still dancing; Isolde was collapsing. I didn't even see him go.' He thought for a moment. 'I didn't even see him come in, but I thought he did. When we looked around, he was gone, and the gateman had not seen him.'

She was pale. 'So where is he now?' she demanded.

Silently, as if he could not bear to speak, Freize nodded back to the rabbi's house. 'That's what's worrying me. I think I just saw him,' he said. 'At the upper window. I think he closed the shutters. I think he is upstairs.'

Ishraq made a little frightened sound and turned and stared at the smart, brightly painted house with the tightly closed shutters. 'Isolde is downstairs,' she said. 'And that thing is up there?'

'Let's get out of here,' he said with a nod. 'Let's get her away.'

'Do you think we have brought the Being down on them? Should we warn them? Should we tell Lord Vargarten?'

Freize looked blank. 'I don't know,' he said. 'I don't know anything any more. Did he save us by bringing us here or did he bring us to them? Has he trapped us here? Is he as bad as they are said to be? Are they holding us as prisoners? Should we ask Lord Vargarten to get us out before he does anything else?'

217

'We've got to get out. I'll fetch Isolde.' Ishraq turned and hurried back to the house with the riding boots in her hand.

She tapped on the door and called: 'It's only me – let me in.'

The door swung open. Ishraq stepped inside as the rabbi's wife closed and bolted it behind her.

'Are you afraid of Lord Vargarten and his men?' Ishraq asked her.

The woman nodded. 'They are brutes,' she said quietly.

'Are you going to hide?'

'We can't take you with us into hiding,' the woman said at once. 'I am sorry, but you cannot come. They would say that we had stolen you away and burn down the village to rescue you.'

'I know, I know,' Isolde said. 'We'll go now. We'll go at once.' To Ishraq she said: 'We're endangering her by staying here. We should go. What's happening out there?'

'Lord Vargarten is getting drunk and ordering dinner,' Ishraq said shortly. 'Freize thinks there will be trouble. And there's something worse . . .'

'What?'

'I don't understand it, but we should get away from here.'

Isolde shook her head. 'They say that this happens often. At Christmas, at Easter. It's terrible, Ishraq. I didn't know.'

'Oh, didn't you?' her friend countered. 'Really? For I knew that Jews are feared and hated, even at Lucretili.'

Isolde looked ashamed. 'My father used to tax Jewish travellers when they passed through his lands and they were sometimes treated roughly. Sometimes their goods were stolen from them and they couldn't get justice, I knew

218

that. But I didn't know that their villages were attacked. I didn't know that their children were taken. This lady, Sarah, has told me some terrible things.'

'We must let her get into hiding,' Ishraq said quickly. 'And we must leave.'

She knelt before Isolde and helped her pull on the riding boots. Isolde cried out in pain as her bruised feet were squeezed, but she managed to stand. 'I'm all right,' she reassured her friend. 'I can't walk, but I will be able to ride.'

She turned and took Sarah's hands. 'I am so sorry. I hope you are safe,' she said. 'I shall pray for you.'

Sarah bowed her head and opened the door for them. As they stepped out into the street, they heard the door close behind them, the bolt slide, and then a creaking sound as a table was dragged across the floor to block the doorway.

Ishraq supported Isolde as she limped across the cobbles to where Freize was waiting with the horses. He beamed as he saw them together, and then glanced down the street to where Lord Vargarten was now seated at a trestle table with a jug of wine before him and men serving him food. The village gates had been opened wide and the girls could see that the soldiers outside were eating too, and drinking deeply of the special ale that the Jews brewed for their feasts. It was strong, sweet ale, brewed from hops and honey, and the soldiers called for more and more as they broke the bread and ate cheese and bellowed that the meat must be roasted by now, and if it did not come at once then they would roast Jewish babies and eat them instead. It was rough and bullying talk, but Vargarten's men laughed as they shouted abuse, and the Jewish men did not respond, but went on bringing more jugs of ale and more bread.

Luca and Brother Peter were seated on either side of Lord Vargarten, not drinking but talking quietly with him, as if they hoped that their presence would keep him calm.

'Tell Luca we're leaving,' Isolde said to Freize, looking at the drunken soldiers. 'It's not safe for Ishraq and me if those men get rowdy.'

Freize handed the reins to Ishraq and went the few steps down the village street, bent to whisper into Luca's ear and listened to his reply.

He came back, looking grave. 'He says I am to take you away, and then come back for him. He wants to stay here till the soldiers leave.'

'Surely he doesn't think he can stop them? He can't countermand their lord.'

'He says that he has to try.'

'Where are we to go?' Isolde asked. 'Back to the inn?'

'Yes, I'll go with you, see you safely inside, and then come back for Luca and Brother Peter.'

Ishraq took a look at the men, who set up a great growl of a cheer as some fat roasted chickens and a big bowl of butter and gravy were brought to their table. 'Let's go,' she said. 'Perhaps they'll eat themselves sick.'

'I'm sure that's the intention,' Isolde said.

Ishraq helped Isolde onto her horse and mounted her own, but was surprised as Freize handed her the reins to his horse Rufino. 'What are you doing?' she demanded. 'Freize, we have to go now.'

'One moment,' he said, and turned back to the rabbi's house. He knew the front door was barred so he tapped on the shutters and they opened a crack and the rabbi's wife, Sarah, peered out.

'I am sorry,' Freize said awkwardly. 'Forgive me. I am afraid of something, afraid for you. When we came to your town, I think we brought a Being in with us, and I think he is in your rooms upstairs.'

Sarah looked at him as if she could not understand his speech. 'A Being,' Freize said again, feeling more and more of a fool before her dark, frightened gaze. 'A great, growing boy.'

She looked at him as he struggled to explain. 'He spoke Hebrew to the gateman,' he said. 'On his forehead is the word *EMET*.'

She knew that word – he could tell by the flicker of recognition in her eyes. She did not speak, but opened the shutter wide and swung open the window behind it in a silent invitation. Freize pitched himself in over the windowsill head first and scrambled to his feet. Inside the darkened house, she stood to one side and gestured that he might go up the twisting stairs to the upper floor. Freize bent his head beneath the low beams and climbed up.

The first room that he came to was a bedroom with a broad bed, piled high with feather mattresses and clean white linen sheets. On the doorway was the mezuzah. Freize looked at it without understanding, thinking it was some kind of pagan icon that might poison him if he went through the door; but he ducked his head and went past it, his neck prickling. The only furniture in the plain room was a chest at the foot of the bed. Certainly, there was no place that the giant Being could hide.

The rabbi's wife crossed the room ahead of him and showed him the smooth, unbroken linenfold panelling on the wall. Freize tapped on it, but it did not yield and it did not sound hollow. He looked at Sarah and, with a little smile, she stepped to one side, and pressed her foot down on a floorboard. There was a tiny click, and a hidden doorway in the panels swung open.

It looked like nothing more than a cupboard. Any searcher might conclude that it was a hiding place for treasure, or for a single man to stand still and silent, and that they had found all there was to discover. Sarah went into the small space and pressed an unmarked place on the ceiling and all at once it slid back, and a wooden ladder descended on a pulley. She gestured that Freize might go up.

Slowly, he climbed through the hatch into the attic and found that it adjoined the roof vault of the next-door synagogue. The women and the children of the village were hiding here, seated, holding each other, in complete silence in the darkness. As Freize's head slowly emerged through the open hatch, their faces turned towards him, but nobody said a word. Freize took in the golden-skinned, dark-eyed faces of a dozen children, the blaze of treasure of the case holding the scrolls of the Torah, the beautiful brocade cover, the silver yad, the rolls of the sacred texts, the golden menorah, and before it all, on guard, his head brushing the very top of the steeply sloping rafters, unsmiling and silent, was the Being.

On his forehead, shining as if in gold, were the letters that Freize had seen on the head of the little Being in the glass jar in the alchemists' room in Venice: *EMET*.

Freize's compassion for the strange Being overcame his superstitious fear. 'I saw you at the window,' he explained. 'And you saved us last night. Thank you. So I came to tell you: there's going to be trouble. You might not be safe here.'

He looked around at the little dark heads of the children, at their trusting faces and the dark eyes fixed unblinkingly on him. 'I'll come back,' he said, as if the words were being forced from him. 'I'll come back for you.'

He reached out for two of the nearest children. 'I'll take two now,' he said.

Silently, as they had promised their parents they would be silent, they yielded themselves to him, and, one under each arm, he went carefully backwards down the ladder, through the hidden door, across the bedroom, and down the stairs. The rabbi's wife saw him lift them through the window and squeeze through the opening himself. She said nothing, but watched him from the window as he put one child on the horse behind Isolde and one child on the horse behind Ishraq, then drew their long riding capes down over the children to hide them. As Freize mounted Rufino, he heard the shutter slam and bolt.

~

The gateway stood wide open: there was no point in securing the village with Lord Vargarten inside. Its safety would depend on his whim, not on its defences. Ishraq led the way through the open gates with Isolde alongside her, Freize bringing up the rear. The soldiers glanced up indifferently as they passed. Ishraq felt the silent child's arms tighten round her waist and spurred her horse onward. Freize glanced back. All the shutters were barred; all the doors were bolted. It was so quiet and it felt so doomed, he thought, that it was like a town with the plague.

Once through the gate, the girls rode side by side, letting

the horses walk up the stony path to the forest and then urging them forward in a canter where the track was smooth.

'As long as we don't meet the fiddler,' Isolde said.

'I think he would have no power over you now,' Ishraq said. 'It was the pedlar who persuaded you that the shoes would make you dance.'

'It felt like the music.'

'It was a trick of the wits, by the pedlar. He was hired by Giorgio to kill me, to get rid of you, and to steal the sword.'

'And he poisoned you?' Isolde demanded. 'On my brother's orders?' She looked grim. 'I will never forgive Giorgio for this,' she said. 'I knew he was my enemy before – I had sworn to recapture my lands from him – but to poison you! You could have died. We could both have died. I will see him dead at my feet for this.'

Ishraq told her friend that she had been in a deep sleep, perhaps a faint, very like death, but Luca had brought her round. She did not say how; she did not describe their tranced night of joy together. She thought that she would never tell anyone – she would never even think of it herself. Luca would never speak of it to her; even now, it felt like a dream, part of the death-like experience: too strange and too secret ever to be spoken of.

'He held you?' Isolde asked.

Ishraq glanced sideways at her friend, looking for signs of jealousy, but saw none. It was as if they had all been too close to death to worry about anything but their survival. 'He warmed me through,' she said. 'He breathed for me. Truly, I think he brought me back to life.'

'Thank God he was there and knew what to do,' Isolde said. 'Think if he had not searched the inn for you?'

224

'He and Freize saved each of us,' Ishraq said. 'We owe them our lives.'

'And, as well, I owe my life to Radu Bey,' Isolde told her.

'No!' Ishraq exclaimed. 'What was he doing here?'

Isolde told her how Radu Bey had appeared in the village, and saved her from the red shoes, how he had lifted his scimitar and whirled down on the shoes, that she had felt the wind of the blade as he slashed it down but nothing but the sudden cool on her feet as the shoes fell off.

'And did he just cut them off and leave?' Ishraq wondered. 'Did he say what he was doing here in the first place? Did he say anything about the fools' gold and Luca's father in slavery?'

'No,' Isolde said. 'I should have asked him. I just couldn't think. He was . . .' She broke off.

'He was what?' Ishraq asked her.

'He was a lord,' Isolde said, incapable of finding words to describe the presence of Radu Bey, his quiet power. She said nothing about the stranger's claim that her father had converted to become a Muslim, and had been married to Ishraq's mother. She said nothing about her own furious denial. She felt she was not ready to tell Ishraq that all the time that her father had brought them up together, he might have known they were half-sisters. She had to consider what she was to her father, and he to her, if he could have raised her with a sister and never told her. She did not know what to think if her father had died without telling her that he had another daughter, or if he intended her to be considered as the co-heiress to the Castle of Lucretili. Isolde did not

225

think she could possibly claim the castle for herself if Ishraq had some sort of right. She could never disinherit Ishraq. But equally she knew she would never hand over Lucretili to another, not even Ishraq.

'But what was he doing here?' Ishraq wondered. 'You don't think he followed us? You don't think he is tracking Luca, hoping to turn him to work against his lord and the Order of Darkness?'

'They said he was trading,' Freize volunteered, coming alongside them.

'That's not very likely, is it?' Ishraq pressed. 'He didn't look like a small trader when we first saw him on his great galley. He said he was exploring the boundaries of the Ottoman Empire with old maps. He's probably doing that on land now.'

'Spying?' Isolde suggested. 'Obviously, the Ottomans are planning to advance from the east into all these towns and villages. They hope to take over all of Christendom – he said as much. Their army will be coming this way if we don't stop them; perhaps Radu Bey was learning the lie of the land. He told me that they hope to get to Rome.'

Ishraq nodded. 'They must plan to take Rome. They have Constantinople – it is the next obvious objective. And that is one of the signs of the end of the world.'

'He knows of Count Vlad,' Isolde said quietly.

'He would do: the count has led one of the few armies that can stand against them.'

'He spoke of him with hatred.'

'Did he?' asked Ishraq. 'He warned me too when we talked at Piccolo. And he warned me against a man who looked as much like him as a twin brother.'

'Shall we canter?' Freize suggested. He was anxious to return to Luca and get him safely away from the village.

The two girls pressed the little children closer to their backs, tightened the little arms around their waists and put their horses at a fast pace down the dusty track. With relief, Freize saw the jumbled roofs of the town of Mauthausen and the guarded gate.

'Here,' he said. 'I don't think I've ever been so glad to see a poor inn before. Please God I will be back in time for my dinner.'

~

The landlady had returned only a little earlier, walking slowly on painful feet. She was in her bedroom resting, but her daughter had come from her farmhouse outside the town and was running the inn.

The girls dismounted wearily in the stable yard. Freize turned his horse. 'I'll go and fetch Luca and Brother Peter and meet you back here,' he said to them.

'Make sure you do,' Ishraq said to him with a smile. 'I won't feel safe until we are all under the same roof again.'

'I won't feel safe till we are far from here,' Isolde said.

'I don't ever feel safe.' Freize capped their complaints. 'Why don't we all go home and wait for the end of days, comfortably, in our own beds?'

Isolde laughed. 'Godspeed,' she said, reaching up and lifting the child down from the saddle.

The ostler recoiled when he saw them. 'I don't think the mistress will let these come in,' he said, taking the horses' reins. 'I'd better tell her.'

He tapped at the kitchen door and said a few words to the young woman who appeared, her hair pinned up and her face flushed from baking.

'Who are these?' she demanded, stepping out into the yard and looking from one child to another. The youngest one, a boy, shrank back from her stare and took Ishraq's hand.

'These are children from the village,' Isolde said. 'We are taking care of them. Lord Vargarten's men are there, so they are safer with us.'

The woman made a disdainful face. 'Jews,' she said flatly.

Ishraq pulled back her hood and unwound her scarf from her face so that the landlady's daughter could see the tumble of her black hair and her olive skin. 'And my mother was Arab,' she said challengingly. 'What of it?'

The woman looked embarrassed. 'My mother was happy to serve you and your travelling companions, but the children could carry a sickness,' she said awkwardly. 'They have all sorts of diseases, these people.'

'They are not sick,' Isolde overruled her. 'I am the Lady of Lucretili and they are under my protection. They will sit with me, in my rooms, and dine with me tonight. I hope they will be able to return to their families when the village is at peace again. I hope you will cook a good dinner for all of us: my friends when they return, and these children. We will pay a fair price, and I will talk with your mother in the morning. She and I went through a terrible ordeal together. I know that she will understand.'

'No, it's you who don't understand,' the young woman said. 'We're not allowed to take them in, even if we wanted to. They're not allowed to come into our houses. It's for their own safety. We have to live apart.'

'Your mother locked out the dancers, but then she danced with them,' Ishraq said. 'She was no better than any of them. If someone is ill, they should be cured; if they are mad, they should be cared for. If they are children – whoever their parents are – they should be safe. You're not a human being if you don't know that.'

'Well, they're not coming into my kitchen.'

Isolde raised her eyebrows, at her most grand. 'Of course not,' she said. 'They are not servants to wait at the table. They are my guests. There is no call for them to go to the kitchen. And I am sure that they are allowed in a house if I vouch for them.'

'Very well,' the woman said grudgingly. 'But if you had to live near the Jews and see their wealth and their prosperity, when we know that they killed Our Lord, you would feel as I do.'

'They're little children,' Ishraq exclaimed. 'The children of good people! How can they be blamed for a crime that happened a thousand years ago?'

'Was it so long? It wasn't a thousand years,' the ostler suddenly remarked. 'It cannot have been, for the priest speaks of it as if it were only the other day.'

Ishraq looked at him thoughtfully. 'It was more than a thousand years ago, and the Jews have been in exile for hundreds of years. And it was thousands of miles away from here. Did you not know that?'

'In the Holy Land,' he blustered. 'Of course I know that. Did I not start off on crusade myself when Lord Vargarten called us? Was I not going to Jerusalem with my friends?'

'Didn't get beyond Amstetten,' the young woman sneered. 'Did nothing but attack the synagogue at Amstetten, kill all the Jews and steal their treasures.'

'A crusade against the infidel,' he said firmly. 'Here or the Holy Land, it is the same thing. It's still blessed. I am still forgiven my sins for going. Amstetten or Jerusalem, it's the same to the Holy Father. It's still killing Jews and Arabs and anyone who is not of the True Faith, so it's blessed work.'

'It's not the same thing,' ruled Isolde, the daughter of a crusader lord. 'It's not the same thing at all.'

'And how can you be so certain that your faith is better than anyone else's?' Ishraq demanded. 'Since your Bible is the same as theirs, and since Jesus Christ is in the Koran?'

The ostler and the young woman looked uncertain. 'Priest said so,' the young woman said. 'And Josef was just following orders.'

In the Jewish village, Lord Vargarten had completed his dinner and washed it down with a flagon of wine when he beckoned the rabbi to the table. 'I'll take my lads away before they become too boisterous,' he promised. 'There's no need for you all to hide in the woodstores and tremble this time. But I must give them something, you know.'

The rabbi bowed his head. 'You know we are a poor farming village,' he said.

'Don't lie – you trade as well. You have a fortune tucked away somewhere.'

'We trade as we can, but at the moment we have more notes of debt than we have gold to lend. We will be repaid after the harvest has come in. That's why we pay your taxes then, my lord. As you know.'

'Of course I know!' his lordship said irritably. 'Tell me something I don't know. What do you have in your storeroom?'

The rabbi looked surprised. 'Flour, a little sugar, some spices, some dried fruits . . .'

'Not that store!' Lord Vargarten raised his voice and the men at the dining table beyond the gates looked up, like hounds hearing the hunting horn. 'Your treasure room, your gold store.'

The rabbi spread his hands. Luca saw that they were trembling slightly. 'I don't keep a treasure store,' he said. 'I wish that I did. I lend money out, and that in only small amounts, as your lordship knows. When your lordship needs a large sum of money I borrow it from my brethren.'

'Why, how much do I owe you?' Lord Vargarten demanded in sudden irritation. 'Let's see your debt book if there is no treasure to be had.'

'Let's see the debt book!' someone repeated from the soldiers' table, and a man got to his feet, kicked his stool out of the way and came in through the gate towards the lord's table. The rabbi rose to his feet and went into his house using a side door.

'Lord Vargarten, we have no quarrel with the people

231

of this village,' Luca reminded him quietly. 'You came to free the Lady of Lucretili from the dancers and you have done that magnificently. All you need do now is finish your dinner and leave.'

'You don't know,' his lordship said, fixing his eyes on Luca's face. 'Priest, you are too young and you know nothing of the world. I owe a small fortune here, probably several small fortunes. And of course they have to reward me for driving the dancers from their door. What would have happened if we had not arrived?'

Luca fell silent.

'The emperor himself and the Church authorise the Jewish people to deal in loans,' Brother Peter observed, as if to himself. 'They are expected to take the sin of usury on themselves. They are under the protection of the emperor, and so under your protection, my lord. You would be very wrong both in the sight of the emperor and of the Church to molest them.'

'For God's sake, Priest, I'm not molesting them!' his lordship swore. 'I'm just checking on what I owe them. I'm simply hoping to reduce my debt. That's fair enough. I am visiting my creditor to reduce my debt, that's all.'

The rabbi came out of the side door of his house, closing it behind him. In the silence, they could hear the quiet shooting of the bolt from the inside.

'And why do they do that? Why bolt the door if not to hide their treasure?' Lord Vargarten demanded irritably. 'They're hiding something in there!'

'I am hiding nothing,' the rabbi said quietly. 'But my wife is of a nervous disposition. She is afraid of your soldiers.'

'Nothing to be afraid of! They're just lads!'

The rabbi laid his debt book on the table before Lord Vargarten and pointed to an entry. 'This is your debt,' he said quietly. 'Three months ago, and this earlier, last year. This to pay for some losses you had sustained, and this is the price of my lady's emeralds that you asked me to obtain for you.'

'This can't be right!' Lord Vargarten exclaimed, looking at the total. 'What interest are you charging me? This is usurious.'

At the mention of the sinful word, a few of the young men at the table stood and settled their sword belts on their hips. One or two went to untie their horses and swung themselves into their saddles, as if they thought there might be riding or fighting to do.

'No, not at all,' the rabbi interjected. 'I charge you three per cent as we agreed, but I can adjust that if you wish, my lord. Since you are here, and since this troubles you. Shall we say two point five?'

Brother Peter looked up. 'He charges you three per cent?' he asked.

'Is that unfair?' Lord Vargarten asked eagerly. 'Is that not a crime?'

'No,' Brother Peter said hastily. 'I was surprised because it is so low. The Knights Templar charge twenty per cent, and they have permission from the Pope himself. This is very favourable to you, my lord. You would pay far more in Vienna.'

'What? What d'you say?'

Luca could see at once that Lord Vargarten could not calculate his debt, did not understand the concept of percentages, could not even add the simple sums.

'Brother Peter says it is not usurious,' he said. 'He says it is fair.'

'And why write it in heretic script?' the lord said, rounding on the rabbi. 'What does it mean that you write like the infidels you are? Why not write it the proper way? One stroke of the pen means one, two means two, a gate shape means five. Everyone can understand that.'

'Most people use the Arabic numbers now,' Luca said soothingly. 'It's easier to calculate with them than with the old system. But my lord, if this rabbi charges you only two point five per cent then you will owe him nine hundred and forty-three nobles.'

'I can't repay that!' his lordship exclaimed in horror. He turned to the rabbi. 'Are you mad? Are you completely mad to come before me and demand this sort of money? I can't repay that!'

'But you don't repay it!' the rabbi pointed out. 'I don't demand it. I never ask you to repay it. It just stays in my books and I—'

'We can soon remedy that!' Lord Vargarten said in a rage. He grabbed the debt book by the spine and tore out the page. There was a gasp and then a cheer from his men. Brother Peter and Luca exchanged a brief look. The rabbi bowed his head, saying nothing as the lord crushed the paper into a ball and threw it at his feet.

'Now how much do I owe?' his lordship demanded, thrusting the torn book across to Luca.

Luca looked at the next few pages. 'About six hundred,' he said.

'Easily mended!' his lordship said joyously, and ripped out another page. 'What do you think of that?'

The rabbi glanced nervously at Lord Vargarten's guard. More of them had mounted up and were seated on their horses, one hand on the reins, the other on their swords, waiting outside the town, the gates wide open to admit them. The rest were on their feet, standing beside the table, clearly ready to obey orders.

'I can adjust the entire debt,' the rabbi said. 'I can rewrite it to your convenience. We are grateful for your good lordship and happy to have given you a good dinner. I can alter your debt as you leave . . . as you leave . . .' he added quietly.

Lord Vargarten took the book and ripped the whole volume in two, scattering the pages and laughing. He turned to his men. 'You can all take one thing!' he yelled at them. 'One thing only. No more than that. One thing and then back here to ride for home. As an adjustment.' He laughed loudly at his own wit. 'An adjustment, as my friend the usurer here would say.'

'Wait!' Luca said. 'You can't let them loose—'

But the men were unleashed. Those on foot simply leaped over the dinner table and ran into the main street of the town; those on horseback spurred their horses on and followed them, jostling each other in the narrow streets, his lordship bellowing with amusement.

'See what they get!' he shouted at Luca. 'They're such fools. See what they come back with! Ten to one it will be a cooking pot, or a coat.'

'Stop them!' Luca implored.

They saw a man wrenching a set of shutters open and then heard the clatter of breaking glass as he elbowed the leaded panes from the window. He plunged into the room and came out with a beautiful, many-branched candlestick.

One of the horsemen turned his horse in a high doorway and had it lash out and kick at the door. As the door yielded, he ducked his head and rode inside. They heard a scream.

Luca looked at Brother Peter. 'How can we stop this? We have to stop it!'

'We can't,' said Brother Peter grimly. 'We have no authority to forbid it. They are Jews, this is their punishment. We'd better just leave.'

'We can't go!' Luca yelled over the noise of the attack on the village, the splintering of doors, the shattering of windows and the shouts of protest. 'We brought these wolves in! We can't just leave them here!'

Brother Peter grabbed Luca's shoulder. 'This is not the first time,' he said urgently. 'And it won't be the last. This time we brought the men in; but they come whenever they wish. The Jewish people know this: this is what they suffer. They suffer, they endure, and then they patch everything up and continue till the next time. The Church allows this; we, the Christians, allow it. The best thing we can do is urge Lord Vargarten to get his men back with their prizes and leave.'

'Why don't the Jews resist?'

Brother Peter pointed to where a man was desperately running down the street with two guardsmen thundering behind him, easily riding him down. He fell under the hooves of the horses, rolling over and over, bunched up, his face in his hands as he tried to protect his head.

'How would they resist?' he asked. 'A Jew raising a weapon to a Christian would be hanged at once, his household broken up, his children baptised and enslaved. His village would probably be burned to the ground.'

'Why don't they leave?'

'And go where? Everywhere is the same for them, and they have not had a home for more than a thousand years.'

Luca whirled on Brother Peter in a frustrated rage. 'Why do we do this?' he demanded. 'Why do we allow it? Why does the Church not demand that the Jews be left in peace?'

Brother Peter nodded, thoughtful amid the noise and the chaos. 'That is probably the only question,' he said. 'Not why they endure it – for they have no choice – but why we do it, we who have every choice.'

He pulled the hood of his robe over his head as if he would hide the sights of the street from his eyes, and approached Lord Vargarten who was standing, hands on hips, bellowing with laughter at the sight of his men running riot in the streets. The rabbi was nowhere to be seen, his book of debts ripped to pieces and the scattered pages blowing down the street.

'Is it enough, your lordship?' Brother Peter asked calmly. 'Your debts are cancelled and each man has taken a prize. You don't want to kill the golden goose, do you? You don't want to drive them away, or fleece them to the bone.'

'Aye, enough, it's enough,' Lord Vargarten agreed, as if he were coming back to reality from a valorous dream. 'Enough, I suppose.'

He cupped his hands to his mouth and bellowed, 'Enough! To me! To me!'

But the men had not had enough. Two of them came reluctantly away from a nearby house, one of them lugging a bolt of carpet, the other stuffing a silver cup in the front of his jacket. But the others, running down the streets and jumping to kick in windows, were out of earshot and out of control.

'Come on.' Lord Vargarten smiled at Brother Peter and Luca and the two men who had come back to him. 'Better get these varlets back into order before they wreck the place.' He mounted his horse, unsheathed his sword and nodded at the two men. 'Follow me,' he said.

Using the flat of his sword like a flail, he rode down the street, beating his own men about the head and shoulders. His two guards rode behind him, cuffing and shouting until the men broke away from their looting and came back into some sort of order.

'Some are still missing,' Luca said breathlessly to Brother Peter. They had run down the streets behind the horses and now stood to one side.

There was a piercing scream from one of the alleys and Luca whirled round to see a woman desperately running from a man who chased after her, unbuckling his belt as he ran. 'Leave her!' Luca yelled.

He ran towards them both and the woman ducked beneath his arm and dashed through a doorway. Her pursuer rounded on Luca, and slammed a clenched fist into the side of his face. Luca staggered back against the wall as Lord Vargarten bellowed with weary patience: 'Leave the woman, and don't hit the priest! Are you drunk, you fool? Get your damned horse!'

The soldier ducked his head and ran back to the gate for his horse as Brother Peter hauled Luca upright. Luca blinked as Freize, riding down the street to rescue his master, jumped down from his horse and steadied Luca.

238

'Are you all right?' Freize asked. 'I came back as fast as I could.'

'It's nothing,' Luca said. 'But I'm glad you're back. We're trying to stop this; Vargarten is calling his men off.'

Freize looked around at the barred doors and the reluctant drunk men, shouting and boasting and slowly coming to their lord. 'I'll go to the synagogue,' he said very quietly to Luca. 'The children are hiding in the attic. See if you can get Vargarten to leave.'

'Where are the rest of you?' Lord Vargarten was bellowing at the man who stood before his lord, shifting sulkily from one foot to another.

'Someone said there was treasure,' he said sullenly. 'Infidel treasure in their church. They went there.'

A crashing noise and the screams of children from the synagogue made Vargarten wheel his horse around. 'Come on,' he said, and rode towards the sound.

The open door of the synagogue, banging on its hinges, showed half a dozen of the guards pushing and shoving their way up the narrow stairs that led to the women's gallery. Lord Vargarten spurred his horse forward, right through the doorway, into the sacred space of the synagogue, and looked around at the beautifully carved wooden chairs and the central table where the scrolls would be read. Everything was polished clean and bare, but there were no candles, there were not even the sconces for candles on the walls. Everything had been taken down and hidden as soon as the warning bell had sounded for the arrival of the dancers. All the holy things – the scrolls of the Torah, the candlesticks – had been hidden with the children, in the secret attic above the women's gallery. It had never been discovered before, but this time Lord Vargarten's men, running along the women's gallery, had heard a baby cry above.

As Lord Vargarten rode up to his men, crowded on the stairs to the women's gallery, he saw the first one hammering his battleaxe upwards, breaking into the limewashed ceiling. There was a shower of plaster and a hole opened up. 'There's someone up here!' he shouted excitedly. 'I heard them. Lift me up!'

'Get a ladder!' someone yelled. But instead a dozen men lifted one of the heavy carved benches from the gallery and used it as a battering ram against the ceiling, thrusting it upwards, shouting 'One! Two! Three!' until it broke through and was jammed between the floor of the gallery and the rafters of the ceiling above.

They shouldered it into place to serve as a makeshift ramp into the attic, and the first man scrambled up the ornately carved back, pushed on by his fellows, and thrust his sweating head through the hole in the ceiling and looked around. They heard his yell of delight, and he ducked his red face down to shout: 'There's treasure up here! And the children are hiding here! And wenches!'

'Oh Lord, come away,' Lord Vargarten said with sudden weariness. 'You'll break your necks. We've all got something as a reward. Leave the children and the wenches.'

'We'll baptise them!' the man shouted, pushing his head and shoulders into the ceiling space, quite drunk with excitement. 'We'll pull down the children and baptise them and we'll have the women! Come on! Come on!'

'We'll make Christians!' another man yelled, crawling up behind him, boosted by his fellows. 'Christian bastards on the Jew whores!'

The first was hauling himself into the loft space, the second pushing him on, and their comrades behind them yelling encouragement, when there was a sudden warning shout from the first man, half in half out of the plaster hole.

There was a crash as the hole was suddenly widened around him, as if scooped out by a giant hand, and a massive figure, too big to be real, leaned down to look at them all. He was on his hands and knees, bending his great head over the opening, reaching towards the straining men, his eyes glaring like a beast, twice as big, three times as big as any of them. His huge face impassive, the letters on his forehead glowing like fire, he took hold of the first man by the arms and lifted him away from the hole, beyond the bench, his legs dangling. The giant swung the kicking man out over the gallery and released him without any force, dropping him from the ceiling to the stone floor below, and then he leaned out of the hole and pushed the second man firmly in the chest. The men behind screamed in fright, and then the great bench swayed as the men at the top flung themselves off, or slithered down away from the monster. But those at the bottom, who had seen nothing, still tried to force their way up, yelling, and the men on the stairs and in the gallery pushed their way upwards, crushing the others.

'Let me out! Let me down!' the man who was second on the bench was fighting his way to get down, choking on his own blood. Saliva and blood spewed from his mouth and he held his ribs as if they were broken. 'There's a monster! A monster! A giant!'

The men swarming up the staircase to the women's gallery, greedy for plunder and rape, looked up at his

241

terrified shout and saw his face, a white mask of terror, blood foaming from his mouth, screaming a warning. Behind him, terrifying in his calmness, was the great Being who bent down and took hold of the enormous bench, as easily as if it were a plank ladder, and, standing up to his full height, twisted it and flung it down, over the women's gallery, to the stone floor of the synagogue, two storeys below.

The half-dozen men fell with it, spilled to the floor, cracking their heads on the tiles, breaking an arm, twisting a leg, one man breaking his back. He lay there in screaming agony.

'My God,' said Lord Vargarten, shaken into terror. 'What was that thing? Did you see it?'

Luca, horrified, looked up and saw the blank face of the Being, and behind him the frightened faces of a score of children, crowding round to see the injured men howling on the floor. Among them, holding them back from the hole in the crumbling ceiling, arms outspread, was Freize. As soon as Freize met Luca's eyes, he gave a little nod of reassurance, and drew the children back from the edge of the shattered ceiling into the darkness of the attic. A gentle touch by Freize to the back of the Being drew him away too, and when Lord Vargarten looked again there was nothing to be seen but the broken hole and a shower of falling plaster.

'Priest – was that a giant?' Lord Vargarten demanded. 'A monster?'

'I saw nothing but the bench collapse under the weight of your men,' Luca said breathlessly. 'My lord, that man looks as if his back is broken.'

'This one is dead.' Brother Peter knelt beside the first man who was dropped from the ceiling, giving him the last rites in a rapid mutter. 'Poor soul, he broke his neck as he fell.'

'I saw ... I saw ...' Lord Vargarten stammered.

'Terrifying,' Luca said. Those men who could get to their feet scrambled up, groaning from the pain of their fall. Some of them dragged up a comrade and limped out past Lord Vargarten into the open air. Some were too badly injured to move. 'What did you see?' Lord Vargarten demanded.

'The hand of God,' Luca announced, thinking fast. 'That first man,' he gestured at the body and at Brother Peter closing his eyes, 'had put his hand on the Holy Bible, stored up there, in the attic. The Jews hold it sacred, just as we do. It is our Holy Bible, and his blaspheming hand was grabbing it, oaths in his mouth. Then I saw an angel of judgement strike him down for blasphemy against the Word of God.'

'I saw it!' Lord Vargarten exclaimed. 'I saw it too! An angel! Bigger than a man, with burning eyes.'

'Let's get out of here,' Luca said. 'Blasphemy is punished by God. You don't want to be part of it.'

'How could it be blasphemy to attack the infidel?' the lord asked.

'Their Bible is our Bible,' Luca said. 'The very same.'

'Never!' Lord Vargarten exclaimed. 'Who knew that?' He kicked his horse and made it wheel round, through the broken doorway of the synagogue. 'Maybe I shouldn't have taken my horse in there,' he remarked.

In the street outside, his men were painfully hauling

243

themselves into their saddles. A couple of them were hiding away little stolen treasures, but most of them were stunned with shock, nursing a broken arm, or bleeding from the nose. Two were slung on the horses' backs, moaning and cursing with the pain

'You impious dogs!' Lord Vargarten yelled, anger replacing fear. 'Theft and rape weren't enough for you? Oh no! You had to go and try to steal the Jewish Bible. Don't you know that's as good as our Bible? You'll all have to go to confession and your hurts are your own fault.'

'Johann is dead!' someone shouted from the back of the troop.

'And it's his own fault!' Lord Vargarten replied. 'Because he put his hand on the Holy Bible and an angel struck him dead. Remember it. When I tell you to take a little reward for your work, I don't expect you to desecrate our own Bible! Fools that you are. Follow me, we're riding home.'

He glanced down at Luca. 'Are you coming back with us?'

Luca shook his head. 'We'll come later. I thank you for your help. I shall send my report to the Holy Father and tell him that you saved two towns from the dancers.'

'No need to mention desecrating the Bible? It was not me, remember, it was that fool and he's dead. I'd rather not have that marked up against me.'

'Not at all.'

'Follow me!' his lordship bellowed to his men and pushed his horse through his troop, down the narrow street and towards the gates.

Luca and Brother Peter stayed very still, the setting sun burning into their faces, until they heard the gates bang shut behind them, the diminishing clatter of the hooves and then the tocsin sound once, to tell everyone that the village was empty of Vargarten's men, and the danger had gone: this time.

Slowly, people opened their shutters and peered out into the empty streets. Tentatively, front doors opened and people came out to assess the damage.

Householders whose windows had been broken emerged with brooms of twigs and started to sweep up the precious glass. There was the noise of hammering from a nearby street as someone started to repair a shutter, torn from its hinges. A woman began to cry over the loss of an heirloom, a treasure which had been passed down by her family for centuries, which they had kept safe through centuries of raids like this, but lost today.

The young woman who had run from the soldier walked back to her house, holding her ripped gown together at the neck to hide her nakedness, her head down.

'I thank you for your help,' she whispered to Luca as she went by.

He was overwhelmed by her dignity. He could find nothing to say but bowed as low to her as if she had been a Christian lady and not a despised Jewess. Then he turned back and paused at the wrecked doorway of the synagogue.

Freize was underneath the opening to the attic, standing astride, balanced on the arms of one of the heavy wooden chairs in the gallery so that he could reach upwards, to where the children were peering down. As Luca watched, a small boy lowered himself into Freize's arms and was lifted safely onto the floor.

Men and women came into the synagogue, calling out for their children and hearing their voices reply. Others went to the rabbi's house and brought their children down the ladder and through the secret door. The mothers who had hidden elsewhere swooped down on their children and gathered them into their arms, kissing their faces, stroking their hair, patting them all over as if to be sure that they were unhurt.

Many of the children, released from their promise of silence, chattered to their parents that Freize had frightened them at first, suddenly appearing through the secret door in the rabbi's house, but he had ordered them to be quiet and hide at the back of the attic, and that he had stood before them as the soldiers hammered on the floor, breaking through from the gallery in the synagogue below.

'And then he threw down the bench!' one girl told her father. 'When the bad man came in. He broke down the floor and threw them all down!'

The rabbi arrived in the synagogue with his wife. 'That was you?' he asked Freize.

Luca could see Freize struggle to explain. 'Tell the rabbi,' he said shortly. 'Tell him truly what has happened here. For I saw something that I cannot understand.'

Freize spoke quietly to the rabbi. 'There was a Being,' he said. 'Call me a fool, but he joined us in Venice. First time I saw the creature it was no bigger than a lizard. Kept by some alchemists in a jar. I know it doesn't sound like it could be so, but it was. When we put it into the canal, it swam like a fish, like a salamander. When we left Venice, I thought it was walking on dry land, and following us – I kept seeing it from the corner of my eye, looking like a stable lad, like a little boy.'

He broke off and looked from Luca to Brother Peter, then back to the rabbi. 'You'll think I'm a fool,' he said. 'Or drunk and seeing things.'

'Why didn't you say anything to me?' Luca demanded. 'Why didn't you tell me you were seeing such a thing?'

'Because I thought I must be mistaken!' Freize exclaimed. 'Even now, it sounds like madness.'

'Go on,' the rabbi said steadily. 'It is not madness to me.'

Brother Peter looked at him. 'Have you heard of such a thing before?'

'Yes,' said the man. 'Have you?'

Brother Peter nodded.

'Ishraq saw the Being when it was no more than a lizard,' Freize said. 'And then she saw him when he was the size of a little lad. I told her that I thought it was the lizard from Venice and we looked out for it after that. When the dancers took Isolde, and I followed her, then I spotted the Being again – he was following me.'

'Why?' Luca asked. 'Why would he follow you?'

Unhappily, Freize shrugged. 'I don't know. I never knew. He never spoke to me. He never answered when I told him to go away. But he was growing considerable. It was troubling. Anyway, when I tried to get Isolde away from the dancers, it was the Being who saved her. He helped her and pulled her onward, and when I started dancing too he got hold of my hand and drew me away. He ran us down the hill towards the village when our feet were dancing us away, back to them, as if he were a good father and we were silly children. And it was the Being who shouted out the special words and got the gateman to open the gates.'

'He shouted in Hebrew,' the rabbi told Luca. 'He said: "Open the gate in the name of the one and only God!"'

'In Hebrew?' Luca asked.

The rabbi nodded. 'The language of our faith. Of course the gateman obeyed.'

'But when we got in the gates and they were closed behind us, and we were safe, the Being was gone. Slipped away.'

'Disappeared?' Brother Peter asked.

'I don't know,' Freize said. 'I was trying to hold Isolde still, and begging the gateman not to put us out, then this gentleman arrived and we wanted to get her shoes off. I didn't see the Being again, and I didn't think to look for him. What with Arabs with scimitars and Ishraq gone, and being trapped in a village of Jews, and leaving you Sparrow all on your own, I forgot all about him.'

'And I never saw him at all,' the rabbi said. 'Not when they came in, and not afterwards. Though it would have meant everything to me to see him.'

'I saw him at the window.' Freize gave a little shudder. 'I was afraid he was up to mischief, in your house, sir,' he said to the rabbi. 'So I thought I should warn the lady, your wife, since she had been so good to us. She wasn't afraid at all. She knew just who I meant and she showed him to me, in the attic of your house, guarding the children.'

'Above the ceiling of the synagogue.' The rabbi nodded at Brother Peter. 'Guarding the Torah and the scrolls.'

'Then,' Freize went on, 'while I was getting the girls to safety, and coming back here to fetch you, Sparrow, I kept thinking about the children in the attic, with the women and the Being, and I was fearful for them all. When I saw you were alive and trying to get Lord Vargarten's men out of the village, I thought I'd go and see that all was well with the children. Vargarten's men had broken into his house and gone on, leaving the door open, so I went in and ran up the stairs. I knew how to open the secret door, so I went up into the attic. The women were there, but no sign of the Being. The little children were there, as silent as angels. Just looking at me as if I could save them, saying nothing.'

Freize broke off, choked with emotion, and spoke to the rabbi. 'It's wrong, what Lord Vargarten allowed is wrong, whatever your people did in the Bible days. It can't be right. No man could leave little children like that, their eyes wide, listening to their village being wrecked. How could anyone do such a thing? How could anyone allow it?'

'What happened?' Luca prompted him.

'I thought we were sitting snug and safe and we would wait it out, then a little one let out a cry, a tiny cry, but it was enough to alert them in the church below. Then we heard the soldiers breaking the ceiling in the church, thump thump with a battering ram, and then the floor broke away under our feet and up they came. I went to the hole in the attic floor and thought that I'd make a bit of a fight of it, but I didn't fancy my chances – I could hear there were dozens of them coming. I thought, at best, I could just try to keep them delayed so the children could get away – down the other stairs and out through the rabbi's house. It's not the sort of odds I like, and I'm not a fighting man as you know, and I have no taste for trouble; but I shouted to the children to run away and I pushed against the first man that came up, but they were coming on again, and I didn't think much for my chances, nor for the children, when the Being put me aside with his big hand—' Freize could not hide his shudder. 'He has a big, powerful hand, you would not believe it; and he put me aside, as if he were sweeping a kitten off a table. He took my place and leaned out of the gap in the floor and I saw him throw the man down – just lift him off and drop him; he thrust the next in the chest – and then he lifted the whole bench itself that had taken a dozen men to lift up. He raised it, and turned it round and threw it down to the floor below, as if it were no more than a ladder for picking apples.'

'I saw it,' Luca confirmed. He nodded to the rabbi. 'I saw the Being do that.'

'And then?' the rabbi asked. 'Where did he go then?'

'I don't know,' Freize said.

'I didn't see, I was talking to Lord Vargarten and looking at the fallen men,' Luca said.

'I was giving the dead man the last rites,' Brother Peter added.

'He just went,' Freize said simply. 'As soon as the soldiers left.'

'I told them the Being was an angel of judgement,' Luca said. 'Because they had grabbed at the Bible. I don't think they'll come back for him. I think Vargarten believes it was a Christian angel.'

'I jumped down and helped the children down,' Freize finished. 'I didn't see him any more. I don't mind telling you that it was most disagreeable. Really. Frightening and noisy and unlikely to turn out all right. We were lucky he was there.'

'You have both heard of such a thing?' Luca asked, looking at Brother Peter and the rabbi.

'Yes,' the rabbi said quietly.

'I have,' Brother Peter said. 'I think this was a golem.'

The rabbi breathed out and bowed his head reverently towards where the Ark should stand, the scrolls of the Torah safely stored.

'What's a golem?' Luca asked.

'We have a story, that it is possible to make a Being from clay, from dust,' the rabbi said quietly. 'And to bring that Being to life.'

Brother Peter nodded. 'As God did with Adam.'

'That's what the alchemists in Venice said they could do,' Freize muttered to Luca. 'They said they were studying how to make life. They said they could create gold from muck and life from dust. And we saw that they could make gold.' He patted the pocket in his shirt where he carried his golden penny.

'Such a Being grows in power and strength,' said the rabbi. 'On his forehead he carries the word *EMET* which in our language, Hebrew, means truth.'

'That he does!' Freize exclaimed. '*EMET* – I saw it myself. He had it from the very beginning.'

'It is said that he is a servant of the Jewish people, that in our time of need he will defend us.'

'He did that today,' Luca observed.

'And he saved Isolde and me,' Freize agreed.

'He saved the children,' said Brother Peter. 'And the sacred things.'

251

'But where is he now?' Luca demanded.

The rabbi shrugged. 'The story says that he can disappear. The story says that the golem can return to dust and come back again to us, in our time of need.'

'Is the presence of such a Being a sign of the end of days?' Luca asked. 'Do you have the end of days in this story?'

'Not in this story,' the rabbi said. He gave Luca a weary smile. 'But we too are waiting for the days to end. Sometimes we think they are here for us. Some days – like today – we think the end has come. But still we wait, and still a worse day comes, and still it is not the end.'

'We should still report it to Milord,' Brother Peter said. 'This has been strange and uncanny.' He looked at the dead man on the synagogue floor, his neck broken, his head smashed. 'And dangerous,' he added.

~

Freize, Luca and Brother Peter rode out of the Jewish village, back to the town of Mauthausen, the mother of the two rescued children behind Freize.

The inn looked warm and ordinary in the dusk, and the children came running out to greet their mother and set off with her to ride home on a borrowed horse.

'Will you be safe?' Freize asked her. 'Should I ride with you?'

She shook her head. 'I will be safe. It is over for now. It will be quiet until the next time.'

'You know,' Freize said confidentially. 'If I were you, I think I would say I was Christian and go and live in Vienna. Would you be safe there? If you lived alongside Christians and did not keep to your ways?'

She looked at him and it was as if she could see the future. 'I don't know,' she said. 'Do you think Jews will be safe in Vienna?'

~

Freize saw to the horses, rubbing them down and turning them out into the twilight field to graze, as Luca and Brother Peter fetched the travelling writing desk to the dining room, with Ishraq and Isolde, and started to compose their report to Milord, the lord of the Order of Darkness.

'Difficult to know where to start,' Brother Peter said, trimming the nib of the quill with a penknife. 'I have never attended such an inquiry. It was not an inquiry at all, it was a riot. We have reported on the dancers, but we should say that they were dispersed in the end.'

'The pedlar told me that the dancers convinced themselves that they could do nothing but dance,' Ishraq offered. 'He put Isolde in a sort of trance so she went out to them. But he said that others convince themselves.'

'So it is not a sickness of the body but a conviction?' Luca asked her. 'A sickness of the mind?'

She nodded. 'Like the hatred of the Jews,' she observed. 'It is as if people are so poor, and their lives so hard, that they have to escape from their reality into an illusion. Sometimes they break out dancing; sometimes they break out in hatred. Either way it is a madness.'

'And the dancers are the same as the Jews to Lord Vargarten,' Luca suggested.

Brother Peter waited, his pen poised. 'How so?'

'People fear and hate the dancers just as they fear and

hate the Jews. Just as they drive out travelling Egyptians, or attack travelling players. Just as they hate people who think differently, or those who look strange. Sometimes people cannot bear others who are different from themselves. They fear anything that is other.'

'Other,' Brother Peter repeated.

'Like me,' Luca said bitterly. 'A changeling. Like Ishraq: a half-Moor.'

Isolde's head went up at the thought of Ishraq's parentage and she blushed scarlet at the memory of what Radu Bey had said to her that she had denied, that she would not repeat.

'You can't blame them,' Brother Peter said. 'We all feel comfortable with our own. I would rather live in my monastery than out in the world.'

'It's understandable,' Luca said thoughtfully. 'But we all have to stop ourselves from hating what we don't know, just because it is strange to us. Lady Vargarten hates the dancers, yet her own sister danced away. Lord Vargarten hates the Jews because he borrows from them and never repays them. They hate them because they are strange and yet they are close; they work together – they are neighbours.'

'Do you want your report to say that people must live together in kindness?' Brother Peter asked with a little smile.

Luca shrugged. 'Oh! No! I was warned against being imprecise by Milord himself. He said benevolence without hard detail is a waste of time. But you can write that the dancers were not a sign of the end of days for though it was very terrible, it did not get worse. They dispersed; some of

254

them were cured and went home. If I was thinking of the end of days from what we have seen here, I would say that the treatment of the Jews was the worst sign.'

'You think that the cruelty might get worse?' Isolde asked him.

'I think that if a people think that a community living among them is evil or sick then they will need very little convincing to destroy them. When you call someone an animal or less than animal, it is the start of the end. What if the next Lord Vargarten blames the Jews for his debts and instead of destroying the debts thinks he will destroy the lender? What if someone like Lady Vargarten takes power? What if, instead of complaining that Jews are here, people decided to drive them away, or drive them to death?'

Brother Peter looked at the young man. 'What you are describing could never happen,' he said. 'People are cruel and unreasonable; someone like Lord Vargarten is a brute. But nobody would destroy a whole race. It could not be done, there is no way that it could be done. It is unimaginable.'

The innkeeper's daughter tapped on the door and said that dinner could be served if they would move the writing box from the table.

'Come in!' Freize said eagerly. 'Let me help you with the plates.'

Luca laughed as Freize swept away the papers. 'Forgive me, Sparrow,' he said. 'But I don't want to inconvenience this lady as she brings the plates from the kitchen. It would be wrong to delay her, when she has gone to all this trouble to make a good dinner.'

She brought them roasted and cold meats, fresh bread,

cheeses, and a rich, warm syllabub in a great bowl. Freize drew up his chair, waited for Brother Peter to complete the long Latin grace and then lowered his head, eating steadily, hardly drawing breath.

They were all exhausted by the events of the long day. Luca kissed the hands of both the girls as they went up to their bedroom without saying a particular goodnight to either of them. Ishraq smiled at him as she left the room, but said nothing.

The two young women combed and plaited each other's hair, just as they did every night, then dressed in their nightgowns.

'Are you afraid to sleep here?' Ishraq asked Isolde.

'No. I know that I am safe now. I know the dancers have gone away. Are you afraid?'

'No. I'm not afraid of the pedlar; I am sure he is on his way back to Giorgio. And I don't fear the dancers. I think that has burned out. I think the worst thing was as Luca says – what will happen? Not to us but to the Jews?'

Isolde knelt at the foot of the bed for her prayers, as Ishraq lay down and pulled the covers to her chin with a sigh of relief.

'I am so tired,' she confessed.

Isolde got in beside her. 'Now you must tell me everything that happened,' she commanded. 'About the pedlar and about you chasing him.'

'Where shall I start?'

Isolde yawned deeply. 'Tell me from when you went upstairs to look at the earrings in the landlady's mirror.'

Ishraq made her voice deliberately quiet and slow. 'I went up the stairs to look at the earrings ...'

Within moments, Isolde was asleep, her breathing quiet and regular. Ishraq lay on her pillow, looking up at the limewashed ceiling, listening to the creaks of the old house settling down for the night. She closed her eyes. She slept.

～

Late in the night, just before dawn, as the moon dipped slowly below the horizon, Isolde started to dream. It was a dream that meant nothing, not drawn from her experience of the day, not a wish that she longed for. It was as if it were someone else's dream. She tossed in her bed and started to cry out, as if to shout a warning to people that had not yet been born.

In her dream, she saw a road that was not like a road at all. It was the road that she had danced so wearily, the road to Mauthausen. But it was not like a road, for she could see the moonlight gleaming on two parallel lines in the road – narrow tracks of metal, shining like silver, snaking along the river valley, going to the town like a poisoned arrow travelling towards a beating heart.

Along the tracks, terribly, came a monster of a machine, dark and smoking, sparks of fire spurting from its great chimney, with a roar like that of a dragon, pounding in the night with metal wheels turning on the silver tracks, overwhelming in its speed and threat and horror.

Isolde turned in her sleep and started to moan. She had never seen anything like this in her life before; she could not comprehend the speed at which the machine was travelling, faster than any horse, faster than a river in spate. She could not imagine where it was going, with such direct and terrible purpose. She tossed and turned, but she could not free herself from the dream.

She saw the smoking chimney at the front of the monster, and then she heard the scream and the whine of the metal brakes as the wheels locked; she saw the slide of the long line of closed carts along the silver tracks in the road. The carts came to a juddering halt before a raised stone platform like a quayside, but there was no reassuring splash of waves. There was a terrible silence. Waiting on the platform were men, with faces as hard as Lord Vargarten's, with dogs like wolves on leashes beside them that gave tongue as if they had sighted prey.

The doors of the first wagon slid open and scores – perhaps a hundred – of starved, frightened people who had been packed inside the closed carts, gasping like fish for air, licking the rainwater from the sides of the cart, stepped unwillingly, sometimes falling to their knees, into the cold, hard moonlight of the stone platform. They looked around with dread, not knowing where they were, nor what was going to happen to them, but recognising the time and place of their death.

Isolde flung herself upright with a scream of terror. At once, Ishraq was at her side, patting her back, hugging her shoulders. 'Wake up! Wake up! You're all right. It was just a dream! You're safe, Isolde. What was it?'

'A dream,' Isolde said slowly. 'I had a most terrible dream.'

'What was it? It's no wonder that you are dreaming of horrors.'

'I don't know what it was,' she said, her voice trembling. 'I don't know where it was. It's something – but there are no words for it. It's something so terrible that it is beyond description. I don't know what I dreamed, and, if I could say it, you would not believe me. That was what they knew – the people in my dream – that they would tell of it, and tell of it, but that nobody would hear them, and, if anyone heard, they would not believe. I dreamed of Jews, but they had been transformed into ghosts in striped jackets, and they were walking to their death. The people around them had been transformed into monsters, men and women without hearts. And I cannot tell you, and they cannot tell you: it is something beyond words.'

Ishraq shuddered at the depth of horror in her friend's blue eyes. 'It was just a dream. It wasn't real.'

'It was here!' Isolde cried out with sudden conviction. 'It was here! In this town, in Mauthausen!'

'Hush, hush. No, it was a dream. It was nothing. You're all right, Isolde. You're safe. We're safe.'

'Oh yes, I am all right,' the girl said quietly, coming to herself and looking around the limewashed walls of the room and the quiet dawn starting to lighten the window. 'But what about them?'

AUTHOR'S NOTE

The dancing sickness that is the subject of Luca's inquiry can be seen in various outbreaks from medieval to modern times. There have been a number of attempts at explanation. Current theories call this 'mass hysteria' – which suits our thinking, but may be no more useful to our understanding than labelling it 'possession by demons'.

The legend of a golem who protects the Jews is a traditional Jewish story. The laws against Jews, their enforced separation in villages, the prejudicial traditions against them and the regular assaults and killing are part of the history of antisemitism that has disgraced Christendom for 2,000 years.

It is that track of thinking which leads from medieval persecution to the indescribable Holocaust, like the train tracks of Isolde's dream, that ran to the village of Mauthausen – which was a hub of Nazi concentration

261

camps, where prisoners worked until they were killed from 1938 to 1945. How many died is still unknown – it is estimated that between 122,766 and 320,000 died at the Mauthausen complex alone.

In the Holocaust itself, up to 6 million Jews were killed, 5.7 million Soviet citizens, 2.5 million Soviet prisoners of war, about 1.9 million Polish civilians, 312,000 Serb civilians, about 275,000 people with disabilities, 196,000–220,000 Roma, 1,900 Jehovah's Witnesses, 70,000 so-called criminals, an unknown number of German political opponents and resistance activists in Axis-occupied territory, hundreds, possibly thousands, of homosexuals. These were not wartime deaths of combatants. This was the Holocaust, the deliberate mass murder of millions of people innocent of any crime. History approaches this topic with difficulty – how to define it? How to understand it? How to explain it? Fiction is, I think, incapable. Fiction pulls out one story or one aspect from the whole and can tell a tragic, potent, individual story; but it is the whole of this that should be told: and the whole of it is unimaginable.

I drew Isolde's nightmare from a recurring dream described by Primo Levi who survived Auschwitz. He dreamed that he would go into a room of friends and be unable to tell them what he had seen, what had happened. He thought that his own experience was – in real life – beyond description, beyond belief.

The prejudiced, fearful track of medieval hatred led to this destination and everyone who walked it through the centuries has some responsibility for treading it deeper into the mind. The fear and hatred of the other followed its old twisted course beneath the Enlightenment, beneath modernity, almost forgotten, until it re-emerged with such terrible force. We must never tread these ways again. Any time that we are invited to hate someone, any time that we are filled with self-righteous anger or fear, we should remember where this road can lead.